Family Shoes

Family Shoes

Noel Streatfeild

A YEARLING BOOK

Published by
Dell Publishing Co., Inc.
1 Dag Hammarskjold Plaza
New York, New York 10017

Yearling ® TM 913705, Dell Publishing Co., Inc.

ISBN: 0-440-42479-8

Printed in the United States of America
First Yearling printing—April 1985

CW

Written for
Josephine Plummer,
who produced the Bell Family series
on the air in Children's Hour

*I am afraid only half the story is here,
but perhaps, if anybody wants to
read the other half, I might write
another book about the Bells.*

Contents

1

About the Family

The Thames is a very twisting sort of river. It is as if it had to force its way into London, and had become bent in the process. First there is a big bend to the right, then a little one to the left, then a great bulge to the right, followed immediately by a smaller bulge to the left. In that smaller bulge to the left is the part of southeast London in which the Bells lived.

The people in that part of London are not rich; they live mostly in small row houses—houses joined together with no space in between. It is a very noisy part of the world. People shout a lot, and bang a lot, and laugh a lot. In the High Street there is an almost continuous street market of a very shouting sort, for not only are there the usual men calling out "Tomarrs ah ri" for "Tomatoes all ripe," or "Whelks luv-er-ly whelks" (whelks are snails, and Londoners love to eat them), but there are a lot of stores behind the market selling radios and television sets, and these are tuned in all day and blare music out into the streets. All day long buses flow like a slow red stream through the crowded roads, and in addition there are delivery trucks, pickup trucks, private cars, and many bicycles, all trying to move along and all hooting at each other.

People who do not live in southeast London might say to themselves that it was a crowded, dirty, noisy place to live in, but the people who live there do not feel like that at all. They are as true Londoners as the London pigeons: they like roaring to make themselves heard, they like street markets, they like living so close together that they know each other's business, they like the jostling jolly life of the streets; they have lived in that part of London all their lives, and they would not move even if you offered them a flat in Buckingham Palace.

Right in the middle of the main street is St. Mark's Vicarage. It is not joined on to the houses next to it like other houses in the neighborhood, but stands by itself with, quite close to it, the parish hall, and next to the parish hall St. Mark's Church. When the Bells first came to St. Mark's Vicarage, Mrs. Bell—or Cathy, as Alex Bell, the Reverend Alexander Bell, calls her—felt quite ill, the neighborhood made her so depressed. Her father had been a country doctor, and she had been brought up with a big garden, and outside the garden plenty of fields and woods to wander in. When she married Alex he had been a curate, working not exactly in a country parish but in a not very built-up one, so she had not felt cramped.

St. Mark's Vicarage was an ugly Victorian building, with a lot of space wasted in passages. The front door opened on a long passage, with first the study and then the dining room on the left, and on the other side an enormous, sunless, chilly room, which the previous vicar had used as an extra parish room, to save himself going out on wet evenings, but which Cathy could see she would use as a drawing room. The kitchen was a tremendous size; it was at the far end of the passage and must, Cathy supposed, have been meant to house a cook and several kitchen maids. With only her working in it she thought it would feel rather like cooking in St. Paul's Cathedral. Upstairs there were three quite nice bedrooms, a bathroom, a linen closet without any windows, and yards more passage.

There never was a house, Cathy decided, that wasted more space than St. Mark's Vicarage, but it was not the house that depressed her, but what was outside the house. Whichever way she looked there were chimney pots; the gravely scrap of earth around the house would never make a garden; there did not seem to be a tree within miles. Perhaps it was there being no trees that gave her that sinking feeling inside. Alex was a very clergyman sort of clergyman: he thought the place where he was most needed was the loveliest place to be. Cathy knew it would be no use saying to him "Oh, Alex, do tell the bishop we won't come here," so she resolutely turned her back on the view outside the windows and concentrated on the house.

At that time the old vicar, who was going to retire, was still living in the vicarage. He and his old wife were devoted to dark red wallpaper, large mahogany furniture, Indian brassware, and potted ferns. Cathy tried in her mind to strip the red wallpaper off the walls, throw out the furniture, brass, and ferns, and put in their place the Bells' own shabby but much nicer possessions, and their nicest possessions of all—their three children. But it was not easy to do, and she was looking so depressed when she got into the bus to go home that even Alex noticed it.

"Cheer up, darling. I'm sure we're going to be very happy there."

Cathy's reply tried to sound hopeful, but only succeeded in sounding doubtful.

15

"I suppose we shall. But, my goodness, Alex, what a lot wants doing."

At that time there were three Bell children: Paul, who was six; Jane, who was four; and Virginia, who was two. Another baby was expected. Of course Alex and Cathy did not know what sort of a baby it would be, but it eventually turned out to be a boy, and they called him Angus.

Most of the planning of what was done in the vicarage had to be by Cathy, for Alex was not at all a practical man. He had been born in a home with plenty of money, and had not been taught by doing without what money was worth. His father owned woolen mills, and it had been his idea that his two sons, Alfred and Alexander, should join him in the wool business. Alfred had joined him, and had been so successful that he not only managed the London end of the business but was director of several companies as well. Alex had known from the beginning that he was not a bit interested in wool, and was determined to be a parson. There had been a dreadful row when finally he told his father about it, and when at last his father saw that Alex had made up his mind he said:

"You must be daft, lad; there's not a penny of money to be made in the Church. If you make a fool of yourself and go into it none of my brass'll keep you."

Alex's father had kept his word. He had sent him to Cambridge, and paid all his expenses until he was accepted into the Church, but from that moment on he never gave him another penny. Alex did not mind a bit, but then he never thought they were poor, which made it very difficult when it came to things like moving house.

Not a great deal could be done to the vicarage. The

16

Bells were helped by something called "Queen Anne's Bounty," which lends money to make vicarages habitable, but that mostly had to go on things like plumbing and a gas stove—dull but frightfully important. The red paper was of course stripped off the walls, but paint is expensive, and so are wallpapers, so what most of the vicarage walls got in exchange was a good coat of whitewash.

Before the Bells moved in, two very important people came into their lives: the first was Mrs. Gage. Cathy had asked one of the churchwardens to recommend somebody to come and give the floors a good scrubbing before the carpets were laid. She came to see the house while the scrubbing was going on. As she opened the door of the vicarage she heard a strange noise, half-tune half-puff. It was Mrs. Gage scrubbing the hall while she sang the hymn "Pleasant Are Thy Courts Above." It was a cold, beastly sort of day, in what ought to have been the beginning of spring and wasn't. Cathy was tired after a long bus journey and was looking bluish-greenish. Mrs. Gage raised her face from her scrubbing brush, took one look at Cathy and said firmly:

"What you want, dear, is a nice cuppa."

Over that first cup of tea Cathy learned quite a lot about Mrs. Gage. Mr. Gage was in a nice way of business in the vegetable line.

"Always been in the veg line, 'is family 'as," Mrs. Gage said, "seems to 'ave a proper talent for it. If there's a good line in celery goin' Mr. Gage's nose will tell 'im of it from 'ere to Covent Garden."

Cathy learned that Mr. and Mrs. Gage had five children, all married except the youngest, Margaret Rose, who was still at school. She learned that the Gages had a little house not far from the vicarage, evidently beautifully

17

kept, for when Cathy admired the way the house was scrubbed Mrs. Gage said:

"I'm treatin' the vicarage like me own place. I'm always tellin' Mr. Gage you can eat off me floors anywhere, 'ceptin' when 'e brings in 'is great dirty feet, without wipin' 'is shoes."

Mrs. Gage learned a lot about Cathy which Cathy did not tell her. She knew, because Cathy told her, all about Paul, Jane, and Virginia, but she also knew, although Cathy did not tell her, about the new baby, which was expected in the summer. She thought Alex, "the reverend" as she called him, a very nice-looking gentleman, but though Cathy did not tell her, she found out there were drawbacks to being the vicar's wife. It might sound all right, but when it meant running a largish house with very long passages on very little money, it could be more of an anxiety than a pleasure. Another thing she knew, though Cathy said nothing about it, was that Cathy had a great deal to learn about management. Cathy thought she had been brought up in a not very well off home, and so she had—compared with Alex; but Cathy's idea of not very well off and Mrs. Gage's were two different things. Mrs. Gage knew what it was for every penny to matter, and she thought it would be something that Cathy would have to learn. She knew that Cathy would need someone to help her to learn to manage, and to help her run the vicarage—at any rate, for the first few months. So suddenly she said:

"I'll pop in for an hour or two to start with, dear. I don't work regular, but I don't mind now and again to oblige."

Cathy said cautiously that she was afraid she would not be able to have Mrs. Gage often, because they would not be able to afford it. Mrs. Gage had a glorious roaring friendly laugh; she laughed now.

"Don't worry, dear. We'll manage some'ow. If you can't pay me, I'll 'ave to pick Mr. Gage's pocket, and not for the first time neither." Then she added more seriously: "Tell you what, I've always been meanin' to do a bit of good works like, so once a month I'll give the reverend's study a good cleaning. It'll be me good deed like."

Cathy knew that Alex, who was never cross about anything, got the nearest thing he could be to cross when people cleaned his study, but even meeting her for the first time she had got very fond of Mrs. Gage and certainly wasn't going to hurt her feelings. So she only said: "That'll be lovely," and hoped Mrs. Gage would forget about her good deed, or at least be careful to choose suitable days on which to do it.

The second person to come into the Bells' lives walked, or rather blew, into the house uninvited. He would perhaps have been shown out again, only the day he blew in was the day Alex had borrowed a friend's car and brought the three children over to see the vicarage. Paul was the only one who was old enough to realize the house they were looking at was to be their new home. The home he had left behind had all their furniture in it, which, though old and shabby, he had always known and loved. This house had no furniture at all and smelled nastily of whitewash. There was a garden around the house which they had left. Facing them across the road, almond trees were in bloom. Paul's face as he looked around the vicarage and out of its windows was revolted. He did not so much speak as words burst out of him.

"Mummy! We can't live here, this is an awful place. I don't never want to live here."

19

Cathy thought Paul was so very right (for she did not want to live there either) that she had to think before she answered him. It was while she was thinking the stranger blew in. A small, wriggling red cocker spaniel puppy. There was a strong wind that morning, the front door had not been properly shut, it had flown open, and the puppy had blown in with all his fur going the wrong way. Jane was the first to get hold of him. She knelt down beside him and hugged him to her.

"Look, Mummy, a fairy dog. He's come to live with us, forever and ever."

Cathy did not want any more family just then. Moving was quite enough without a not-yet-house-trained puppy added to the party, but fate was against her. The puppy was one of three belonging to an assistant churchwarden, who was looking for a good home for it and thought nothing could be better than the vicarage. Being parson's children the Bells were, of course, properly brought up on the Bible, and a suitable name for the puppy was at once thought of by Paul.

"We'll call him Esau, because Esau was a hairy man." Suddenly the vicarage stopped looking awful, and Paul stopped minding moving into it. He gave Esau an enormous hug. "Good morning, Mr. Esau Bell, we're very glad to have you in the family."

When the Bells had lived at St. Mark's Vicarage for seven and a half years Paul won a scholarship to a very good day school. This was an important day in the vicarage, for Paul needed a special education, as he was going to be a doctor. From their first summer in St. Mark's Vicarage, when Angus was only a new baby, the whole family had been invited to stay with Cathy's brother, Uncle Jim.

Uncle Jim had taken over his father's practice, and he and his wife, Aunt Ann, and their children, Ricky and Liza, lived in the rambling house with the large untidy garden that Cathy had known when she was a child. Quite near them lived Cathy's father and mother, whom the children called Mumsdad and Mumsmum. Mumsdad had mostly retired from being a doctor, but he still did some work for the small local hospital. Paul, age six, driving around with Uncle Jim or waiting outside the hospital for Mumsdad, thought the most glorious thing that could happen to anybody was to become a country doctor and live among trees and fields, and not in stuffy, noisy, dirty southeast London. But as the years went by and he grew older, his ideas changed. First, though he would not admit it and still grumbled about them, he got fond of both St. Mark's Vicarage and southeast London. Secondly, he knew he did not want to become a country doctor, that he meant some day to be a specialist and work in one of the great London hospitals. Being a specialist, or training to be a doctor of any sort, is a very expensive business, and Paul knew, without being told, that it could only be done with scholarships. So it seemed to him his first real step toward being a doctor when he heard he had won his school scholarship.

Jane and Ginnie, as everybody called Virginia, went to a school called St. Winifred's. St. Winifred's had been built out of money left by a rich old lady "to provide girls with a Christian education, and to give free education to the daughters of poor clergy." The free education for the daughters of poor clergy was too good an offer for Alex and Cathy to turn down, but there were disadvantages about St. Winifred's. The girls had to wear an absolutely hideous uniform: shirt blouses with ties, very bunchy navy gym tunics, absolutely atrocious black stockings, no socks after your eleventh birthday, and black shoes, navy blue overcoats, and the most unbecoming hats, with the school ribbon around them, that anyone had seen. Miss Newton, the headmistress, did what she could to modernize the school, which had very old-fashioned rules, but it was uphill work, as the board of governors liked the old-fashioned rules and tried to make the school stick to them. Jane's great interest in life was dancing. There was a dancing class at St. Winifred's which, as the daughter of a poor clergyman, she attended free. The dancing mistress, Miss Bronson, had been well trained and did her best to pass on her training to the girls, but you cannot do much with two classes a week, and large classes at that. She had done what she could for Jane, having at once spotted she had talent. Sometimes she kept her after a class to give her private lessons, and she taught her exercises to do at home every day. In addition, though Jane did not know this, she had been to see Miss Newton about her. Jane, she said, in her opinion had outstanding talent and should be properly trained. Miss Newton promised to pass on the message but said she held out no hope.

"They're desperately poor, I'm afraid, and not being a government school we can't get special scholarships for our girls, but I'll tell Mrs. Bell the next time I see her."

Cathy, when she heard what Miss Bronson had said, looked miserable.

"I know she has talent, bless her, but I'm afraid a dancing school is out of the question. It wouldn't be only the fees, it would be special clothes, and fares, and goodness knows what all. My children do grow so, and clothes are so expensive, and something always seems needing doing at the vicarage—it absolutely eats money, that house.

22

I do hate saying no, but it really is impossible at present."

Jane was the sort of girl who always worked hard at anything that she did. It worried her to be behind in her class, it even worried her that she was no good at athletics, and she tried very hard to make up for not being good at them by sounding extra keen about them, which she was not. St. Winifred's was the sort of school where hard-working girls like Jane got on very well, so she was as happy there as she could be in any school which was not a dancing school.

Ginnie was the exact opposite to Jane. Jane was thin, small for her age, and unusually pretty, with dark blue eyes and brown hair curling to her shoulders. Ginnie was almost as wide as she was long, so wide that sometimes when family members were feeling mean they called her Queen Victoria, because she had the same sort of shape that Queen Victoria had when she was an old lady. Nobody could call Ginnie pretty; she had greenish eyes and very straight mouse-colored hair that stuck away from her head in two stiff plaits. The nicest thing about her appearance was her smile: she had the kind of smile that nobody could see without feeling they had to smile too. Ginnie was the opposite to Jane about work too. She never cared how badly she did.

"It's simply idiotic for Miss Virginia Bell to slave and slave to be at the top of the class. All that would happen would be that she'd be so dead from exhaustion by the end of the week she couldn't work anymore, so she'd be bottom the next week."

Ginnie thought dancing the most disgusting waste of time. She had to go to the dancing classes, but she never learned much, for she spent most of her time in the back row, making her friends laugh by imitating the girls in the front row. Ginnie adored athletics. Sometimes she dreamed of being the captain of a team, but it was only a dream, for she was not really outstanding, and in St. Winifred's you had to be outstanding to be a champion at anything, for it was a big school with over seven hundred girls.

Angus was at a choir school; he had a really lovely voice and had recently been promoted to sing solos. Angus despised his voice; he thought nothing of being able to sing. His ambition was to own a private zoo. In the bedroom which he shared with Paul, as a start toward this ambition there were always at least six boxes of caterpillars.

"Once Mummy's got used to seeing these caterpillars, Paul, I bet she won't notice if larger things come. I could start with a mouse or two, work through to rats, and then quite soon something perhaps as large as a monkey."

Paul was not enthusiastic about Angus's daydream.

"You don't keep to your end of the window ledge as it is, and if you think I want a monkey scratching for fleas all night you've got another think coming."

2

Curiosity

The summer after Paul got his scholarship was the summer that Angus was eight.

On a streaming wet day three weeks before the birthday Cathy was getting tea and listening for her family's return from school when the telephone bell rang. She stopped spreading jam on bread and waited to see if Alex would answer it. It was sure to be for him, but sometimes when he was writing a sermon or a difficult letter he was such miles away he did not hear it. This time he did hear so Cathy went back to her jam spreading, but since the telephone was in the hall, half-listening to what Alex said.

"Hallo. Oh, it's you, Alfred." Then there was a long pause in which his brother Alfred's voice could be heard growling like a far-off thunderstorm. Then Alex said: "How nice of you, old man. Of course we will all come. It will be a red-letter day for us, and the best birthday Angus ever had."

Before Alex had put down the receiver Cathy was standing beside him with a piece of bread in one hand and a jammy knife in the other.

"What did Alfred say? What'll be a red-letter day? What's happening on Angus's birthday?"

25

Alex came back to the kitchen with Cathy.

"My father and mother are coming to stay with Alfred and Rose in three weeks' time. As it coincides with Angus's birthday, they thought they would have a birthday party for him, and a family party for all of us."

"What sort of a party? Tea?"

"No, a theater party. They're taking us to Covent Garden to see the ballet. Veronica's never seen one, and they think she should. There's to be a birthday supper party afterwards."

"Ballet! Won't Jane be excited!" Then Cathy's face changed and wore the anxious look mothers' faces have when their children are invited to something and have not the right clothes to wear. "Oh, dear! Must it be an evening party? Why couldn't it be a matinée?"

Alex thought Cathy was worrying about bedtime.

"One late night won't hurt Angus."

Cathy sighed.

"You are the nicest man in the world, Alex, dear, but you are too unworldly to live. Can't you see that party? Everybody in evening dress. Your mother upholstered in good silk. Rose in her latest model. Veronica wearing a new fluffy dress for the occasion. And us looking like very, very poor relations."

Alex put an arm around Cathy.

"No matter what they wear they won't look a patch on you, they never do."

Cathy made a face at him.

"In my old black day dress, which years ago was a castoff of Rose's!"

"It isn't evening dress. Rose sent you a special message she was wearing an afternoon dress." Alex stopped, for Esau had run barking to the front door. "That'll be Miss

Bloggs. I met her delivering parish magazines, and I want to see her so I asked her to tea."

Most parishes have ladies attached to them who are sort of unpaid curates. Miss Bloggs was that sort of lady at St. Mark's. She had wishy-washy hair, which had been reddish, but was now mostly gray, a scraggy body, and an eager expression, like a dog who hopes everybody is glad to see him but is not sure. She was, as Ginnie often said, "So good she couldn't be good-er." All day she slaved for Alex. Much of her time she spent on her bicycle, which she called her steed, peddling around the parish, leaving messages, begging for subscriptions, asking for clothes for rummage sales, or delivering parish magazines. Alex often said he did not think he could have got through all the work that he did if it were not for Miss Bloggs. Cathy liked Miss Bloggs because she was so useful to Alex, but she was not really her favorite person. Hearing Alex open the front door and let Miss Bloggs in, she called from the kitchen:

"What a day to deliver magazines! You must be soaked. Hang up Miss Bloggs's raincoat to dry, Alex, and take her into the dining room and light the gas fire. Tea won't be long."

Miss Bloggs had the sort of voice that sounded as if she had taken elocution lessons.

"Don't bother about silly me, Mrs. Bell, dear. We never catch cold, my steed and I; never trouble trouble till trouble troubles you."

Cathy knew by the way the front door opened and shut which of her family was coming in. Angus slammed it, Jane shut it by leaning against it, Paul, who was usually carrying books, used his knee to hold it open. Ginnie and Alex never shut doors after them. So as Esau excitedly

27

skidded down the passage, and the house shook as the door slammed, she did not need to hear him speak to know it was Angus.

"Down, Esau. My goodness, you are a wet boy! Have you been out?"

Cathy came to the kitchen door.

"Don't let Esau climb all over you, darling, he's very wet. Take off your boots before you come into the hall, and hang up that raincoat."

Angus's mind was not on boots and raincoats.

"Mummy, have you got a match box?"

Cathy waited until she heard the boots removed.

"Have I got what? Hang up your raincoat before you come to the kitchen. I don't know what Mrs. Gage will say if you drip all down her hall."

Angus had a passion for long words, though he did not always get them quite right.

"It's per-pos-terious for Mrs. Gage to mind my drips. Anyway, Esau has made so many footmarks it's like the hall had a mud floor. Can I have a match box?"

With thrilled yaps and barks Esau again skidded toward the front door; this time it was Jane and Ginnie. Cathy, who, because of Miss Bloggs, had opened a can of pâté and was making some thin pâté and lettuce sandwiches, laid down her knife and went again to the kitchen door.

"Take off your boots, darlings, before you come into the hall, and hang up your raincoats."

Jane was kneeling beside Esau.

"You blessed lamb, you're sopping. I'll get a towel and dry you. Poor angel, I can't think why you don't get pneumonia!"

Ginnie grunted as she pulled off a boot.

"To hear you talk people would think you were the only person in this house who cared for Esau, wouldn't they, Esau, my most exquisite darling?"

Cathy waited to hear the boots removed, then she went back to her sandwich spreading. Esau, Jane, and Ginnie came running down the passage. She looked up smiling, pleased they were home.

"Had a good day, darlings?"

Jane sat on the table.

"Something simply marvelous is going to happen. I'm going to dance a solo in the school play."

Cathy's eyes shone. Always she felt miserable about Jane's dancing, and any chance Jane got for an extra lesson, or, as now, a chance to show what she could do, was as if somebody had given her a present.

"I am glad, darling. What sort of a dance?"

Jane had taken a towel and was drying Esau.

"A nymph. Stand still, angel boy. How can I dry you if you wriggle like that?"

Cathy looked doubtfully at the towel.

"Is that his you're using?"

Jane nodded.

"I ought really to wear only a tiny bit of something, but being St. Winifred's I should think it would be long and thick for decency."

Ginnie was chewing the ends of lettuce Cathy cut off the sandwiches.

"Who's coming to tea, Mummy?"

"Miss Bloggs. She's here already. You must go and wash, darlings."

The children looked reproachfully at her. Angus said:

"That Miss Bloggs comes to tea abs'lutely every day. Mummy, will you listen? Can I have a match box?"

Cathy laid another sandwich on the plate.

"I don't like the way you children speak of Miss Bloggs. She's a wonderful help to Daddy."

Jane raised one of Esau's ears and whispered into it:

"Esau, angel boy, according to Daddy Miss Bloggs is the cream of his parish workers."

Ginnie picked up another bit of lettuce.

"If Miss Bloggs is cream, I hope I'm skim."

Cathy meant to speak severely.

"Ginnie . . ." Then she saw Ginnie's leg, which was sprawled out behind her. Above her sock was a large strip of pink plaster. "What have you done to your leg?"

Ginnie glanced at her leg as if the news there was plaster on it surprised her.

"It's that old cut. The top came off, so Matron put a new plaster on."

Cathy looked at the plaster with a professional eye.

"What did Matron say?"

Ginnie sighed.

"You know what a fuss she is. She said, 'Keep that plaster on until I see that leg again.' Do you know, Mummy, I bled and bled so much I thought I'd bleed to death."

Cathy finished the last sandwich.

"These sandwiches are for visitors only. Now, do go and wash, darlings. Poor Miss Bloggs and Daddy have been waiting ages for their tea."

Angus in desperation pulled at Cathy's arm.

"It's un-possible for me to wash until I've got a match box."

Cathy, arranging the sandwiches on a plate, suddenly realized that Angus had been talking about match boxes ever since he came in.

"What do you want a match box for, pet? You haven't got a new caterpillar, have you?"

"Yes. It's a woolly bear one—I got it for Paul. I swapped it for that book of songs that Grandmother gave me for Christmas."

Cathy was used to her children's swapping habits, but Grandmother's Christmas present had been a lovely book of old English songs.

"Oh, darling, you didn't!"

Angus was pleased with himself.

"A woolly bear caterpillar will be much nicer to have. All those solos, and I ab-nor singing solos."

Ginnie finished the last piece of lettuce.

"You can't hate singing solos as much as we hate hearing them, my boy. At that concert for the parish mothers I thought I'd be sick in the middle of 'Cherry Ripe.' "

Angus thought that most unjust.

"I didn't ask to sing, and I don't ask to go to a choir school. Mummy, could I have a match box now?"

Jane, who had finished drying Esau, hung up his towel. As she turned she saw what was in Angus's hand.

"What a dear little caterpillar."

Angus was not tall, but now he drew himself up to all the height he had.

"A woolly bear caterpillar isn't a dear little anything, it's a me-ter-lodg-ical experiment."

"Who says so?" asked Ginnie.

"Paul." Cathy took a full match box off the shelf and tipped the matches out. Angus carefully put his caterpillar into it. "It's only till Paul comes home. I'll move him into a proper box with muslin on top after tea."

Cathy looked at the caterpillar.

"Couldn't it go in with the silkworm? Or that green

31

caterpillar with the red tail? You keep such a lot of boxes in the bedroom, and I don't think it's healthy."

"You'd better be careful. I'm sure I've heard somewhere that sort of caterpillar's hairs are poisonous," said Jane.

Ginnie pretended to look knowledgeable about caterpillars.

"It looks odd, as if it might turn any minute. It wouldn't surprise Miss Virginia Bell if it was a cocoon before Paul got in. What sort of an experiment did Paul say it was?"

Angus frowned, trying to remember exactly what Paul had said.

"He'll be able to tell by that caterpillar exactly what the weather will be like next Christmas."

Ginnie gave the caterpillar a gentle nudge.

"How? Does it sing 'I'm dreaming of a white Christmas'?"

Cathy put the plate of sandwiches on a tray.

"Will you children go and wash? Those that don't wash don't get any tea."

With a clatter and a rush the children ran upstairs, Jane and Ginnie to the bathroom, Angus to introduce his caterpillar to the rest of his pets. Over hand washing Ginnie whispered:

"You know, Jane, I told Mummy the top came off that cut, and that's why Matron put a plaster on it. Well, the top didn't come off; I pulled it off on purpose."

"Whatever for?"

Ginnie lowered her voice still further.

"You know that new girl Alison in my class. Well, she only just sat down this morning when Matron came in and began mutter-mutter with Mam-zelle, who was teaching us French. Then Mam-zelle nodded and said '*Vraiment*' and pushed her hands and eyebrows into the air the way she does, and then Matron took Alison away. And she never came back."

Jane was using some pumice stone on an inky finger.

"I expect she was wanted at home."

"That's what I thought at first, but I asked everybody and nobody saw her leave. So I had an idea. I thought perhaps she'd done something awful, and was being kept in Matron's room till the police came. That's why I pulled the top off my cut to find out."

Jane laid down the pumice stone and went to the towel.

"What was she doing?"

"At first I thought she wasn't there, because she wasn't in Matron's ordinary room, but when Matron went to get some plaster I looked in that other special room where the bed is, and there was Alison asleep. She was really asleep, because I leaned right over her to find out."

Jane finished drying her hands.

"You're a terribly nosy girl, Ginnie."

"I'm glad I was nosy, for I'm positive there's a mystery, and I'm going to discover it."

Jane raised her voice.

"Angus, do come and wash, you know I have to wait and see you're clean." Ginnie took advantage of Jane's back being turned to let the water run away, and to hide her hands in the towel, but Jane was too quick for her. "Hold them out, let's see them." Unwillingly Ginnie held out her hands. "Look at your wrists!"

Ginnie scowled.

"Mummy said 'Wash your hands.' She said nothing about wrists."

Jane put the plug back in the basin and turned on the water again.

"Get a move on."

Ginnie and Angus bent over the basin. Ginnie nudged Angus with her elbow.

"I don't know about you, Angus, but seeing I never like washing my hands, giving them an extra special wash for Miss Bloggs offends me all over."

Jane leaned against the bathroom wall, waiting for the other two to finish.

"I wish I could like Miss Bloggs more. Sometimes I feel awfully mean about her. Look at the way she gives us presents for Christmas and birthdays, and I'm sure she hasn't much money. I bet she's giving you something nice for your birthday, Angus. What a miserable thing it is that you can't like people just because you know you ought to." She went back to the basin. "That's better, Ginnie. Let's look at yours, Angus. Yes, they'll do. Now, do get a move on, both of you. I'm hungry."

Cathy, Alex, and Miss Bloggs had started tea when the children came down. One thing both Alex and Cathy were very strict about, and that was manners. All the children shook hands with Miss Bloggs, and Jane apologized for their being late. Miss Bloggs was always delighted to be in the vicarage. She smiled in a pleased way at the children.

"Well, little people, what's the news?"

Jane helped herself to a jam sandwich.

"I'm going to dance the nymph in the school play."

Ginnie, hoping no one was looking, stretched out her hand toward the pâté and lettuce sandwiches. Cathy was on the lookout.

"Bread and jam. They're more substantial."

Ginnie knew she was beaten, but she had to have the last word.

"Meat is more nourishing."

34

Miss Bloggs tried to say something helpful.

"What won't fatten will fill."

Angus paused with his sandwich halfway to his mouth.

"Will it? I gave my green caterpillar cabbage to fill it, because I hadn't lettuce to fatten it, and it didn't fill. Instead it burst and turned abs'lutely inside out."

Alex knew only too well how descriptive Angus could become when describing misfortunes that happened to his caterpillars.

"Get on with your tea, old man."

Cathy was only half listening to what everyone said, for her mind was still on clothes for Angus's birthday party. If Jane had nothing fit to wear than somehow a new dress must be found for her, and Ginnie must wear Jane's old dress. It really was very unfair that when anything new was bought Jane always had it. Poor Ginnie had scarcely had a new dress since she was born. If Jane could still be squeezed into the yellow, could Ginnie wear the green velvet, or that cast-off spotted blue of Veronica's? Cathy's thoughts were interrupted by the sound of the front door, and Esau barking.

Paul's rain-splashed face came grinning around the door.

"How do you do, Miss Bloggs? Hallo, Dad. Shan't be a second, Mum, I must get my shoes off, they're sopping."

Angus got out of his chair.

"Paul, I've got you a woolly bear caterpillar."

Alex said:

"Sit down, Angus, you know there's no jumping up at mealtimes."

Miss Bloggs leaned across the table to Angus.

"Is Paul collecting caterpillars too?"

Angus took another sandwich.

35

"Course not. This caterpillar is a met-er-lodg-ical experiment."

Alex laughed.

"Any interest Paul takes in caterpillars, Miss Bloggs, is supposed to be scientific. He says he has outgrown keeping them as a hobby. I am afraid before long he'll have turned his bedroom into a dissecting room. That's the worst of having a son who intends to be a doctor."

Cathy, thinking of party dresses, spoke more fervently than she felt.

"I wish he wouldn't want to be a doctor—that's my family's fault. I wish he'd take after Alex's family and make money in the wool trade."

Jane looked reproachfully at her mother.

"You don't, Mummy. Look at that lovely, lovely house Mumsdad and Mumsmum brought you up in, and look how simply gorgeous it is for Uncle Jim and Aunt Ann and Ricky and Liza to live in now."

Cathy nodded.

"I know. It's a lovely house, and being a doctor is a fine job, even if you don't earn much, but it's such a terribly expensive training. From the time he starts, even if he's lucky, it'll take Paul five years before he's through."

Ginnie spoke with her mouth full.

"Course it's worth it. Do you know, Miss Bloggs, they've got a pony and a car, and a gorgeous garden with simply masses of fruit. And all we've got is one scrubby-looking vicarage and one dog. Oh, Daddy, I do wish we could have a car."

Alex laughed.

"You'll have to go on wishing, Ginnie. There are so many things we need that even if we had a windfall, and that's not likely, a car's the last thing we'd bother about."

36

Ginnie began counting on her fingers.

"If it was me, first I'd have a car, and then I'd have a television set, and then, because Mummy wants it and it can make ice cream, I'd have a freezer."

Cathy held her hand for Alex's cup, which was being passed up the table.

"If we had a windfall, the first thing we'd have is new carpets—ours are a disgrace—and secondly a freezer, and thirdly new clothes all around."

Jane leaned across to her mother, her eyes shining.

"Oh, Mummy, couldn't a little of the windfall pay for me to go to a dancing school?"

Alex turned to Miss Bloggs.

"My poor family don't know it, but if we had a windfall we'd have the house painted and the roof seen to." Then he looked at Jane. "But if there was any left over I think Jane's dancing school would come next. That's something I do wish I could manage, Jane, darling."

Jane took another sandwich.

"Silly Daddy, you know it's only wishful thinking. I've long ago got used to knowing it can't be, but I think wishing it could does me good. After all, miracles can happen; you said so in a sermon once."

Alex gave a pretending groan.

"The way Jane harbors my sermons, Miss Bloggs, and quotes them against me, is enough to break her father's heart."

Paul was hungry. He drew his chair up to the table and helped himself to a sandwich.

"Nice specimen, Angus."

Praise from Paul was praise indeed. Angus glowed with pride.

"Did you have time to speri-ment to see if it will snow next winter?"

"I told you some people say they can tell next winter's weather by woolly bear caterpillars, but I never said I believed it. Have you fixed anything for your birthday, Angus?" Paul turned to his father, trying to keep pride out of his voice. "Starting next Thursday I'm to stay late to have coaching at the nets."

Alex, too, was a cricket enthusiast.

"I say! That's fine!"

Paul was cautious.

"Shouldn't think anything would come of it, but they're looking for bowlers."

"No good counting on it," Alex agreed; "but if you bowl as well as you did last summer, and your batting improves, there is a chance, you know. If I could make time I might come along next Thursday and have a look at you."

To Cathy it was always amazing how an otherwise sensible man like Alex could forget important things.

"Alex, dear, next Thursday is the party."

"What party?" asked Paul.

Alex looked ashamed of himself.

"Of course. What an idiot I am."

Jane glanced from her father to her mother.

"Out with it, darlings. We don't want any of the little-pitchers-have-long-ears stuff."

Between them Alex and Cathy told the children the news. It had a mixed reception. Paul said gloomily:

"Ballet's not much in my line. It seems a bit off to miss coaching at the nets to see that."

Jane felt so happy it almost hurt.

38

"The ballet! Galosh galoosh, goody goody goody. The ballet! How scrumdatious!"

Ginnie leaned across to her father.

"I hope you won't think Miss Virginia Bell rude, Daddy, dear, but she does wish it was Mumsdad and Mumsmum who were coming instead of Grandfather and Grand-mother."

Alex felt this needed some explaining.

"My father is what is known as an outspoken man, Miss Bloggs; Ginnie prefers Cathy's father's softer approach."

Miss Bloggs wagged a finger at Ginnie.

"Hard words break no bones." She turned to Angus. "And what does the birthday boy think about it?"

"I've never seen a ballet, so I don't know what it is, but I hope the birthday supper's good."

Miss Bloggs got up to go.

"I hope it is too." She leaned over Angus. "An elf has whispered in my ear a little something that a birthday boy might want."

Ginnie waited until Miss Bloggs, followed by her father and a barking Esau, had left the room. Then she leaned across the table to Angus.

"Clap, my boy, and Tinkerbell won't die."

Cathy said reprovingly, "Ginnie!" but her mind was once more on clothes.

"You haven't grown much, Jane. I should think that yellow dress would still fit."

Ginnie took advantage of her mother's absorption in clothes and snatched the last meat sandwich, scowling at the rest of the family to prevent them from giving her away. She spoke with her mouth full.

"And what's Miss Virginia Bell to wear?"

Cathy spoke carefully, knowing there might be a row.

39

"There's Jane's green velvet."

Ginnie was not fussy about clothes, but that was too much.

"I won't wear it, so it's no good talking about it. It came in a secondhand bundle of clothes for needy clergy. All that fluffy stuff that made it velvet is rubbed off. And whoever wears velvet in June?"

Jane spoke for the honor of the family.

"It's absolutely true, Mummy; nobody does. And it doesn't meet across the back on her, and when she leans forward her underwear shows. We'd all be embarrassed if she went to Covent Garden dressed in it."

Cathy's voice was full of doubt.

"There's that pretty blue spotted dress."

Ginnie gasped.

"Pretty! Mummy! D'you think I'm going to a party with Veronica, wearing a dress that was an everyday dress of hers last year? If that's all you've got for Miss Virginia Bell she'll wear her school uniform, thank you."

Cathy shuddered.

"That she certainly won't. It's hideous."

"Not half as hideous as green velvet with the fluff gone, or one of Veronica's everydays worn as a party dress."

A sudden glorious idea came to Jane.

"If the yellow dress is too short for me, Ginnie could wear that, couldn't she? Then I'd have to have something new, because there's absolutely nothing else. Oh, Mummy, suppose it doesn't fit! Suppose the gorgeousness of having something new!"

Alex was in the doorway, Cathy said:

"Before you sit down, get the money box. I think we may be going to need one new dress for this party."

Alex hesitated.

40

"Ought we to open it for that? There's summer vacation and . . ."

Cathy was firm.

"I know. But it's your family's party, and you know what they are."

The thought of the possibility of a new dress had brought color to Jane's usually pale face. She clasped her hands.

"Oh, Mummy, could it be something really long and partyish?"

Cathy hated to say no, and she sounded as if she did.

"I'm afraid not, darling. You know it's got to be suitable for all the parish things, as well as this party. Besides, it's not going to be evening dress; Aunt Rose sent a special message to say it's day dresses."

Paul thought of his missed cricket practice.

"Pity really. If it had been evening dress we couldn't have gone, because none of us have got any."

The money box was kept in a corner of Alex's big roll-top desk. It had been started when Paul was a baby. The idea had been to open a postal savings account. No postal savings account had ever been opened, for something was always needed. One of the family got ill and had to have special food, shoes wore out, clothes wore out, windows got broken; it seemed as if no sooner was there a little money in the money box than an evil spirit with a big appetite came and ate it up. A space was cleared in the middle of the dining-room table and Alex took the top off the money box, which was made like a letterbox, and tipped the money onto the table. It was mostly small change, but there was one folded-up bill, which Angus pounced on with surprise.

"Goodness, however did a 'normous sum like that get in?"

Ginnie was putting pennies in piles of ten.

"Mummy had it as a birthday present from Uncle Jim." She pushed a small coin into the middle of the table. "That was mine. I remember wondering if it was still good being rubbed so thin."

As the children finished counting, they pushed the money over to Alex, who added it up and gave about a third of it to Cathy.

"Will that be enough to buy material for Jane's new dress?"

"Oh, I should think so. Now, could you three men clear the table and wash up if we three women went to my bedroom for a big try-on?"

Clearing the table, Angus wore a worried look on his face. Alex noticed it.

"What's bothering you, old man?"

"What is ballet, Daddy? I know Jane does it, but that's just dancing class. Is that what we're going to see on my birthday?"

Alex had seen very little ballet himself, so he was rather hazy as to what was in store for them, but he always liked to give the children a sensible answer if he could.

"It's a story told in dancing."

Angus scowled more than ever.

"A proper story like *The Wind in the Willows*?"

Paul was listening too.

"It's more sloppy stuff, about love and all that, isn't it, Dad?"

Alex felt he was getting out of his depth.

"No, they dance real stories, *Cinderella, Sleeping Beauty*, all sorts. I don't know what Uncle Alfred's taken tickets for, it depends what they're dancing on that night. Sometimes I think they do three ballets in an evening."

Angus put a plate on the top of his pile.

"When I'm an uncle and I'm going to arrange something for my nephew's birthday I shall say to him: 'This is your party, what would *you* like to see?' "

Angus went out of the room with some plates. Paul nodded at his departing back.

"I must say it is rather bad luck, Dad. I daresay he won't like ballet at all."

"I'm not sure. He's a funny little boy. In spite of all this fuss he makes about singing in the choir school he's an unusually musical child. I shouldn't wonder if he enjoyed ballet, for, after all, music's a large part of it. It'll be interesting to find out. It might give us a line on the way to use his talent; perhaps he ought to be learning the violin or the piano instead of singing."

Paul was sweeping the crumbs off the table.

"Sickening it's a Thursday. The only ballet I ever saw I was bored stiff—a lot of girls prancing around. They did it in the middle of a pantomime."

Alex laughed.

"The Royal Ballet is in rather a different class, I think. I'm sorry I can't let you off, old man, but your grandfather will want to see you."

"Trying to get at me again, I suppose."

Though Alex had chosen a career of which his father did not approve, he was fond of the old man and could see his point of view.

"You're the eldest grandson. You can't blame him for wanting you in the wool business."

"But he knows the answer, so what's the good of going on nattering?"

Alex was carrying a tray to the door, but at that he stopped.

"Be just, old man. Your grandfather is a great believer in common sense winning in the end. He thinks he's making you a good offer. He can't believe that in the long run you'll be such a fool as to turn it down. Although he's failed with me, he's not lost faith in you. He's a stubborn old man, your grandfather, but he knows what he wants, and usually he gets it."

"You've done all right without him—I bet he hates that."

"It may seem to you that I'm doing all right, but I don't look any great shakes to him. You look at your Uncle Alfred: he's enormously rich, he's been knighted, and here am I barely able to dress my own children."

Alex had not meant this to be taken seriously, but Paul was far more practical than his father. He knew that though this was not literally true there was truth in it. He answered especially quickly.

"Rats! We get along all right."

Alex opened the door with his foot.

"Not by your Uncle Alfred's standards." Then he gave Paul a proud smile. "But I'm lucky with you, old man. That scholarship's made all the difference."

Paul picked up another tray and followed his father.

"I suppose if I wanted to go into the wool trade I could be rich, couldn't I?"

"You bet you could. Your grandfather would adopt you, I shouldn't wonder, but we're not worrying about that. You use the gifts God gave you. You wish to be a doctor, then be a doctor. It's a fine career, and a worthwhile one, and if you don't make much money it doesn't matter, because you'll be leading a worthwhile life."

*   *   *

44

In her bedroom Cathy was crawling around Jane, giving little pulls to her yellow taffeta skirt.

"Yes, it's much too short, darling. It's at least three inches above your knees."

Jane leaned over to examine her skirt.

"I can't think why. I haven't grown much—I'm still the smallest girl in the school for twelve."

"Even not growing much it's some months since you wore it, and girls of your age don't wear skirts three inches above their knees."

Ginnie, watching the trying on, was lying on her stomach across her mother's bed.

"It is too short, Jane. But Miss Virginia Bell's going to look awful in yellow."

Cathy got up and unbuttoned the dress.

"I don't believe it. Let's try it on you. I think you'll look great."

Ginnie climbed off the bed and pulled off her school tunic and blouse.

"You won't think I look great when you see me beside my dear cousin Veronica. She has her hair permanently waved, and a special cut to suit the shape of her head. Not that I mind—I feel superior to Veronica. When I see her at the party I shall think, 'You poor mimsy-pimsy stuck-up minx.' "

Cathy slipped the yellow dress over Ginnie's head and buttoned it.

"You shouldn't think things like that, darling, though I do know what you mean. I hope, though, you'll try to make Angus's birthday party go well—you know how sticky parties with Grandfather and Grandmother can be." She turned Ginnie around and stood her away from her.

"There! Look at yourself in the glass. Anything wrong with that?"

Ginnie crossed to the glass. Nobody could say that yellow was her color, but she did look nicer than usual. She was quite surprised.

"It's not so bad. But you wait—when you see me against Veronica, shame will eat at your vitals."

Jane looked at Ginnie with her head on one side.

"Don't you think it ought to be shorter? She's only ten."

Ginnie unbuttoned the dress.

"No, thank you, I'll wear it the length it is. I haven't got thin legs like you."

Jane sat down on her father's bed.

"I wish you didn't have to wear your old black, Mummy."

Cathy laughed.

"Why? I'm quite fond of it."

Ginnie pulled her uniform over her head.

"I'm not. It was Aunt Rose's once, and it bothers me you're still wearing it."

Cathy hung the yellow dress back in the closet.

"So long ago, I expect she's forgotten she ever gave it to me."

Jane hugged her knees.

"Couldn't the money box possibly manage some stuff for a dress for you?"

Cathy closed the closet door.

"Goose, of course it can't. I shall enjoy the ballet so much I shan't remember what I've got on."

Ginnie tied her tie.

"We shall remember. You know how Aunt Rose is; she says things that sort of sound all right but are meant to be beastly." She minced toward her mother, imitating her

46

aunt. "Do you mean to say you've got that old dress still, Cathy, dear?"

The imitation was so good Cathy and Jane laughed. Cathy said:

"She doesn't mean to be unkind, but she's got what your father calls a difficult nature."

Jane groaned.

"Difficult nature! Daddy's too good to live. He never says worse than that about anybody, but I could say a lot worse about Aunt Rose."

Ginnie bounced onto Cathy's bed.

"And I could about my awful Uncle Alfred, and his whiny-piny mimsy-pimsy daughter Veronica."

Jane was mentally redressing her mother.

"If you had all the money you wanted, Mummy, what dress would you choose? I mean, suppose you could choose absolutely anything."

Cathy sat down by Jane.

"I suppose all women, except very rich ones, have got some special dress they've always wanted. I've always wanted just once to have a really silly dress. You know the sort I mean, soft and very garden partyish. I've never worn anything like that in my life."

Jane rubbed her cheek against Cathy's arm.

"Poor Mummy, what a shame!"

Ginnie wriggled over and patted Cathy's knee.

"Don't worry, Mrs. Bell. If I was Miss Bloggs I'd tell you fine feathers don't make fine birds."

Cathy smiled.

"And Miss Bloggs would be quite right." She turned to Jane. "Not poor Mummy at all. I daresay I wouldn't like it if I had it, but it's always fun imagining I would."

Jane tried to picture her mother before she was grown up.

"Did Mumsmum know you wanted a dress like that?"

Cathy put an arm around Jane.

"Of course she did, bless her, just as I know the sort of dress you'd love to have; but what good would that silly sort of dress have been to the daughter of a not-very-well-off country doctor, and what good would the sort of clothes Veronica wears at parties be to the daughter of a very badly off London vicar?"

Jane looked up reproachfully at Cathy.

"You're getting at me, Mummy. You're trying to make me behave like Queen Victoria and say, I will be good. You're going to try and make me say: 'I'll be pleased with navy blue.'"

Ginnie gasped.

"Mummy! You can't be going to make poor Jane wear navy blue for Uncle Alfred's party, when that awful Veronica will be all pink frills and bows."

Cathy took Jane's face in her hands.

"Navy blue! Why on earth should I dress my daughter in navy blue for a party? Surely we get enough of that loathsome color in your uniform."

Jane smiled.

"I thought from the way you talked about the clothes for badly off London vicars' daughters you meant something useful."

"I only meant something that would wear well and wouldn't fade. What a daughter! Thinking I'd make her wear navy blue! Isn't she a goose, Ginnie?"

Jane flung her arms around her mother's neck.

"You're the most gorgeous mother in the world."

Ginnie got off Cathy's bed.

"Though she isn't sloppy like Miss Jane Bell, Miss Virginia Bell wouldn't change her mother for any other. It's

48

my day to take Esau out. Do you think, as it's so wet, just around the parish hall and back would do, Mummy?"

"Certainly it'll do, and don't forget to put on your raincoat and your boots."

Ginnie moving made Jane remember the time.

"I suppose we ought to go and see how the washing-up goes on."

Cathy was thinking of other things.

"I wish I could be really the most gorgeous mother in the world to you, Jane, darling, and send you to a dancing school. Daddy and I think of it a lot, you know, but we can never see how it can be done, unless of course you won a scholarship, and St. Winifred's doesn't seem to think you have had enough training for that."

"Quite truthfully I don't either, Mummy. Daddy once said in a sermon 'Too late' were the saddest words in the English language. I don't always agree with what Daddy says in his sermons, but I feel it in my bones that those two are true."

"My poor daughter, too late when you're only just twelve!" Then Cathy spoke much more briskly. "As a matter of fact, if we could afford first-class lessons for you it wouldn't be too late at all. You're what's known as a born dancer, and you're just the right build. All that's wrong with you is that you've not been properly trained . . ." She broke off. "That's the telephone. I wonder if Ginnie will answer it. I'm sure Daddy's gone to evening prayer." She went into the passage and hung over the banisters and called to Ginnie, who was struggling into her boots. "Answer that, darling."

Ginnie marched to the telephone and said grandly:

"Hallo, hallo," then, in a very changed voice: "Oh, it's you, Miss Newton. I'll call Mummy."

Cathy went to the telephone. Jane followed her downstairs and looked anxiously at Ginnie.

"What have you done now?"

Ginnie, whose conscience for once was clear, looked proud.

"Nothing. But a headmistress doesn't ring up for nothing. It must be you this time, Jane."

A sort of dim echo of Miss Newton's voice came from the receiver. After listening for some time Cathy said: "Thank you so much for letting me know." Then, after another pause: "No, as you say, under the circumstances very unlikely." Another pause and then: "No, I think we need pay no attention to that. Good night, Miss Newton, and thank you for letting me know."

Jane and Ginnie spoke at the same time.

Jane asked: "What's unlikely?" And Ginnie: "What aren't we going to pay attention to?"

Cathy smiled at their anxious faces.

"It's nothing, fortunately. There's a new girl in your class, Ginnie, Alison something-or-other. Her mother told her not to go to school this morning, as she wasn't well, but she went just the same. Luckily she was fetched out of your class before any of you spoke to her, and spent the day in Matron's room."

Ginnie did not like the sound of that word "luckily"; she felt as though she had swallowed a piece of ice.

"Why luckily?"

Cathy was amused by Ginnie's anxious expression.

"Because she's got mumps."

In a flash, Jane saw all the awful things which would happen if Ginnie got mumps. She said in a wail:

"Oh, Ginnie, mumps!"

Cathy thought Jane was being silly, making a fuss about nothing.

"There's no need to sound so tragic. Ginnie never went near her, so there's no quarantine."

Ginnie, to stop her voice from wobbling, took a deep breath before she spoke.

"If I had been near her, how soon would it be that I caught mumps?"

Cathy was moving toward the kitchen, so she answered vaguely:

"Somewhere inside three weeks, I think."

Jane followed Cathy down the hall.

"If Ginnie had seen that girl, would she have been in quarantine?"

"Certainly. We don't want mumps in the house, she'd have gone into isolation right away."

Jane, in spite of urgent faces from Ginnie, persisted in her questioning.

"No ballet party?"

Cathy stopped, and took Jane by the shoulders and gave her a little shake.

"No, nothing. But she didn't go near the girl, so there's no quarantine. Now, stop asking questions and let me see how the boys have managed with the washing-up. When you've taken Esau out, Ginnie, give him a rubdown. He makes such a horrible mess in the hall."

Ginnie hardly heard what Cathy said.

"How do you feel when you're starting mumps?"

Cathy laughed.

"This girl Alison's mumps is an obsession with you two. I can't remember how I felt, it's years since I had it, but I do remember my face swelled up the size of a soccer ball."

51

Jane waited until Cathy was safely in the kitchen. Then she whispered:

"What are you going to do?"

"Nothing. I don't believe I smelled her breath, and that's the way you catch things."

"You said you leaned over her."

Ginnie looked fierce.

"You've got to forget every word I've said. I don't want to have quarantine."

Jane tried to think of something nice about quarantine.

"You'd miss school. You'd like that, wouldn't you?"

Ginnie shook her head furiously.

"I missed school when there was scarlet fever, and all that happened was I had to sleep by myself in the drawing room, and was sent to bed directly when you came in from school, and the rest of the day I did housework with Mrs. Gage and Mummy. It was simply awful."

Jane tried one last effort.

"But if you get mumps you'll give it to all of us. There wouldn't be any ballet party, most likely I wouldn't be able to dance the nymph. Think how awful you would feel if that happened, Ginnie."

Ginnie knew how awful she would feel, but she was not going to give in.

"I won't get mumps. I tell you I don't think I breathed her breath, but as you're fussy, I tell you what I will do. Every day I'll measure my face, even if it gets a quarter of an inch bigger I'll tell Mummy."

Jane was not comforted.

"But you'll have got it by then."

"Only the beginning of it. Now you absolutely promise you won't say anything, don't you?"

The rules about tale-telling were very strong in the Bell

family. It was one of the things it was impossible to do. But this mumps business was different. Jane knew there were times when tale-telling was right. Was this one of them?

"Could I ask Paul what he thinks?"

"No. You're not to ask anybody. I'll be very careful to sleep with my head the opposite way to your bed, and I'll measure my face every day. Nobody could do more to be careful who isn't even sure they smelled the mumps person's breath."

Jane was still worried.

"I do wish you'd let me talk to Paul."

Ginnie stamped her foot.

"You're a very selfish girl, Jane. Here I am almost with mumps, and you keep bothering me. As a matter of fact I don't believe you're thinking about me at all. I think you're only thinking about not seeing the ballet and not dancing that silly nymph. Anyway, I don't mean to have mumps, so stop fussing."

3

Clothes

It was impossible for a person as cheerful as Ginnie usually was to be worried about something without people noticing she was being unusual. Of course she did not worry all the time, but only when she remembered, so it was not so much the worrying Cathy noticed as the interest Ginnie was taking suddenly in her face. When Cathy did not understand something about her children she often asked advice from Mrs. Gage, for Mrs. Gage was very sensible.

After nearly a week of rain Saturday was fine. Cathy, happy because of the sun, felt in the mood to talk. She was cooking kippered herrings for breakfast.

"Have you noticed anything odd about Ginnie, Mrs. Gage?"

Mrs. Gage looked up from scrubbing the kitchen floor.

"She's always a caution. Seems a bit quieter off and on like."

Cathy gave the kippers a prod with her fork.

"She's never been a vain child, but quite suddenly she's taken to staring at herself in looking glasses. Did any of your children do that when they were ten?"

Mrs. Gage thought the matter over.

54

"Come to think of it my Margaret Rose was chronic at it. But then she had 'ad the looks, which Ginnie 'asn't. Shouldn't wonder if something 'asn't been said at the school. Children often acts up after somethin's been said that way."

Cathy left the kippers and put some tea in the teapot.

"Ginnie's never been a child to care what was said about her. She's always made fun of her appearance."

Mrs. Gage went back to her scrubbing.

"She's taken a vain fit, maybe, but what I say is you've got the face 'eaven sent you, and no amount of thinking about it won't alter it, so it's no good makin' a fuss."

Cathy thought of her fat, plain little Ginnie, and smiled.

"I don't think we need take quite such a gloomy view as that. Lots of girls have started fat and without any looks have grown up with figures like film stars, and lovely faces. Ginnie has got plenty of time to become beautiful. I wonder whether you'd have a talk with her. You'll have her to yourself while Jane and I are out buying the stuff for her dress. If something has been said at school which has upset her you're the right person to find out about it. She thinks a lot of what you say."

Mrs. Gage in her scrubbing had reached the trash bin. She pulled at a piece of newspaper which was sticking out of it.

"Right-o, dear." She opened the bin and took out the paper. "Funny how the paper things comes wrapped in always seems to 'ave better bits in it than the paper what you buys to read. Look at this piece the kippers come in. Isn't that a smashin' dog?"

Cathy moved around and looked over Mrs. Gage's shoulder at a large photograph of a poodle.

"He's beautiful."

Mrs. Gage folded the paper so that she could read it.

"Oh, it's a competition. Look what's wrote. ''Ave you got a camera? Enter your dog now for the most beautiful dog in Britain competition.' And look at the list of prizes! Well, I never! Better show this to young Paul. 'E's got a camera."

"I daresay the competition's over—you know how old fishmonger's newspapers often are. Is the date still on it?"

"No. It's come off where the fish stuck, but you could buy today's copy and see."

Cathy's mind was not really on the competition but on the day ahead of her. How lucky it was such a lovely morning! They so seldom went to the west end of London to shop, it would have been cruel luck if it had rained. Going with Jane to choose new stuff for the dress would be fun, for their clothes were usually altered from secondhand ones that came in bundles for needy clergy. If there was one job Cathy hated more than another it was turning other people's old garments into clothes for her family. How nice to ride on the top of a bus, crossing the Thames, watching the tugs and the seagulls, and seeing Big Ben. She said, answering her own thoughts:

"Oh, what a lovely morning!"

Mrs. Gage was more practical.

"I said to Mr. Gage as I woke up this mornin': 'Nice it's fine for Mrs. Bell and Jane for their shoppin', but it's a funny thing, the day I do the vicar's study as my good deed, the sun always shines after a wet week.' "

Cathy looked fondly at Mrs. Gage's back.

"It's angelic of you to do it, and I'm glad the sun shines, as a reward."

Mrs. Gage sniffed.

"Reward nothin'. It 'appens regular as clockwork. Out

56

pops the sun, and the parishioners look out of their windows and seein' the sun again says to theirselves: 'I could do with a nice walk after all that rain, now where shall I go? I know, I'll pop along and call on the vicar!' "

"They don't come to see him unless there's something to see him about."

Mrs. Gage's hearty laugh roared out.

"That's what you think, dear. But you'd be surprised. They 'oard things for a fine Saturday. They know the weddin's got to be fixed or the baby christened, but do they come on a wet Saturday? Not them. They wait till it comes out nice, like this mornin'. Then they march in and sit in our 'all, waitin' to walk with their muddy boots right across the study carpet which I've just washed."

Alex, walking back from early service, was thinking about his study. It was splendid of Mrs. Gage to clean it, she looked upon it as the same thing as giving money to the church, bless her, but he did wish she would choose some other charity. Of course he knew studies had to be cleaned, but he thought it a little hard it had to be on a Saturday. Saturdays were such busy days for vicars. The parish workers came to do the flowers and clean the brass, and of course he had to look in and have a word with them. There were always babies to be christened on Sundays, and the fathers and mothers of the babies came to see him on Saturdays about that. Saturdays, because they were half-holidays for many, were the days when people called who wanted to see him about getting married, or other of their business. And Saturdays were the days when he had to put the finishing touches to two sermons.

Alex had made a rule for himself, which he tried very hard to stick to. It was not to let anybody know when he was feeling cross. So outside the vicarage he stopped.

57

First he pulled back his shoulders, which were feeling rather saggish, because it was before breakfast. Then he gave himself a sort of mental slap to remind himself not to grouse. Then, feeling better, he opened the front door. Cathy was coming up the hall with the breakfast tray, she stopped to give him a kiss.

"Hungry?"

Alex, almost over his bad mood, gave a pleased sniff.

"Kippered herring?"

"Yes. Everybody's charmed except Esau. Sound the gong, Alex, darling."

The family came cascading down the stairs. Paul carrying his books. Angus sliding down the banisters. Jane talking as she came.

"Oh, Mummy, galosh galoosh! Look what a scrumdatious Saturday it is. Do you think pink could be useful?"

Mrs. Gage, coming up the passage, gave Angus a gentle smack.

"If I was your mother I'd take a slipper to you. The shorts aren't made that would stand up to slidin' on them like that."

Ginnie rushed down the stairs and jumped the last four steps.

"Do up my dress, Mrs. Gage darling, while I finish plaiting my hair."

Mrs. Gage made pretense clicking disapproving sounds.

"Late as usual, young Ginnie. Dragon for sleep you are."

Ginnie never minded what Mrs. Gage said.

"I'm much nearer on time than I often am." Then, hearing her father call, she shouted "Coming" and tore into the dining room.

All meals in the vicarage started with grace. Alex knew

that few other homes said grace, and that his children thought it was old-fashioned of him to say one, but he liked a grace said, and paid no attention to what his children thought.

"For what we are about to receive may the Lord make us truly thankful."

Alex had barely said the last word when Ginnie burst out:

"Could Miss Virginia Bell be wrong in thinking she heard Miss Jane Bell ask if her new dress could be pink?"

Jane turned eagerly to Cathy.

"Could pink ever be a useful color, Mummy?"

Ginnie looked at Alex.

"Would you stand up for me, Daddy? Would you make Jane remember that when she has a new dress it's only hers to begin with, and will be mine in two years? I keep hoping I'll get thinner as I get older, but I bulge more and more, and nobody who bulges looks nice in pink. My size is a cross I have to bear."

Alex laughed.

"Poor Miss Virginia Bell." Then he turned to Jane. "Is this the shopping day?"

Jane looked at Cathy.

"I think it's a cross we have to bear to have a father who's so unworldly he doesn't even remember the day when his child is going to have a new dress."

Angus paused, with a spoon of cereal halfway to his mouth.

"When caterpillars change into cocoons Paul says they don't feel odd, but I think they do. I think they feel sort of surprised when they wake up and find that instead of being something that walks, with lots of legs, they've got wings instead. I mean I would."

Alex poured some milk over his cereal.

"Does this mean that there is now a butterfly in the menagerie?"

"Was," said Paul. "We let it out of the window of course. I wish we had a yard. I'd like to keep some animals for diet experiments, rabbits, guinea pigs, and so on. I think it would be interesting to feed them on all sorts of food they never ate before, and see how they get on."

"Like when we were at Uncle Jim's?" Ginnie asked. "And you cooked those toadstools instead of mushrooms?"

Paul remembered only too well, for he had been responsible.

"By the book they were all right."

"That was the only time," said Angus reminiscently, "that I ever knew anybody could be sick fourteen times without eating anything in between."

Cathy, too, remembered only too well the day her children had picnicked on supposedly edible fungi.

"Darlings, please not at breakfast. As a matter of fact, I don't know why you want to remember it at all."

"We only did," Ginnie explained, "because Paul's thinking of giving odd food to rabbits and guinea pigs, and we were standing up for them."

Cathy looked affectionately at Paul.

"You can't become a doctor without having an inquiring mind, but that's the last time you're going to experiment on any of us."

Jane was stroking Esau's ears.

"Mummy, as Esau hates kippers, could he have the littlest bit of cereal and milk this morning?"

The rule was that Esau was not fed at meals. This meant nothing, for all the children fed him under the table, and on special occasions he was allowed something off a plate. But this was not a special occasion, so Alex tried to be firm.

"You know he mustn't be fed at meals. I say that every day. Anyway, it ruins his figure."

Cathy put down her teacup.

"Talking of Esau's figure, Mrs. Gage found something in the newspaper that the kippers were wrapped in. It's a competition for the most beautiful dog in Britain. I don't know what date the paper was, or if the competition is over, but Mrs. Gage thinks that if it isn't over you ought to take Esau's photograph, Paul, and enter it for the competition. They're offering a lot of money in prizes."

A gasp went around the table as she told them about the prizes.

"What will you buy with the money, Paul?" Jane asked.

Ginnie stopped eating and leaned on the table.

"If he wins first prize he can buy almost anything! Will you spend it all on one thing, Paul, or on lots of little things?"

"If it's a photograph of Esau," said Angus, "then the money belongs to him, and it's him ought to decide what it's spent on."

Alex laughed.

"Esau's a very good-looking dog, but I don't think we should start spending that money at the moment. Paul has only a very small camera and it's not in very good condition."

Angus looked anxiously at his father.

"Esau mayn't like being the most beautiful dog in Britain. Hundreds of people will come and look at him, and he won't care for that at all."

"I don't think we need worry at the moment about admiring crowds, old man," said Alex.

Mrs. Gage brought in the mail. She handed a pile of letters to Alex.

"The usual for you, Vicar." Then she passed one letter to Cathy. "It's from your brother, Mrs. Bell, dear." Paul told her they had just heard about the competition. Mrs. Gage looked affectionately at Esau. "Bit of all right if our Esau were to win us a lot of money, wouldn't it? Mind you, though, it don't always turn out for the best. There was a woman up my street took a prize in one of these newspaper competitions for the best-looking twin babies."

"What happened?" asked Jane.

Mrs. Gage saw the children were listening. Her voice became full of drama.

"The day they won the prize the newspaper sends a photographer, and what do you think 'ad 'appened? The twins was swelled up so you wouldn't 'ave known them from a coupl'a soccer balls. It was the mumps."

In the second after Mrs. Gage had said the word "mumps" Ginnie threw an appalled glance at Jane, and Jane an equally appalled one at Ginnie. Each day before breakfast Ginnie measured her face with a tape measure. So far there was no difference in the measurement, though Ginnie had worried moments when in looking glasses she thought she looked different. Jane's worry was in case Ginnie was not measuring in the right place, and the mumps might swell up without their noticing it. Now they said in frightened voices:

"Mumps!"

Mrs. Gage was charmed to have so good an audience.

"That's right. Their mother thought maybe it was a judgment for puttin' the babies' photos in the paper."

As the door shut behind Mrs. Gage, Ginnie asked in a voice which, try as she would, sounded scared:

"Can you get mumps as a judgment, Daddy?"

"Of course not. Can you believe that heaven would inflict mumps on two defenseless babies, just because their mother entered their photographs for a beauty competition?"

Cathy, who was reading her letter, gave a pleased squeak.

"Oh, what fun! There's going to be a medical conference the week after next, and both Uncle Jim and Mumsdad have to come to it, so Aunt Ann and Mumsmum are coming too. It will be nice to see them all."

Such a chorus of approval greeted Cathy's news that Alex had to laugh.

"I notice much more enthusiasm when your family appear than when mine do, Cathy."

Jane, who sat next to him, patted Alex's hand.

"It's much easier when they come, no dressing up like there is for Grandfather and Grandmother, or the fuss that goes on when Aunt Rose and Uncle Alfred ask us to things. Mummy's family like us as we are, and don't care what we wear."

Cathy was still reading her letter.

"Oh, and imagine, Ricky and Liza are on vacation, so they're going to come too. They say, if it's fine, would you all like to go to the zoo on the Saturday."

"Goodness," said Jane, "the things that happen to this family. Imagine, the ballet party for Angus's birthday one week and the zoo the next. Aren't we getting festive?"

Jane saw Ginnie had sunk into silent gloom, and she did not wonder. She knew that Ginnie must be feeling awful inside, thinking you could get mumps as a judgment, and though she thought Ginnie ought to have had quar-

antine she was sorry for her. Nobody else noticed anything was wrong. To Paul it was always a day to remember
when he could talk to Uncle Jim. Uncle Jim took his
being a doctor for granted, and made the years before he
could be one shrink. To Angus a day at the zoo was the
perfect day. He had once said that his idea of a perfect
life would be to live in an empty cage at the zoo, and he
meant it. Alex was not noticing Ginnie, because he was so
pleased for Cathy. Her father, though he was retired, was
still on many committees, and Cathy did not see nearly
enough of her parents. It was nice to see her so pleased
she had pink cheeks and shining eyes. He came around
the table and kissed her.

"Good-bye, darling. I hope you and Jane have a good
morning shopping. I must go and get on with my work,
before Mrs. Gage lays her claws on my study."

After Paul had gone, and while Cathy was talking food
with Mrs. Gage, Jane, Ginnie, and Angus cleared the
breakfast table. Ginnie, unable to hold back her worry
anymore, burst out:

"Jane, I know Daddy says you can't, but do you think
you can get mumps as a judgment? I mean, could you if
you weren't a poor defenseless baby?"

Angus was scraping kipper bones onto a plate.

"I don't think Esau can get mumps as a judgment,
because I don't think dogs get mumps."

Jane tried to sound hopeful.

"Perhaps there isn't any such thing as a judgment;
anyway, perhaps you can't catch mumps if there is." She
saw she was not being very encouraging, so she changed
the subject. "I wish that photograph was taken, and Esau'd
won the prize money now; then Mummy could have a
new dress as well as me."

Angus was disgusted at such casual treatment of other people's money.

"If Esau had all that money you don't know he'd want to spend it on a new dress for Mummy. I expect he would, because he's got a lovely nature, but you can't just go spending his money without asking."

Jane patted Esau.

"Of course that's what you'd spend your money on, wouldn't you, Esau?" She knelt down and hugged his red-gold body to her. "Angel boy, you would buy Mummy a new dress, you're as embarrassed as we are to see her going to Aunt Rose's party in Aunt Rose's castoff, aren't you?"

It was not like Angus to pay attention to clothes, but because Jane had spoken to Esau about Cathy's dress her words had sunk in. He watched her leave for the kitchen with a loaded tray. Then he said to Ginnie:

"Esau hasn't any money yet, but if he ever has, and if Mummy needs a new dress, I'm perfectly certain he would buy one."

Ginnie was glad to think of other things than judgments.

"Of course she needs a new dress. She's only got Aunt Rose's old dress. You know how despising Aunt Rose can look. Well, we think she looks despising when Mummy wears it."

"Isn't there enough money in the money box to buy her a new one?"

Ginnie looked scornfully at Angus.

"Of course there isn't, my boy. There's only just enough to get Jane one, if there's to be anything for the summer holidays."

Angus, though he quarreled with her a great deal, had faith in Ginnie.

"Couldn't you do something to get her one? You usually think of things."

It was at that moment that Ginnie's glorious idea was born. Everybody spent their time saying "Your old black dress" and "Aunt Rose's castoff" and things like that, but nobody did anything about it. Yet there must be things that could be done. Perhaps not a whole new dress, but there must be some way to make it different. She, Ginnie, would find that way.

"I believe you've got something there, my boy. I'm not sure yet exactly what. Miss Virginia Bell will wait for guidance."

There was always trouble if Cathy went out when the children were at home without stating clearly what each was to do while she was away. The Bells were not a quarrelsome family, but it would not be natural for any children to offer to make beds, wash up, or do any other chore unless they had been asked to. Before Cathy left with Jane on the shopping expedition she arranged that Angus would give his caterpillar boxes a real cleaning out, and while this was going on Ginnie would help Mrs. Gage make the beds. Later, while Mrs. Gage was doing her good deed to the study, Ginnie and Angus were to be trusted to do the shopping. The reward for all this hard work was money for ice cream.

There was no need for Mrs. Gage to look for a way to ask Ginnie if anything was worrying her, for before they were halfway through the first bed Ginnie said:

"Mrs. Gage, do you really believe things can come as a judgment? I mean, like you said those twins had mumps?"

Mrs. Gage laid down her side of the sheet. Then she sat down on the bed and told Ginnie to come and sit beside her.

"What are you worryin' about judgments for? What you been up to?"

Ginnie turned her face away.

"Nothing."

Mrs. Gage was not having that. She turned Ginnie's face around so that she could see it.

"I saw you lookin' in the glass just now. Is it somethin' to do with your face?"

The pupils of Ginnie's eyes grew large with fright.

"Why? Does it look different?"

Mrs. Gage hugged Ginnie to her.

"Is it somethin' to do with the mumps? Now, come on, dear, the beds can wait. I know you've somethin' on your mind, and what I told you about them twins brought it to an 'ead like. Troubles shared is troubles 'alved."

Because Ginnie was really so terribly worried, Mrs. Gage's being so nice was the last straw. She flung her arms around her neck and started to cry. She cried so hard that for quite a long time, though she told Mrs. Gage the whole story, Mrs. Gage never heard one word she said. So presently, when the crying had reached the sniff and hiccuping stage, she said very gently:

"Come on, stop cryin'. When you go out shoppin' you don't want the 'ole 'Igh Street wonderin' what you been cryin' about. Now, start at the beginnin', and tell me slow what the trouble is."

Out came the story, how Alison had been taken out of class, pulling the top off the cut, the leaning over Alison, and the awful end when Miss Newton had called.

"It's my 'satiable curtiosity that did it. I simply had to know what the secret was."

Mrs. Gage stroked Ginnie's hair.

"I'm the same meself, dear. See a telegraph boy and

you can't 'old me, it's fidget, fidget till I know who it's for and what's in the telegram."

Ginnie felt much better after having told Mrs. Gage her awful secret, but she was not at all sure that Mrs. Gage realized the full terribleness that might happen if she caught mumps.

"You see, if I get it it won't be only me who has quarantine, it'll be everybody. There won't be any party for the ballet, Jane won't dance her nymph, Paul will miss his cricket coaching, and now Mummy heard today that Mumsmum, Mumsdad, Uncle Jim, Aunt Ann, Ricky, and Liza are all coming to London, and we're going to the zoo. If I have mumps that won't happen either."

Mrs. Gage made worried clicking sounds, her tongue against her teeth.

"This is a mess, this is. Mind you, never say die. I knew a lady once that 'eld a baby all the way from Liverpool to London, never knowing the baby 'ad a disease. She never caught it."

"But I'm afraid I shall catch it. I'm afraid it'll be like you said, a judgment."

Mrs. Gage got up.

"Judgment or no judgment we'd better finish these beds. Rightly I did ought to go to your mother. Still, the trouble's done now so to speak. Maybe we'd better 'ope on."

Ginnie went around the bed and picked up her side of the sheet.

"Every day I measure my face, and it isn't a tiny weeny bit bigger than it ever was."

"Maybe you're not goin' to 'ave it. I always said you was born lucky. Fall in the sea and you'd come out dry. Nor do you want to pay too much attention to what I said about a judgment. I'm curious meself, and I must say I never expected no judgment to come from it. But one thing I can tell you, young Ginnie; I've 'ad the mumps, and you'll know fast enough if you're gettin' 'em."

"How?"

"Oh, you feel proper rough, not yourself at all, and your face pains somethin' fierce, so I tell you what we'll do. If you don't feel yourself, you keep out of everyone's way, and call me. If I'm not about, you go straight to your Mum and tell her everything just as you've told it to me. And maybe, now I know, you'd better let me 'ave a look at your face every day. Mind you, you got to act honest. Tell me the moment you feels the least bit off."

Ginnie felt wonderfully better after this talk with Mrs. Gage, and as it never needed much to turn her from despair to gaiety she set off shopping with Angus and Esau in the wildest spirits. It was not difficult shopping, so soon the children were coming out of the ice cream shop with double-sized ice cream wafer sandwiches. They put down the shopping bag to make eating easier, and to leave their hands free to give Esau his taste. It was while they were feeding Esau that Miss Bloggs saw them. She got off her bicycle.

"Good morning, dears. What are you little people doing?"

It was so obvious they were eating ice cream, Ginnie decided that Miss Bloggs could not mean that, so as it was rude to say nothing, she told her about Jane's new dress, and that Mrs. Gage was cleaning out the study, and they were helping by doing the shopping. Angus added:

"This ice cream is our reward."

Miss Bloggs seemed pleased about what happened to other people; she said, as if she were eating an ice cream herself:

"Splendid! Splendid! Many hands make light work. And what are you wearing to the birthday party, Ginnie? We expect you all to do us credit when you go to Covent Garden."

Ginnie took a big lick of her ice cream.

"We won't. Jane's the only one who will. All I've got to wear is Jane's old yellow, which you've seen often. Mummy's wearing her black of course."

Miss Bloggs smiled happily.

"I've always liked her in that."

Ginnie gave Esau another little bit of ice cream.

"You may, but it's really only an old dress of Aunt Rose's, and we're all sorry that she has to wear it to a party given by Aunt Rose. You don't know our Aunt Rose—she's an expensive-looking woman."

"The sort that smells," said Angus.

Ginnie saw Miss Bloggs looked puzzled.

"Angus means scent, and sometimes of flowers too. She often wears those."

Miss Bloggs had no dress sense at all. She considered clothes were coverings; winter and summer she wore a dark blue coat and skirt. In the summer with a cotton blouse, in the winter with a woolen sweater. She seldom saw well-dressed people, and had the mistaken idea that smart people wore fussy clothes. So when Ginnie said flowers, an idea sprang into her mind.

"I wonder if your mother would like some flowers to brighten her dress for the party. Somebody sent a box of artificial flowers for the last rummage sale. I didn't put them into the sale, because I thought they were quite unsuitable, and an occasion might turn up when they would be useful. Now the occasion has turned up. I'll put some money into the rummage sale fund, and if you little

70

people will come with me I'll give you the box to take to your mother."

Miss Bloggs's house was not very far from the vicarage. She asked the children and Esau to come into the dining room and to wait while she fetched the flowers. It was not very nice waiting in the dining room, because it was a very brown room, and the pictures were dull, and Esau sniffed at the fireplace, which had paper folded like a fan in it, pretending he could smell a mouse. Luckily, before he tore the paper fan out, Miss Bloggs came down with a cardboard box. She put it on the table. Inside it were artificial flowers that had been good once, but had become old and tired looking. There were some very red roses, some forget-me-nots, some daisies, and several bunches of faded violets. Ginnie, staring at this flower garden, saw the flowers, not as they were, but as they might be. She was so carried away by the vision inside her head that she caught hold of Miss Bloggs's hand.

"Miss Bloggs, dear, would you let *me* have these flowers? They're *for* Mummy, but I don't want her to see them until I've sewn them on. It's to be a surprise."

Miss Bloggs could see no harm in the request.

"Of course, dear. Very sweet of you to think of it. I am sure your mother will love a surprise for the party."

Ginnie put the box under her arm.

"Come on, Angus. I want to get home and hide these before Mummy sees them."

That evening a very important event took place. Esau was photographed. For Esau it had been a nasty afternoon. Paul came home at lunchtime, with a copy of the paper with the competition in it. It was not too late to send a photograph, so immediately after lunch Esau was given a bath. The family took turns at bathing him, Paul and Jane one time, Ginnie and Angus the other. This time it was Paul and Jane's turn, and a very thorough bathing it was. Afterwards Esau was dried by the dining-room gas fire, and then he was given a tremendous brushing and combing until he glistened like a ripe horse chestnut. Over tea there was a family discussion. Against what background, and in what position, should Esau's photograph be taken?

"I think he looks simply angelic sitting in the armchair in here," said Jane.

Alex's eyes twinkled as he looked at Cathy.

"I thought we agreed Esau wasn't to get on chairs. You said his hairs were such a job to brush off."

"I did," Cathy agreed, "and we did say he shouldn't, and I'm sure he does, but he certainly shan't in a photograph. That would look as if we approved."

"I should think coming out of the front door would be best," Paul suggested. "If somebody said 'walk' he would wear his best, pleased, excited face."

"Seeing he's a vicarage dog," said Angus, "I think he should be coming out of church."

"Miss Virginia Bell thinks that a very silly suggestion, seeing Esau is never allowed inside a church, and hates us going because he's left alone at home."

"All the same, the steps are a good idea," Cathy pointed out. "He would look enormously distinguished sitting at the top of them."

In the end the top of the church steps it was. Esau was bribed with biscuits to sit in six different—but to his admiring family, equally engaging—positions. There was no doubt about it, he was an unusually good-looking dog, and when he had just had a bath and a brush, quite irresistible.

"Such a pity," said Cathy, "it's not in color. His red-gold coat looks so lovely against the dark oak of the church door."

Jane hugged Esau.

"Adorable boy! I only hope, if you win, you don't get offered a film contract. You easily might, and we couldn't let you go and live in Hollywood."

"I should think he'd certainly win," said Angus. "There couldn't possibly be a more beautiful dog than him in Britain."

Ginnie skipped over to Cathy and put her arm through hers.

"Were you thinking if he won first prize you'd have a new dress, Mummy?"

Cathy squeezed Ginnie's arm to hers.

"Of course not, goose. Plenty of other things would come first."

"But you would be glad if you looked so different at the party that everybody, especially Aunt Rose, was absolutely astonished."

Cathy smiled.

"It certainly would make a startling change."

4

The Birthday

There is a very special smell that belongs to a birthday. Angus woke up early, sniffed, and wondered for a moment why the morning smelled exciting. Then, in a second, he remembered and in one bounce was out of bed and hopping around the room.

"Wake up, Paul. It's birthday day. I'm eight."

Paul rolled over, and would have told Angus what he thought of him for waking him up, but he remembered in time what day it was.

"Many happy returns. I wanted to buy you some white mice, but Mum said you'd nowhere to keep them. But I've bought something I know you want. You'll get it at breakfast."

The thought of parcels on his plate made Angus hurry. He rushed out into the passage to see if he could be the first in the bathroom, but Jane had beaten him to it.

"Sorry," she shouted through the door. "Many happy returns. You should have had it first, you're a king today and can do what you like, but I didn't know you wanted it. I couldn't get up early enough on this gorgeous day. Imagine! The ballet and a new dress!"

The girls' bedroom door was open so Angus walked in,

for it was as good a place to wait for the bathroom as any other. Ginnie was sitting on her bed with her back to the door, very busy working at something, but she heard Angus come in.

"Hallo, happy birthday and all that." Then she turned and made a this-is-secret face at him.

Angus tiptoed across the room.

"What are you doing?"

"Sewing the flowers on Mummy's dress of course. Imagine, Angus, I could only start last night, because she didn't press it till yesterday afternoon, and I couldn't start till she'd done that, or she'd have seen the flowers and the surprise would have been spoilt." Ginnie held up the dress. "Look, isn't it gorgeous!"

Cathy's dress was a very plainly cut black crepe de chine. Ginnie had sewn the violets around the neck, the daisies on the cuffs, and was finishing sewing the last of the bright-red roses round the waist. Angus was full of admiration.

"It does look cheerful! Won't Mummy be pleased!"

"I stayed awake simply ages to do it. I thought Jane would never go to sleep. I never would have kept awake only I stood up to sew. You can't really go to sleep standing up because you fall over if you do. I'd better put it away now in case Jane comes. I'm hiding it behind our raincoats. I'm going to put on the last of the roses when Jane's doing her dancing practice." Ginnie got up and opened the closet door and hung up the dress. "I simply can't wait for this evening to see Mummy's face when she sees what I've done for her."

Jane came bounding into the bedroom.

"The bathroom's all yours, Angus." Then she saw Ginnie beside the closet. "Has Ginnie been showing you my lovely

75

dress? Mummy finished it last night. I think it's too beautiful to be true."

It was a charming silk dress with little flowers all over
it. Ginnie looked at it gloomily.

"It's all right for you, Jane, but each time I see you
being fitted in it I shudder. I can see me in it in two years'
time. Unless my shape changes very much by then I'm
not going to like me in it at all. I'm not the sort of girl to
wear dresses that stick out and rustle." Jane closed the
door behind Angus. Ginnie's voice became muffled, for
the tape measure was across her mouth. "Still not swollen,
thank goodness, but I knew it wouldn't be." She rolled up
the tape measure. "Mrs. Gage says before you have mumps
you feel rough and your face pains you something fierce.
I don't feel rough at all, I feel very smooth this morning,
and my face doesn't hurt the teeniest weeniest bit."

"I should stop worrying about your face. Mrs. Gage
said yesterday she'd never seen a face less like having
mumps."

Ginnie put away the tape measure.

"As a matter of fact this morning Miss Virginia Bell
wasn't worrying about her face. D'you know what I'd
have done, Jane, if I had the tiniest feeling of mumps this
morning?"

"Gone to bed of course."

"Not me. What'd be the good? You'd have all had
quarantine if I'd had it, and then nobody could go to the
ballet. No, I'd have gone to the ballet, and I'd have spent
all the evening taking deep breaths, and breathing them
at Veronica."

On birthdays the place of the birthday person was
decorated. For Angus's birthday Cathy had made a ring

76

of early summer flowers, and in the middle was his pile of birthday presents. On birthdays breakfast had to be half an hour early, to allow time for parcel opening before school. Angus had some lovely presents. Esau always gave the same present, a birthday card marked with his footprint. There was a camera from Mumsdad and Mumsmum, a box of tools from Cathy and Alex, a flashlight from Paul, a platform for his railway from Jane, a magnificent magnet from Mrs. Gage, a china goat and a little plaster rabbit from Ginnie, and a Morse code buzzer from Miss Bloggs.

They were all full of admiration when they saw the buzzer, it really was such a good idea. Ginnie said:

"I would never have thought Miss Bloggs was a Morse code buzzer sort of person. When she said an elf had told her what you wanted for your birthday, Angus, my bet was that a hymn book was coming."

Alex tried to look stern-fatherish.

"You children are very unjust to Miss Bloggs. She doesn't have much money, and it seems to me she always gives you lovely presents."

Angus was eating his breakfast with one hand and playing with the buzzer with the other.

"Actually this buzzer is almost the nicest present I've had."

"Not nicer than Mummy and Daddy's tools," Jane protested, "or the camera from Mumsdad and Mumsmum."

Angus gazed affectionately at the buzzer.

"This is an immediate nice present. I can take it to school. The tools will be nice for always, and so will the flashlight and the platform. The camera would have been more useful if it had come last week. It's newer than

Paul's, so it would have taken a much better picture of Esau."

"One would think," said Ginnie, "that Miss Virginia Bell had not given Mr. Angus Bell a birthday present, for he didn't mention it."

Angus looked gravely at Ginnie.

"I'm pleased to have that little goat, and I'm glad to have the rabbit, but I can't help knowing that you didn't buy the rabbit, because I saw you with it at Christmas."

"You're a very ungrateful boy, Angus, isn't he, Mummy? When Jane told me she'd bought you a new platform for your railway I said that I'd buy you a little goat, and I'll not only buy him a goat but I'll give him the rabbit as well. They can both stand on the platform as luggage."

Cathy smiled at Angus.

"So they can, darling, and even birthday boys must eat their breakfast."

Angus took a mouthful, but he had not finished his argument.

"Goats and rabbits don't stand on platforms as luggage much."

Ginnie turned to her father.

"That a child of yours should be so ignorant, Daddy!" Then she hissed at Angus: "In the country they do all the time."

Before the family left for school Cathy said:

"Now listen, darlings. Everybody is to be completely ready by twenty past six. Uncle Alfred is sending a car, which will be here at half past, and you know how fussy he is about punctuality."

Usually, of course, there was a special tea with a cake on birthdays, but because of the party Angus's tea and cake were saved for Saturday. Instead there was a high tea, with an egg each to keep them, Cathy said, from rumbling during the performance.

In the contrary way things like boilers always behave, that day the vicarage boiler chose to do what Mrs. Gage called "act up." She came to the tea table to warn the children.

"Nothin' for it, dears, if you're to 'ave baths before you dress, same as your Mum said, you'll 'ave to share the water. It won't 'ot up more'n the once."

It was decided that Angus, because it was his birthday, would have first bath. Ginnie, because she was slow, second, and Jane third. Paul was not home from school when the discussion started, so he was clearly the fourth.

"Oh, Mummy," pleaded Jane, "must I have a bath? I want to feel gorgeous all over under my new dress, and I can't all messed up with Angus and Ginnie's dirty water."

Ginnie was so indignant she choked over her egg.

"I like that. Mr. Angus Bell and Miss Virginia Bell are just as clean as Miss Jane Bell. As a matter of fact, when I get out of the bath nobody will ever know anyone has bathed in the water."

Cathy laughed.

"Painfully true as a rule, I'm afraid, but not on this occasion, because Mrs. Gage is going to be in the bathroom seeing that every corner of both Mr. Angus and Miss Virginia Bell is scrubbed." Then she turned to Jane. "If you come to my bedroom before you have your bath I'll give you some of those eau-de-cologne bath crystals I had for Christmas. They ought to make you feel worthy of the new dress."

"Do you think I could take my Morse code buzzer with me to the theater?" Angus asked. "Then I could practice it if I didn't like the ballet."

Nobody refused requests, if they could help it, made by the person whose birthday it was, but Alex very quickly turned that suggestion down.

"Certainly not."

Jane saw Angus thought Alex was being mean.

"But you could take the flashlight Paul gave you." She saw her father looked like arguing. "It'll help you find the keyhole when we get in."

Angus was glad he might bring his flashlight, but it was a poor substitute for his buzzer, so it seemed a good moment to present another idea. He adored a swap, but seldom had something really good to bargain with.

"That camera Mumsmum and Mumsdad gave isn't any use to me. I'll get an increase in allowance now I'm eight, but I have lots of things to buy, so I could hardly ever buy a film."

Pocket money in the Bell family was earned money. On the principle that the older you were the more help you should be, Jane, Ginnie, and Angus had an increase in allowance with each birthday. Paul had his own spending money as part of his scholarship.

Cathy felt sure Angus was planning a swap.

"There is a film in the camera, and I think in the summer holidays films for it can come out of the money box, because we all like family photographs." She saw Angus was going to argue. "Now run along, darling, and have your bath."

Much barking from Esau announced Paul was home.

"The only miserable thing about the day is Esau being left at home," Jane said. "I'll hate seeing his sad little face when we leave."

"If we say 'church,'" Ginnie suggested, "he'll think we'll soon be back."

Jane looked scornful.

"Why should he think we were going to church, in an expensive car? He's not a fool."

Cathy looked at her watch and then at Jane and Ginnie.

"You better go up, Ginnie. I shouldn't think Mrs. Gage will take long scrubbing Angus."

Paul came in. Cathy gave him his egg, which she was keeping hot.

"I'm going to clear all around you, Paul, and start the washing-up. Mrs. Gage is bathing the family."

Jane stopped in the doorway.

"And you, my poor boy, have to have fourth used water. We have to share because it won't get hot. I should think your bath will be pure mud."

Paul and Alex, left alone, sat in companionable silence. They heard through the open door Mrs. Gage at work on Ginnie in the bathroom. They heard a discussion carried on in a shout between Jane upstairs, and Cathy in the kitchen, as to the whereabouts of the eau-de-cologne bath salts, and another louder conversation between Angus and Cathy about a shirt. Presently Paul said:

"What a fuss, Dad!"

"Your mother wants her family to cut a dash. Anything said about your missing your cricket practice?"

Paul cut himself another piece of bread.

"Nothing much. Just he hoped that it was the only Thursday I'd miss, as they got their eye on me. He didn't say anything about my chances of course, but he did say they were on the lookout for bowlers."

"Too early yet to tell your Uncle Alfred I suppose." Paul thought talking of something that might never happen a bragging sort of thing to do. He made a protesting

81

noise. Alex nodded. "Quite right. Pity, though. He'd be interested. He was quite a bowler at school."

Cathy, holding a steaming kettle, stood in the doorway. Her face was wearing the sort of despairing face mothers' faces wear when the men of her family do idiotic things.

"Look at you two! Talking about cricket as if you had all day before you. Do you know it's well after half-past five?"

Paul hurriedly swallowed the rest of his tea. Alex, looking rather hangdog, got up.

"Sorry, darling. What's the kettle for?"

Cathy tried not to sound irritated.

"For you to shave. I thought you knew the water'd gone wrong. The children are sharing the only bath."

Upstairs there was the gay rushing about of a family getting ready for a party. Angus, already dressed in a clean shirt and his best shorts, was hopping up and down the passage, tapping his Morse code buzzer. Alex caught hold of him to have a look at him. Mrs. Gage had done a remarkable job. His hair, which usually stood on end, was beautifully parted and smoothed flat with water. His face, neck, and ears shone as if they had been polished. His tie was neatly tied and pinned into place.

"My word," said Alex. "I didn't know you could look so clean."

Cathy called to Paul.

"See Angus doesn't touch the caterpillars. He's beautifully tidy and he's to stay like that."

Jane, in her dressing gown, danced out of the bathroom.

"Smell me, Mummy. Did you ever know anyone smell so gorgeous? I'm coming in to show you as soon as I'm dressed."

Mrs. Gage, grinning, came out of the bathroom.

82

"Look a bit of all right, don't they? You seen young Ginnie?"

Ginnie came out of her bedroom.

"I'm so clean I couldn't be cleaner."

Ginnie was always last, but now, except for her dress, she seemed ready. Cathy was surprised.

"How quick you've been."

"I hurried. Could I come and watch you dress, Mummy?"

Cathy, knowing no reason for Ginnie's request, thought she meant to be funny.

"Very interesting I'm sure, to watch me put on my old black."

"Please, Mummy."

Cathy could not imagine why Ginnie was interested.

"Goose. Of course you can't. We haven't much time, and Daddy has to shave. Thank goodness I did make time to have my hair set."

Ginnie frowned at the shut bedroom door. It had been such work putting on the flowers. If only she could be there to see her mother's face when she saw them.

In the bedroom Cathy was getting on with her dressing and Alex was shaving. Suddenly Cathy gasped.

"Oh, Alex! Look!"

Alex looked. He saw Cathy at the closet, holding what seemed to him to be a fancy dress.

"What on earth's that?"

Cathy spoke in a stunned voice.

"My old black. Violets around the neck. Very, very tired roses around the waist, daisies on the cuffs."

Alex, his face covered all over with soap, came across the room and examined the dress.

"Who sewed them on?"

"Must have been Ginnie. Angus can't sew, and Jane

83

would never be so silly. Oh, Alex, I do hate hurting Ginnie's feelings, but they must come off. I'll look like the Goddess of Spring."

Alex was not thinking of the dress but of Ginnie.

"Would it have taken her long to sew them on?"

"Ages I should think, and she must have done it in the night, for the dress was all right when I pressed it yesterday afternoon. Oh, dear, it's meant to please me. What shall I say to her?"

Alex did not see the dress as a problem.

"Wear it. It was a labor of love."

Cathy gazed at him in horror.

"Wear it! It'll ruin the evening. Can you see the expression on your mother's and Rose's face if I walk into Covent Garden covered in flowers? Can't you imagine the way everyone who looked at me would laugh?"

Alex thought clothes unimportant and hurt feelings, especially hurt feelings of a child, very important.

"Does it matter whether people smile or not?"

"Not to you perhaps, but it does to me."

"Well, wear a coat over it."

Cathy got cross.

"Oh, get on with your shaving. The temperature has been seventy all day, and as you well know, I haven't got a coat fit to go to Covent Garden in. Besides which it wouldn't help. Ginnie would be very hurt if I covered this flower garden with an old winter coat."

Jane banged on the door.

"Can I come in, Mummy? My dress is scrumdatious."

Cathy opened the door, shut it behind Jane, and watched her horrified expression as she saw the black dress.

"Isn't it ghastly! Ginnie must have done it as a surprise for me."

84

Jane saw even more clearly than Cathy had done Aunt Rose's and Grandmother's faces. She could hear the giggles and see the nudges.

"You can't wear it. You simply can't."

Alex had finished shaving. He joined the group around the dress.

"I'm afraid she must. You see, it was a labor of love."

Jane did not care whether the flowers were a labor of love or not, she only knew her mother must not wear them.

"I can't help what they are, Daddy. Mummy simply couldn't go to Covent Garden wearing them. It looks like a very, very bad fancy dress."

"Exactly." Cathy sat on her bed. "Oh, Jane, can't you think of some way I could take them off without hurting Ginnie's feelings?"

Jane fingered the weary-looking flowers.

"If they weren't three sorts they wouldn't be quite so awful."

Cathy jumped up.

"Clever girl! I believe she's got it, Alex. I shall tell Ginnie I can only wear one sort of flower. That vicar's wives never wear three kinds at once."

Jane did not see that one kind would help much.

"But which will you wear? Those dreadfully flabby violets at the neck? Those dirty daisies at the wrists or those ghastly roses?"

Cathy smiled bravely over Jane's head at Alex.

"Ginnie shall choose. I'm not going to hurt her feelings more than I must."

Alex had been a little shaken by Jane's horror when she saw the dress.

85

"That does seem a solution. I do hope she understands, bless her."

"She will," said Cathy. "She's a very sensible child. Oh, dear, I do pray she chooses the daisies—my gloves will cover most of them. Call her, Jane."

Ginnie had been waiting for that call. She bounded into the bedroom as if off a springboard.

"Did you want me, Mummy?" Then, seeing the dress in Cathy's hands. "Are you pleased? They took simply ages to sew on. I had to do it standing up because I went to sleep sitting down."

Cathy kissed Ginnie.

"So pleased I could hug you to bits. But I'm afraid I can't wear it quite like this. I'm afraid three sorts of flowers at once wouldn't look suitable, and you know what Uncle Alfred is about things being suitable. Vicars' wives don't wear three sorts of flowers at the same time."

Ginnie could not believe her flowers were to be taken off the dress.

"But, Mummy, they took simply hours to sew on."

"I'm sure they did, darling, but you wouldn't want me to go to a party unsuitably dressed, would you?"

Ginnie felt a great lump swell up in her throat. After all, wasn't her mother pleased? Wasn't it a lovely surprise? Her voice sounded as if there was a lump in her throat.

"I don't think you'd be unsuitably dressed. To me you'd look like a queen."

Alex took a hand.

"Uncle Alfred doesn't expect Mummy to look like a queen—he expects her to look like a vicar's wife."

Cathy saw Ginnie was near tears.

"Look, darling, you must accept that vicars' wives only

wear one sort of flower. The question is, which? You must choose."

Ginnie gazed first at the violets, then at the roses, then at the daisies. They had all taken so long to sew on. They all looked so perfect. It was dreadful to think of any of them being cut off again.

"If it can be only one sort, then I know which it must be. The roses. I think they are the crimsonest roses there ever were in the world. You can see them for miles and miles."

5

The Party

Grandfather, Grandmother, Aunt Rose, Uncle Alfred, and Veronica were waiting in the foyer of Covent Garden Theatre. Grandfather was rather a fierce-looking man, with a red face and bristly white hair.

"What time are you expecting Alex and his family, Alfred?"

Alfred was important-looking. The sort of man you could guess made a lot of money. If you looked at him carefully you could see he could be Alex's elder brother, for he had the same brown hair and eyes; but there were two great differences. Alex was very thin, and Alfred was growing fat, especially in front. Alex was pale, but Alfred's face was red. It was extra red as he looked at his watch, for he hated anything he had arranged not to happen exactly on time.

"Should have been here five minutes ago. If there's one thing I dislike more than another it is to be kept waiting."

Grandmother was a plump little woman with neat gray hair. She looked as if her clothes were made by an upholsterer rather than a dressmaker. She had rather a sharp way of speaking, but it was mostly a way of speaking, for inside she was very kind in a bossy way. Her eyes were full of amusement as she looked at Alfred. He might seem a successful businessman and a knight to other people, but to her he was still her boy Alfred. She had lived all her life in Bradford, and was proud everyone should hear it when she spoke.

"Don't fuss, Alfred, lad. You always fussed as a child. That's one thing I will say for your brother Alex, he was never a fusser."

Rose was a fair-haired, pretty, most beautifully dressed woman, but she was spoiled by her voice. It was the whiny voice of someone who has had far more nice things in her life than she expected, and has grown whinier each year, as she found there were no new things to wish for.

"I suppose they were none of them ready when the car came. You know what a muddle they live in."

Veronica took after her mother only more so. She was prettier than her mother had ever been, and she had a far whinier voice. She had on a blue dress made of organdy. Over it she wore a little ermine cape. She twisted around so that her very full skirt billowed out.

"I'm never late, am I, Mumsie?"

Grandmother thought Veronica looked a picture, but she also thought, if she had her to herself, she would get her out of her affected ways, or know the reason why. She said briskly:

"Don't mess that dress up, Veronica. It's sweetly pretty."

Veronica grew more prancy than ever.

"Mumsie says blue's my color."

Rose looked dotingly at Veronica.

"You look nice in anything, pet." Then she turned to Grandmother. "I really wanted her to wear her new long dress, she looks a dream in it, but it was no good suggest-

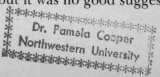

ing evening clothes, Alex and Cathy haven't any. The only decent clothes Cathy has are my castoffs."

Grandfather tapped Alfred on the shoulder.

"Don't forget Paul is to sit next to me. You take the rest of them out for refreshments at intermission and give me time to have a word alone with him. I don't believe he'll stick to this doctor nonsense when he hears what I have to say."

Veronica put her hand in her grandfather's.

"Don't you wish I was a boy, Grandfather? Then I could come to Bradford."

Alfred for a second stopped looking at his watch and looked instead at Veronica. He thought she was perfect.

"I wouldn't change my little girlie for a son. Dada's proud of his pet."

Grandfather ran a finger through one of Veronica's curls.

" 'Twouldn't have done no good if you had been a boy. You'd have gone in with your father at the London end."

Grandmother's voice rang out sharply.

"Got too grand for Bradford, haven't you, lad, now you're Sir Alfred, and director of City companies and all?"

"Look! There they are. There are the cousins." Veronica jumped in the air and waved. "Oh-oo!"

Grandmother was shocked.

"Never thought to hear you making a noise like that, Veronica. You sound as if you were at fun fair at Blackpool."

Rose took Veronica's hand.

"Stand quiet, pet. They've seen us."

Alex and the children pushed through the crowd; Cathy hid herself behind them. There were kisses and handshakes and "Happy birthdays" for Angus. Then Cathy came into view. Rose had her face forward to kiss her. When she saw the flowers her mouth opened in a gasp. Cathy pulled her to her, and while pretending to kiss her whispered fiercely:

"Don't say anything about them. I know how they look, I'll explain later."

Veronica held both hands over her mouth and giggled.

"Oo. . . . Aunt Cathy, you do look funny!"

Jane saw Aunt Rose's face and heard Veronica's giggle. She had never looked prettier, her eyes were shining as if there were stars in them, but suddenly the stars went out and she flushed. Grandmother was the only other who had seen and heard what happened. She was not having Jane's evening spoiled by anything so ridiculous as a few flowers on a dress, however terrible they looked.

"What a pretty dress, Jane. I don't know when I saw a prettier. It's new, isn't it?"

Back came the stars.

"Isn't it gorgeous? Mummy made it. We bought the stuff together."

Alfred flapped around like an agitated hen.

"Quiet, everybody. No one enjoys an evening's fun more than I do, but what I say is, there is no pleasure without organization. Now this is how you sit. First you, Ginnie, then you, Veronica, pet."

"Where's the birthday boy sitting?" asked Grandmother.

"On the other side of Veronica. That's the right place, isn't it, Angus, next to your little hostess?"

Angus thought Uncle Alfred was honoring his birthday by letting him choose where he would sit. In that case he certainly was not going to sit next to Veronica.

"Well, Uncle Alfred, if I can choose . . ."

Cathy felt as a family they were sufficiently out of favor already. It was not their fault traffic had held up the car, and it was not her fault about the roses; still, there was no need for Angus to make things worse.

"That'll be lovely, won't it, Angus? Who's sitting on Angus's other side, Alfred?"

"His Grandmother. Then Jane. Then me. I've put my-self right in the middle. Then you, Cathy, on my right. Then Rose. Then Alex. Then Grandfather. Then Paul."

Uncle Alfred did everything in the grandest way. As they reached the end of their row of seats, his voice boomed out telling the usher he would have eleven programs.

"What I say is, when you're out to enjoy yourself, let yourself go and enjoy yourself. If programs add to the evening's pleasure, they are worth the extra expense."

Paul caught Jane's eye. Of course they could not say so, but they thought extra money spent on programs a wicked waste, it was so easy to share programs.

Ginnie pushed her way to her seat with her chin stuck in the air. She had promised before they started to be as nice as she could to Veronica, but that was before she knew she had to sit next to her, with nobody on her other side to talk to.

"It's mean," she whispered. "Mean. Mean. Mean. No-body could be nice to Veronica who had to sit next to her only all the evening. I'd sooner be dead."

Veronica, skipping along behind Grannie, called out:

"Be careful you don't put your seat down on my dress, Ginnie. There's so many yards in my skirt really I need two seats."

Ginnie wished she had thought of putting down her seat on the dress. It would have done her good to hear it tear. Instead she sat down with her back half turned to Veronica.

"There's hardly any stuff in my dress, thank goodness. It was Jane's first, and yellow doesn't suit me. So there's nothing you can say will make me feel worse in it. Now, please don't talk, I'm going to read my program."

Cathy leaned forward and looked anxiously at Ginnie, Veronica, and Angus. All seemed well. Ginnie was quietly reading her program, and Angus was talking to Grandmother. It would have been better if one of them were talking to Veronica, but at least they were not quarreling.

"Have you had a lot of presents, Angus?" Grandmother was asking. "Grandfather will give you our present at supper."

Angus beamed at her.

"Do you know, I had a Morse code buzzer. I wanted to bring it to the theater, but Mummy wouldn't let me."

Cathy, satisfied that for the moment her family were remembering their party manners, turned to Rose.

"I want to explain these roses."

Rose listened to Cathy's explanation of what had happened, but she could not understand how Cathy felt.

"But surely you might have thought of us. Imagine if we run into any of my friends. What can I say?"

Cathy could see it was hard on Rose. Nobody likes guests who wear the sort of clothes that make other people laugh.

"I simply couldn't insult Ginnie by cutting all the flowers off."

"If you felt like that I think you might have covered them with a coat."

That made Cathy cross.

"In this temperature? Besides, I've only got a very

shabby one, not a bit suitable for this lovely theater." Cathy saw Rose had some more to say, so she added firmly: "You'll have to put up with me, Rose, flowers and all. I'm not going to let them spoil the ballet for me, and if you're wise you'll forget about them, too, and just enjoy yourself."

Alex had not heard this conversation, for he was talking to his father. He had read his program. They were to see "Les Sylphides," "Symphonic Variations," and "Les Patineurs."

"I'm afraid this won't be much in your line, Father."

Grandfather dug his elbow in a meaning way into Alex.

"You're right, Alex, lad. But it seems smart thing to go to ballet." He pronounced it bal-ett. "Rose and Alfred do nothing but go to the best places. For myself I like a right good laugh."

"So do I, Grandfather," said Paul.

Grandfather was pleased.

"Shouldn't wonder if you and I had a lot in common, young man."

Grandmother could not get over how pretty Jane looked. She stroked her flowered skirt.

"This is pretty, love."

Jane had been straining to hear, through Uncle Alfred's booming talk, how her mother was getting on with Aunt Rose. She could not see Cathy's face because it was turned the other way, but she could see Aunt Rose's and it looked sneering. But on such an evening she could not worry for long. She turned to Grandmother a face shining with happiness.

"Imagine, a new dress and the ballet all on one night! I'm so happy I feel I could float. Do you ever feel floatish, Grandmother?"

Before Grandmother could answer, everyone in the theater was clapping the conductor, who had just taken his place on his rostrum. He tapped the rail in front of him with his baton, and Chopin's Sylphides music seemed to fill the theater with moonlight. Jane felt pleasure that hurt like pain. She clasped her arms to hold the pleasure to her. She spoke in a whisper.

"I think the moments before the curtain goes up are too glorious to be really happening."

At intermission Uncle Alfred, as he had promised, led everybody outside for refreshments. Paul was going, too, but Grandfather stopped him.

"I arranged with your uncle to leave us, as I want a word alone with you, and maybe this is my only chance, for we go back north tomorrow. Now, no beating about the bush. I want you in Bradford in my business. I'm right glad you won that scholarship, but schools can't teach you everything. As soon as you have your general certificate I want you to come to me to learn the wool trade. I'll start you at bottom, but you'll soon work up, and one day a fine share of all I have will be yours."

"But I want to be a doctor. You know that, Grandfather."

"I know you've talked about it since you were a little lad, but you're growing up now, and I reckon it's time you saw sense. It'll cost a pile of brass to turn you into a doctor, and if you have it the others will go short."

Paul hated that.

"But I shan't cost money—I mean to do it all on scholarships."

"It'll take time, and who's keeping you all those years? From what I hear you could take your general certificate next year, and from then on you'd be earning. Think what that would mean to your father's pocket."

Paul felt his will weakening. He wanted to be a doctor, he knew he ought to be a doctor. But it was going to take years, and money was very short. Perhaps even if you were sure you would make a good doctor, and certain you were not cut out for the wool business, you ought to do it if it meant helping your family. What Grandfather had said about the others going short had hit a sore place. When money crises arose at home, or Jane's not being able to learn dancing was talked about, Paul always felt miserable. Everybody else had to do without things and here was he cheerfully going ahead, planning a career which meant he would not be self-supporting for years.

"Do you mind if I say something which might sound rude?"

"I was never afraid of words. They don't break bones."

"I don't want to go into the wool business, you know that. But sometimes, especially now after what you've said, I might. . . . I mean the time might come when I'd think I'd have to."

"Well?"

Paul swallowed nervously.

"This sounds awful. Suppose I ever did think I'd give up the idea of being a doctor, and came to you, would you give Dad an allowance?" He saw Grandfather's face turning purple, so he added quickly: "Only until I am earning enough to give him one myself."

Grandfather made angry, spluttering sounds before he spoke.

"When your father went into the Church I said he'd not have any of my money, and he never has. You little whippersnapper you, trying to get me to go back on my word."

96

Paul was so scared of Grandfather's temper, and that he would raise his voice so the people in the row behind could hear, that he spoke more bravely than he felt.

"I'm not trying to make you go back on your word. But you must see my side. If I give up being a doctor, and leave school as soon as I have my certificate, to help my family, I must feel I *am* helping them. If a person gives up what they most want to do to do something they don't want to do, there must be a reward of some sort. You do see that, Grandfather."

"The reward is that you'll be a rich man some day."

"I don't want to be a rich man, I want to be a doctor, so there would have to be some other reward to make me say I'd do it."

Grandfather, though Paul could not see it, had the beginning of a twinkle in his eyes.

"Is that your last word?"

"Yes."

Grandfather lay back and put his hands in his pockets.

"I like a man or a boy who can state his price and stick to it. Very well. I want you and I'm prepared to pay for what I want. The day you decide to throw up this doctoring nonsense and join me I'll settle a good allowance on you. But, mind you, it's your allowance and not your father's; I said he should never have a penny of my brass and he never shall, but I can't prevent you doing what you like with your own money, can I? Now, I don't expect you to decide tonight, but you think things over. Then you sit down and write me, privately of course. The letter is your bond. On the day I receive it your allowance will start."

Paul saw the others were coming back to their seats. A terrible lot seemed to have happened while they were gone. Grandfather seemed to think everything was more or less settled.

"You do know I haven't decided yet, and quite likely I never will."

Grandfather felt pretty safe.

"There's no great hurry. But the sooner I get that letter the sooner that allowance starts."

Nobody could say Aunt Rose and Uncle Alfred did not give good parties. There was a glorious cold supper waiting, which started with iced soup, then a choice of lobster or chicken, and afterwards strawberries and cream, ice cream, and other frozen desserts. In spite of the splendid food, it was not an easy party.

Jane had been so carried away by the ballet that now that it was over she felt squeezed out like a sucked orange.

Cathy felt nervous. Angus was looking odd. He had looked odd at intermission, but now he looked odder. He would not say a word, in fact he seemed half asleep; she did hope he was not going to disgrace them by being sick. She had asked him three times if he felt all right, and each time he had at first seemed to find it hard to hear what she said, but then had answered, "Of course I am."

Paul had scarcely seen the last two ballets. Questions chased each other round and round in his head. Could he ask his father or mother what they thought? No, of course not, they would only think of him. Could it be right to spend your whole life doing something you didn't want to do, and might not be good at? How soon would he have to make up his mind? What would his school say if he left as soon as he had his general certificate? These thoughts were still nagging at him during supper.

Alex, though he knew well how it felt not to want to

talk, for he often felt like that himself, was afraid Rose and Alfred might think Paul was not enjoying their party.

"You're very silent, old man. I suppose you can't talk and do justice to this magnificent supper at the same time."

Ginnie was in a bad temper. So much party food cheered her up quite a lot, but a whole evening of Veronica could not be got over by food, however splendid. Inside she was still growling.

"Your family are a speechless lot, Alex," said Uncle Alfred, as the last of the strawberries and other desserts disappeared. "Maybe there's something outside will make them talk." He went into the next room and, after a pause to light eight candles, came back with a magnificent chocolate birthday cake. He put it in the center of the table. "How's that, Angus? Never had as fine a cake as that, did you?"

Angus was sitting between Veronica and Aunt Rose, so he could not be nudged by his family. Cathy, from across the table, said urgently:

"Thank Uncle Alfred and Aunt Rose, Angus. Such a beautiful cake."

Jane, who was sitting on the other side of Uncle Alfred, caught the urgency in her mother's voice. She leaned backwards and behind Uncle Alfred's back gave Angus a poke.

"Say thank you, Angus."

Veronica twittered:

"On my last birthday there were pink roses and blue ribbons on my cake, weren't there, Mumsie?"

Rose thought how bright and gay Veronica was, and how dull her cousins.

"That's right, you did, pet, and you had a pink dress with blue ribbons to match the cake."

Ginnie, sitting next to Grandfather, opened her mouth to say something rude, but Cathy, fearing trouble, spoke first.

"We've all eaten so much I'm afraid there won't be much room for cake."

Veronica giggled.

"Terrible if we all burst."

Ginnie thought that a very Veronica-ish remark.

"A girl who burst because of a little bit of birthday cake would be a pretty miserable sort of person."

Grandmother felt the party needed cheering up.

"You must cut your cake, Angus."

"He's got to blow the candles out before he cuts it," said Veronica.

Alex became conscious for the first time that Angus was taking very little interest in his party. He said, in an aren't-we-having-a-good-time voice:

"That's right, old man. All eight in one breath."

Slowly, and without interest, Angus got to his feet, leaned over the cake, and gave a blow that would have disgraced a one-year-old.

"Oh, Angus, you are a silly boy," said Veronica. "Only three. I'm only a girl but I blew out all mine at my last birthday, didn't I, Dada, and I had nine to blow out."

Alfred thought Angus was a poor birthday guest.

"You did, pet. I'm afraid Angus isn't very interested in his cake."

Alex came around the table.

"I'll help you cut it, Angus." He put the knife into Angus's hands and his own over them. "It's a magnificent cake, Alfred. It's like cutting through a mountain, isn't it, Angus?"

Alfred was glad somebody was appreciative.

"The best that money can buy. Give me the slices as you cut them. I'll pass them around."

Grandfather felt in his pocket.

"I've got something for you here, Angus."

Alex gave Angus a push.

"Go to Grandfather and see what he's got for you. I'll finish cutting the cake."

Angus came slowly around to Grandfather, who put his arm around him.

"Your grandmother and I didn't know what you wanted, Angus, so I said I know what I'll do, I'll give him a five-pound note and let him choose something for himself."

The Bells were seldom given presents in the form of money. They all thought Angus very lucky. Jane said:

"Angus! What a lot of money! Imagine what you can buy with it!"

The five-pound note seemed to have woken Angus up. He flung his arms around Grandfather's neck. "Thank you awfully, Grandfather." Then he raced around the table and hugged Grandmother. Grandfather was amused at the effect the money had had on his grandson.

"What are you planning to buy with it, Angus?"

Uncle Alfred, though he was prepared to spend money when there was a reason for it, was a great believer in thrift.

"Saving it, I hope."

Rose thought in a family as poor as Angus's, money should go on necessities.

"I'm sure Cathy knows something Angus needs."

Veronica did not like other people being the center of attention.

"I've got a money box simply full of money I've saved, haven't I, Mumsie?"

Angus was still standing by Grandmother. He looked at Grandfather, his dark eyes shining.

"I know exactly what I'm going to do with this money, Grandfather. I'm going to buy a pair of shoes like those men danced in tonight. Then I'm going to the Royal Ballet School to ask them to make me into a dancer."

This sounded so unlike Angus that everyone thought he was being funny. Cathy said:

"Darling! Imagine you a ballet dancer!"

Alex laughed.

"I think you'll get along better in the choir school, old man."

Angus did not seem to know that nobody thought he meant what he had said.

"I'm going to be a dancer like that one who spun around and around when he pretended he was skating. I'm going to be the best dancer in the world, I abs'lutely know it, and it won't be any good anybody arguing. It's my money, Grandfather gave it to me to do what I like with, and that's what I'm going to do with it, nobody's going to stop me."

As Angus was talking, Jane realized he was not being funny. He meant every word he was saying, and she felt very sorry for him.

"But, Angus, shoes aren't enough. I've had shoes for a long time, you know I have, and you know I've always wanted to go to the Royal Ballet School. But it costs heaps and heaps of money."

Seeing the ballet seemed to have changed Angus; he was quite unlike himself.

"I'll arrange it somehow, Jane. I'm going to be the greatest dancer in the world, so not having enough money won't stop me."

Grandfather, winking at everybody to be sure they enjoyed the joke, beckoned Angus to come to him. He laughed so much he could hardly speak.

"A male dancer, eh? That's something new in our family. I don't remember either your father or your Uncle Alfred showing much talent in that direction."

"But I've got talent . . ." Angus broke off and rubbed a finger in a puzzled way up and down Grandfather's sleeve. "I always knew I didn't want to sing, but I like the noise music makes. Tonight the first moment the ballet music started my feet knew what they wanted to do. You all thought I was sitting still, but I wasn't. Right inside, where you couldn't see, my legs were dancing. Now all I've got to do is to learn steps."

Grandfather let out a great roar of laughter.

"All you've got to do is learn steps! You'll be the death of me, Angus. But I always did enjoy a good laugh, and you've given me one, so I tell you what"—he winked again at the family—"you go to this dancing school and tell them just what you've told me, and if they'll take you I'll pay for your lessons."

Suddenly the joke stopped being a joke. If Grandfather was willing to pay for someone to learn dancing, would he consider Jane? It was almost too much to hope, but it was worth a try. Giving Alex a look to say "Leave it to me," Cathy said:

"We've all been a bit carried away by the ballet. It's wonderful of you to suggest paying for Angus to have lessons, but in a day or two I daresay he won't want them. Jane . . ."

Angus was furious.

"I will, Mummy, I abs'lutely know I will."

"Perhaps, darling, but I think you are old enough to see that if anyone goes to the Royal Ballet School it must be Jane." Cathy turned to Grandfather. "If you really mean you would pay, would you let Jane go for an audition? She's worked terribly hard, and she has talent, honestly she has."

Jane could not speak; somewhere inside her she had always believed a miracle would happen, and here it was, but Ginnie was full of words.

"She dances gorgeously, Grandfather. I simply detest dancing, but Jane's marvelous, everybody says she is."

Alex never had asked his father for help, but this time the offer had been made.

"She is good. It would be money well spent."

Grandfather had stopped laughing and was turning purple. He was sorry he had said he would pay for Angus, but he had not supposed he would be taken seriously.

"You're wasting words, all of you. I'll spend my brass the way I've a fancy. I won't go back on my promise—if Angus can make that dancing school take him, and you say he can go, Alex, I'll pay—but that's my offer and there's no more to it."

Grandmother could not understand why usually reasonable people like Alex and Cathy were being so foolish.

"Father'd never pay for dancing lessons for Jane—you know that, Alex. Letting little Angus have a lesson or two won't hurt anyone, but Jane is a different matter. You don't want to fill a girl's head with silly ideas. If she takes extra classes they should be in a kitchen, where she'll learn to make a good man happy some day."

Uncle Alfred thought his mother so right he almost clapped.

"You never spoke a truer word."

Veronica was puzzled.

"But you never let me go in the kitchen, Dada."

Uncle Alfred was bursting with pride in Veronica. He thought it was a shame how plain, shabby, and dull her poor cousins appeared beside her. That he was bursting with pride showed in his voice.

"Things are different for you, Veronica, pet. When you marry there'll be no need for you to do your own cooking; Dada will see to that."

"All the same, you must know how things should be done," Rose said. "When you leave school Dada will send you to a finishing school, and you'll learn some cooking there."

Since Grandmother had said Grandfather would not pay for Jane to learn dancing, Ginnie had been seething with rage. This talk about Veronica and finishing schools was the end. She said, as if her words were a cork bursting out of a bottle:

"That'll be a waste of time, Veronica. Even if you learn to cook you'll never make a good man happy, or a bad one either." There were horrified hushes and "Be quiet, Ginnie," and "Shut up" from Cathy, Alex, and Paul, and a faint "Don't, Ginnie" from Jane, but nothing stopped Ginnie. "I don't care. I'm going to say what I want to say. I'm glad Angus is going to learn dancing, if he wants to, though goodness knows why he wants to, but I don't see why everybody's siding against poor Jane. . . ."

105

Only by the most terrific willpower was Jane holding back tears. There was to be no miracle. When, for a moment, you had believed one to be about to happen, that was bad enough, but for years to have longed and worked for a miracle and then to see it performed for another member of the family, that was too much. But Ginnie mustn't be cross, it would do no good. She said in a strangled voice, which forced its way through the lump in her throat:

"Don't, Ginnie. Please don't."

"It's no good saying, 'Don't, Ginnie,' and it's no good frowning, Mummy, or saying 'Hush,' Daddy. It was very kind of Uncle Alfred and Aunt Rose to take us to the ballet, but that doesn't mean they can tell Veronica things are different for her than they are for Jane, just because they're rich and we're poor."

Everybody, except Jane, who dare not speak again, and Angus, who was dreaming he was dancing in a ballet, tried to stop Ginnie. Uncle Alfred with a pompous "Well really!" Grandmother with a shocked "Be quiet, Ginnie, love." Grandfather with a roared "Shut your trap, Ginnie." Alex with a sharp "Ginnie!" Cathy with "Ginnie, be quiet." Paul with "Oh, I say, do shut up." Veronica with an excited "Ooh, isn't Ginnie naughty!" But none of them had any effect. Ginnie meant to go on until she had said everything she wanted to say.

"Everybody in our family knows Jane's wanted to go to a dancing school for years and years and years, and when the chance comes you all get grand and despising and say she must go and work in a kitchen. . . ."

Glances exchanged between Alfred and Rose got Paul, Jane, and Alex to their feet. Cathy said:

"I'm sure the car must be here, Alfred."

Uncle Alfred nodded, and opened the door.

"It'll be outside. Can't you keep your child in order, Alex? Pity the evening should be spoilt for everyone by such unpleasantness."

Alex had hold of a still muttering Ginnie, and was pushing her in front of him into the hall.

"It's not meant as unpleasantness. It's just strong family feeling."

Alfred was not having that.

"Call it what you like, but it's downright rudeness."

"Bad upbringing," said Rose.

Veronica skipped into the hall to enjoy the last of the fuss.

"I'm never rude, am I, Mumsie?"

Grandmother was sorry for Cathy.

"You should take a slipper to her, dear. I'd have taken a slipper to Alfred and Alex if they'd behaved this way when they were Ginnie's age."

Uncle Alfred thought everybody was passing off the affair too lightly.

"It's the ingratitude, Ginnie. That's what I can't get over."

Cathy knew Ginnie; in her present state it was no good talking to her. She was thoroughly roused over what she considered a just cause. The great thing was to get her safely into the car, where she could calm down. It was urgent, too, to get Jane into the car: she wouldn't hold out much longer. She turned to Uncle Alfred.

"Ginnie's been very naughty, but you can trust Alex and me to deal with her."

Ginnie thought all this apologizing and scolding was humiliating; it was Uncle Alfred and Aunt Rose who were wrong.

"Don't bother with them, Mummy. Let them talk and sneer and sneer like they do. We don't care, do we? As a matter of fact it's done me so much good telling them what we think of them I shan't care how you and Daddy deal with me." Then she pulled away from Alex's restraining hands and dashed across the hall to Veronica, who was swinging on the end of the banister. "As for you, Veronica, I think you're a spoilt stuck-up mimsy-pimsy minx. I've always thought so, and now I'm very glad I've told you."

In a second Grandfather had picked Ginnie up in his arms and she was outside the front door and in the car.

"You're a bad girl, Ginnie, and I hope your father takes a slipper to you." Then he chuckled. "But you're a chip off the old block and I like your spirit. Your father couldn't say boo to a goose."

Alex, Cathy, and Paul tried to make their good-byes sound as if it was the end of any ordinary party, but they were not successful, and everybody except Angus, who had not known anything was wrong, and Ginnie, who was still bubbling with things she wanted to say, was thankful when the car started.

"Ough," said Paul, "that was a sticky evening! Whatever got into you, Ginnie?"

Alex's voice had never sounded sterner.

"I'm very angry indeed. . . ."

Cathy had her arms around Jane. She could feel her shaking with the sobs she could no longer hold back. Luckily Angus was in front with the chauffeur.

"Shut the windows between us and the front of the car, Paul. Leave scolding Ginnie until we get home, Alex. Jane, Jane, darling . . ."

Jane gasped through strangling sobs.

"I'm sorry, everybody, but I must cry. I did hold back crying while I was there, didn't I, Mummy? They didn't see I was going to cry, did they? Oh, I hope Veronica didn't see. I don't want to be mean or jealous. If Angus wants to learn to dance I'm glad he's going to. But to be paid for! They'll take him . . . I feel it in my bones they'll take him. Him to go to the Royal Ballet School and not me! I can't bear it. I simply can't bear it."

6

Disaster

Every time Cathy remembered Angus's birthday party she shuddered, and try as she would she could not help remembering it, for the effects of it went on and on.

First there was Ginnie. Alex and Cathy hated punishments, so there were as few as possible, and what there were had to be suitable for the crime committed; but what punishment was suitable for being rude to relations? In the end Alex decided Ginnie would not have been rude if she had not been overtired. Of course the cure for that was bed, so for a whole week Ginnie had to go to bed the moment she came home from school. Ginnie was grand about her punishment.

"As a matter of fact Miss Virginia Bell is quite glad to go to bed, she gets bored hearing people talk, talk, talk, all the time."

Of course it was not true, and everybody knew it was not true, and all the family felt miserable for Ginnie, and they missed her as well. Angus missed her for an odd reason.

"It's so dull having no one to quarrel with."

But Ginnie's punishment was a passing trouble. Angus learning dancing instead of Jane hung like a cloud over the vicarage, and Angus made Jane's unhappiness worse. He never realized how terrible she was feeling, and rushed around to everybody showing his letter from Grandfather, saying he had meant what he had said, and if the Royal Ballet School would take him he would pay. His head was so full of the idea of learning to dance that he did not notice that his family and Mrs. Gage were not at all keen to hear the letter read out loud. Alex and Cathy had a long discussion in the study with the door shut.

"If only," said Cathy, "we could find a way to pay for Jane to go too. It'll be heartbreaking if Angus learns and she doesn't."

But they could not think of a way to pay, though they considered everything, from selling their furniture to parting with a life insurance policy. What in the end they decided to do was to go and see Miss Newton, the head of St. Winifred's, and ask her advice.

Miss Newton was a very headmistressy-looking headmistress, with neat hair, severely cut coats and skirts, and rather perched spectacles. She had a cool, brusque, don't-be-foolish-dear manner, but underneath she was a most understanding person. She was glad to see Alex and Cathy, because she had noticed something was wrong with Jane, and when she heard what it was she was really upset.

"Poor child! No wonder she looks so wretched. It really is a cruel business. Everybody knows she has talent, and to see lessons wasted on her brother, who probably will have lost interest in dancing in six months!" She sat silent for a bit, thinking. Then she said: "Let us write to the Royal for you. Miss Bronson knows somebody there. I don't suppose for a moment it's the regular time for auditions, but perhaps, as a kindness, they would not only see Angus to put you all out of your misery, but see Jane too. I'll explain you can't afford the fees, but that we all want to know how much promise she shows."

It was no wonder Miss Newton had noticed something was wrong with Jane, for she was feeling as low-spirited as if she was getting well after influenza. She could not remember a time when she had not longed for proper dancing lessons, but neither could she remember a time when she had not known her father was too poor to pay for them. It had been easy not too mind too much, because good dancing lessons were like a television set, or a car, terribly wanted but things they all knew they could not have. But now good dancing lessons had come off the list of things nobody could have, and at once not having them became an injury that never stopped aching. Supposing the Royal Ballet School took Angus, how was she to endure seeing him go there while she went to dancing lessons at St. Winifred's? To make Jane's life more difficult, Angus spent every waking moment doing what he called dancing, and of course it was not remotely like dancing. Clumsy efforts to imitate the dancers he had seen, great leaps in the air, arms waving, feet anywhere, usually finishing in a crash with him on the floor, and chairs overturned. Cathy said it was nonsense Miss Bronson bothering the Royal to audition him, they would only laugh, but Jane thought she was wrong.

"If he was a girl it would be different, but I wouldn't wonder if they let him have lessons for a bit, just to see if they can do anything with him. There is always a shortage of men dancers."

As if Jane being sunk in gloom and Ginnie being punished were not enough for one family to endure, Paul seemed to Cathy and Alex to be behaving peculiarly.

112

Usually he came home from school full of talk about the day's doings, but that week he came home looking, as Cathy complained to Alex, bowed with worries, which of course he was. It was all right as long as he was doing something, either work or games, but the moment he had nothing to do it was as if a door in his brain opened and in popped a question mark. Should he give up the idea of being a doctor? Should he write to Grandfather? Each day he went to bed deciding to write in the morning, and each morning he woke up deciding to think a little longer before he wrote.

Cathy was always glad to see her relations, but she had never looked forward to seeing them as much as she looked forward to seeing them that Saturday. Mrs. Gage, who of course knew all about the Jane trouble, was almost as glad as Cathy when Saturday arrived. It was a lovely morning, and she came in beaming.

" 'Ere's Saturday at last. And very nice too. Do you good, dear, to 'ave a look at your Dad and Mum. 'Eard from that dancin' school yet?"

Cathy was cooking kippers for breakfast. She gave one of them a gloomy prod.

"No. We might hear from Miss Bronson this morning."

Mrs. Gage tied on her scrubbing apron.

"I was talkin' to Mr. Gage about it last night. Won't 'alf be cruel, I said, if our Angus goes to that school, while our Jane keeps on at St. Winifred's, and do you know what 'e said?"

Cathy did not know, and did not really care, for what Mr. Gage thought would not help.

"What?"

" 'E said if 'e was the vicar 'e'd preach about it in church, and 'ave a collection took."

Cathy nearly upset the pan of kippers.

"Mrs. Gage! What an idea!"

"Well, why not? Ask for things for anybody but 'is own family the vicar will. Foreign missions, churches eaten by beetles, and I don't know what all. If I 'ad the gift what the vicar 'as, I'd lean right out of the pulpit and I'd say: 'This mornin' I'm goin' to preach a sermon about me daughter and 'er dancin'.' "

Cathy laughed a real proper laugh for the first time since Angus's birthday party.

"Get along with you! Go and sound the gong; the kippers are ready."

The gong was under the stairs. Mrs. Gage picked it up and was just going to beat it when a hand came through the banisters, and Ginnie's voice whispered:

"Mrs. Gage! Mrs. Gage! Look!"

Mrs. Gage looked. She almost dropped the gong. The face looking over the banisters was swelled out on one side like a soccer ball.

"Oh, my goodness! No need to measure this mornin'."

Ginnie was nearly crying.

"I thought I was safe. If I was going to get mumps I ought to have by now."

Mrs. Gage was making plans.

"Anyone seen you?"

"No. Not even Jane. She got up early to do extra dancing practice, in case they'll see her at the Royal Ballet."

"Well, back to bed quick, and lie on the side what's swole."

"If I don't come down to breakfast Mummy'll come up and see me."

Mrs. Gage gestured to Ginnie to hurry.

"I'll tell 'er I've seen you. I'll say you've one of your

bilious turns, which is all it may be. I'll say I've give you some salts to sleep it off. Soon as I can I'll be up. 'Op it now."

Cathy accepted Mrs. Gage's statement about Ginnie quite calmly. She did sometimes have bilious turns, and usually was quite all right after a dose of salts. In any case there was something else to think of that morning. There was a letter from Miss Bronson. As it happened there was an audition on the following Wednesday. The school had written to say that Cathy could bring both Jane and Angus to it.

As soon as breakfast was safely started Mrs. Gage crept up the stairs and into Ginnie's room. Ginnie raised a very hot-looking swollen face, and tears rolled down her cheeks.

"I never knew mumps would hurt so awfully. I suppose I've got them as a judgment like you said."

Mrs. Gage sat on the bed and made clicking, worried noises.

"Funny it comin' on now. This is a nice caper, this is. Whatever will your poor Mum say? No good worritting 'er before we need. Just as soon as she goes out shoppin' you an' me'll slip 'round to the doctor's."

Ginnie choked back a sob.

"I don't feel like slipping anywhere. You wouldn't believe how it hurts. It's like a bear biting and biting."

Mrs. Gage got up.

"I better go down before I'm missed. I'll catch Jane. She'll 'ave to see to the front door. Directly I tip you off you get your clothes on. We'll 'ave to find a big scarf to cover that face. We don't want the 'ole parish askin' what's wrong."

Jane found the news she was to go to the Royal Ballet School for an audition made her feel a tiny bit less low-spirited. It would not be any good, but she would have been inside and seen what the school was like, and that was something, and if by any glorious chance they said she showed promise, it would be a great deal. Feeling more like dancing than she had for days she went into the hall after breakfast to get in some extra practice before she helped Mrs. Gage with the beds.

Mrs. Gage, scrubbing the hall, kept track of all the family. She heard Alex shut himself in his study to finish his sermon, Paul take his books to his bedroom, and Cathy, Angus, and Esau start out with a list and a shopping bag. Then she came to Jane. She spoke in a whisper.

"Keep on with your dancin', dear, but you'll 'ave to answer the bells an' that. I got to slip out for a minute. It's Ginnie." Her whisper became dramatic. "Her face is swelled up somethin' fierce."

Jane stopped dancing.

"It can't be! We'll all be in quarantine! No audition on Wednesday! No zoo!"

Mrs. Gage looked anxiously at the study door.

"No need to make a fuss, dear. It may not be the mumps, but I'm takin' 'er to the doctor in case. Now, if your mum comes 'ome before we're back, whatever you do keep 'er downstairs. No good 'er gettin' upset before she needs, poor dear."

Jane sounded bitter.

"Of course it's mumps. Nothing else makes you swell. Does it?"

Mrs. Gage tried to sound hopeful.

"Could be other things I s'pose. But from what you and me know it looks peculiar like. Still, never say die."

Ginnie, muffled in a big scarf, was hurried by Mrs. Gage out of the back door.

"Now, look, dear. Whatever 'appens, keep your face covered, you don't want to get cold in it. Nor you don't want to speak to nobody, in case you're infectious like. So if anyone tries to speak to you, don't open your mouth."

Although many people knew Ginnie, they were mostly busy and did not notice that only Mrs. Gage answered when they called out "Good morning." Then suddenly there was the sound of a bicycle braking, and Miss Bloggs stood in front of them.

"Good morning, Mrs. Gage. Good morning, Ginnie, dear. Is your father in?"

Mrs. Gage gave Ginnie a nudge to move on.

"The vicar's in 'is study."

Miss Bloggs was a chatty person.

"Looking forward to the zoo this afternoon, Ginnie?"

Mrs. Gage gave Ginnie another push.

"Lookin' forward to ridin' on an elephant she is."

Miss Bloggs peered curiously at Ginnie and her scarf.

"You're very silent, dear. Is anything wrong?"

Mrs. Gage tried to sound pleasant.

" 'Er and me are out on a bit of a secret like. So we'd take it kindly if you didn't tell the vicar you'd met us."

Miss Bloggs was charmed .

"A secret! What fun. I love secrets. You can trust me, Ginnie. I never saw a sign of you this morning."

Miss Bloggs was in the study with Alex when Cathy, Angus, and Esau came back from shopping. Cathy, knowing Mrs. Gage would want the vegetables for lunch, gave her a call. Paul heard her and came down the stairs.

"I don't believe Mrs. Gage is in, Mum. Jane's been answering the front door."

Cathy could not have been more surprised. In all the years they had known Mrs. Gage she had never been out until her work was finished, unless it was to do the shopping or something like that.

"Out! How very odd." Alex held his study door open for Miss Bloggs. Cathy turned to him. "Have you sent Mrs. Gage out for something?"

Alex was just going to answer when Jane came flying down the stairs.

"Oh, Mummy, I was doing the beds. I didn't hear you come in."

Cathy was even more puzzled. The beds should have been finished by Jane and Mrs. Gage long ago.

"Is Mrs. Gage out?"

Jane hesitated.

"Just—well, just for a moment."

Cathy supposed Mrs. Gage was out on some private business that Jane knew about but did not want to discuss before Miss Bloggs, so she changed the subject.

"How's Ginnie?" Then, thinking that perhaps this family talk sounded rude, she turned to Miss Bloggs. "Ginnie wasn't well this morning, she's in bed. We hope she's going to be all right in time to go to the zoo this afternoon."

Jane tried hard to think of something truthful to say.

"She's asleep. I mean, she might be, mightn't she?"

Miss Bloggs was so worried her eyes wobbled. She looked first at Jane, then at Alex, then at Cathy, then at Paul. Oh, dear, she thought, how very distressing! Jane is not telling the truth. I do dislike being a tell-tale, but this time I must be. Feeling fussed made her voice come out in a squeak.

"Oh, Vicar! Silence is golden, but there are times when one must speak. I mean—"

She was interrupted by Angus. He had been trying to spin on one leg and had not apparently listened to what

118

was said, but Miss Bloggs's remark attracted his attention.

"I wouldn't have thought silence was gold; it looks more purple to me."

Alex put a hand on Angus's shoulder to keep him quiet.

"Shut up, old man. What must you speak about, Miss Bloggs?"

Paul thought everybody was behaving very oddly.

"What's up?"

Jane, behind her family's back, made an I'll-tell-you-afterwards face at Paul. Cathy began to have the sinking feeling inside that mothers get when they suspect someone in their family is going to get into trouble.

"What is it, Miss Bloggs?"

Miss Bloggs felt terrible. She had promised not to tell Alex she had seen Ginnie, and here she was telling the whole family.

"I'm betraying a confidence, a thing I never do. But, you see, Ginnie's not in bed. I met her out with Mrs. Gage. It was rather odd. The child had a scarf around her head, and never spoke a word. Mrs. Gage said they were out on secret business. She asked me not to tell you, Vicar, that I'd met them but . . ."

Cathy felt irritated. What stupid nonsense was this? There was no reason why Ginnie should not get up and go out if she felt better. By why this secrecy? Why with Mrs. Gage? Why the scarf?

"What's all this nonsense, Jane?"

Jane saw it was no use hiding the truth any longer. Sooner or later everybody would have to know. Mrs. Gage thought she was helping by keeping the mumps a secret, but it was not helping really.

"You'd have to have known in the end. Mrs. Gage didn't want to worry you till she was sure it was."

Cathy could have shaken Jane.

"Was what?"

Jane thought the answer so terrible her voice trembled.

"Mumps!"

There was a shocked silence. Then Cathy said:

"Why should Mrs. Gage think Ginnie has mumps?"

Jane shook her head.

"I can't explain that. Ginnie will tell you."

"Do you think she's got mumps?" Alex asked.

Jane nodded.

"I'm awfully afraid she might have."

Jane saying that made her family see how awful mumps would be.

"No zoo!" said Cathy. "I must telephone my family."

Angus kicked angrily at the stairs.

"I won't have quarantine. I abs'lutely won't. I'm going to my audition."

Paul looked at his father.

"Sickening luck if I'm in quarantine just when I was getting a chance to bowl."

It was Esau who heard Ginnie and Mrs. Gage sneaking in at the back door. He skidded down the hall, barking excitedly. Mrs. Gage gave Ginnie a friendly push.

"That's done it. They'll all 'ave to know where we been."

As Ginnie and Mrs. Gage came into the hall the whole family surged toward them. Cathy looked questioningly at Mrs. Gage.

"Is it?"

The others did not need to ask, one look at Ginnie's face was enough. A sort of wail of "Oh, Ginnie!" went up. Angus added:

"It's mean of you, Ginnie. You always have things the wrong time."

This was just the sort of thing Ginnie was hoping one of them would say. She raised her chin as high as her swelled face would let her.

"What does Miss Virginia Bell have at the wrong time, Angus?"

"Mumps," roared her family.

Ginnie, with a struggle, managed to look amazed.

"Mumps! Why should I have mumps? If you want to know, I've been to the dentist and had a tooth out. I was very brave, Daddy, so you owe me a reward."

Cathy had so believed in the mumps she found it hard to accept good news.

"Is it true, Mrs. Gage? Was it only a tooth?"

Mrs. Gage was not letting Ginnie down.

"But of course, Mrs. Bell, dear. What else? Why should young Ginnie 'ave the mumps? It was the bad tooth what the dentist said you knew about. Poor child, she was in such a state I couldn't wait for you to come in, I took 'er right away."

Alone with Ginnie, Jane learned that the doctor had laughed when he saw her face and sent her to the dentist, but no one else ever found out why she had thought Ginnie had mumps.

Alex said to Cathy:

"I think there's a mystery somewhere."

Cathy laughed.

"I'm certain there is. But give Ginnie her reward and ask no questions. This is one of those sleeping dogs that wise fathers and mothers let lie."

7

The Zoo

It's surprising how often troubles can be sorted out, if only there are the right sort of people about to sort them out with. The afternoon at the zoo was a sorting out time for Paul and Jane, and in a way for Cathy too.

The trouble, as a rule, about a family going to the zoo is that everybody wants to look at different creatures. With the Bells and Cathy's family there was no trouble, for they behaved like animals going into the Ark. Uncle Jim and Paul had a passion for snakes, and never wanted to look at anything else, so the moment they arrived at the zoo they rushed for the snake house. Ricky's and Ginnie's passion was riding on the elephant. They were given enough money for three rides each, and at once they disappeared in the direction of the elephant house. Liza had Angus were almost exactly the same age, and their ambition was to visit every creature in the zoo, and give food to them all, so loaded with packets of stale buns, nuts, and fruit they ran off together. Cathy's father, Mumsdad, didn't mind what animals he saw, but he was especially fond of Jane, and Jane's passion was bears, so they went to the bear pit.

As soon as they were all scattered, Mumsmum, Aunt

Ann, and Cathy found a place to sit down. Mumsmum said:

"What a pity Alex couldn't come, Cathy."

Cathy hated doing things without Alex.

"Saturdays are bad for him. He's always behind with his sermon."

Mumsmum did not want to sound interfering but she was worried.

"Jane looks pale dear, doesn't she?"

Cathy was glad to talk things over. She explained about Angus's birthday party, and Grandfather's offer. Her mother and Aunt Ann saw at once what a dreadful business it was for Jane. Mumsmum, who always spoke her mind, said:

"Angus learn dancing! What nonsense! His Grandfather must be mad. It's no career for Angus. It'll be throwing money away."

Aunt Ann was fond of Cathy, and also sorry for her, for she could see how difficult things must be.

"Do you mean to say, knowing about Jane and how good she is, the old man actually chose to pay for Angus? What a mean old beast."

Cathy tried to explain.

"He isn't really; he's quite nice. Much nicer than Alex's brother, Sir Alfred Bell. It's just he doesn't approve of dancing for girls. He thinks they ought to learn to cook, and useful womanly things like that. But one good thing is coming out of this muddle. Jane is going to the audition with Angus, so that'll mean we should know where we are. We know she has talent, but what we don't know is whether it's too late to train her."

"What good will knowing do?" Mumsmum asked gently. "You couldn't pay for her to learn."

Aunt Ann was so sorry about Jane she sounded cross.

"I wish we could help. It's a shame Jane shouldn't have a chance, but Ricky and Liza have to go to boarding schools soon."

Mumsmum patted Cathy's hand.

"I wish we could help, but it's a bit of a squeeze making ends meet as it is."

Cathy felt warm all through with knowing she was loved.

"Bless you darlings, but none of you can help. You don't suppose I've told you my tale of woe to ask for help, do you? I only wanted to explain why Jane seems under the weather, and to feel you sympathize. You both know I wouldn't change Alex, bless him, but I wouldn't be human if I didn't wish he could earn a little more money. I hate to see the children doing without things they need."

While watching the bears Mumsdad was watching Jane. He might not be in practice anymore, but he was still a doctor. Jane was always small for her age, and rather frail, which did not worry him a bit for he knew that was how she was meant to be, but now she looked more than frail. He tried to think what could be wrong, and suddenly he knew she was not ill but was unhappy.

He waited until she had thrown her last piece of bun to the bears, then he tucked her hand under his arm.

"And how's my favorite granddaughter been getting on?"

Jane hesitated. It was a lovely sunny afternoon—should she spoil it by talking about what had happened? She knew if she talked about it she would feel a whole lot better.

"I'm doing all right outside, at least I hope so, but I'm doing very badly inside."

"How that?"

"I'm jealous. I read somewhere jealousy is the worst of the seven deadly sins."

Mumsdad squeezed Jane's hand against his side.

"So it can be. What has made you jealous? I shouldn't have thought you were a jealous person."

Out the story poured. The party. What everybody had said. Miss Bronson's letter to the Royal Ballet. The coming audition.

"As a matter of fact I'm glad about the audition. I know I can't go to the school, but just seeing inside will be something to remember always."

Mumsdad was quiet for quite a bit; then he said in a thinking-it-over voice:

"I don't fancy it would be possible for you not to be a little jealous of Angus."

Jane, having started confessing, decided to tell everything.

"If it was only a little jealous I wouldn't despise myself so much. If I tell you something awful, would you be ashamed of me forever?"

Mumsdad chuckled.

"I shouldn't think so. What is it?"

"When I'm at my most jealousish I hope and hope the Royal Ballet will say they won't train Angus."

"What good is that going to do you?"

Jane gave Mumsdad's arm a little shake to make him understand.

"If nobody goes it won't be any different to what it was. But imagine me year after year, learning at St. Winifred's, getting older and older, and worser and worser, while Angus goes to the Royal Ballet School."

"Poor granddaughter! You have all my sympathy. I can't say whether, if you had a chance, you would make a dancer, and at the moment I can't see where the money is coming from to give you an expensive training, but one thing I have learned in a long life, and that is never give up hope."

Jane gave a rather sad laugh.

"If you were Daddy's Miss Bloggs you would say 'While there's life there's hope.' She's always quoting things like that."

"If she quotes that she's quite right, but what I would quote is this: 'Honor lost, much lost. Money lost, little lost. Hope lost, all lost."

Jane repeated the words.

"I like the last bit. I'll write it down. Hope lost, all lost. I'll make a vow, Mumsdad, no matter how despairing and wormlike I feel I'll never give up hoping."

Over the snakes Paul was talking to Uncle Jim. He had not meant even to hint at his problem, but a chance remark started him off. Uncle Jim said:

"Let me know if there are any books I can lend you. I had read up no end of stuff while I was still at school."

Paul did not want to sound grumpy, but the last thing he wanted just then was books about medicine.

"Thank you. I'll remember if I want any."

Uncle Jim looked at Paul out of the corner of his eyes. He wondered what was the matter with him.

"How're things going at school?"

"Fine, thank you."

126

There was no doubt about it: Paul was in a funny mood.

"What's wrong, old man?"

Paul, his eyes on the snakes, blurted out:

"Nobody knows this, but I've more or less decided not to be a doctor."

Uncle Jim knew it was impossible that Paul, who had never swerved from his longing to be a doctor, could suddenly have changed his mind. There must be some desperate reason.

"What's this about?"

Paul had agreed Grandfather's offer should be kept private, but he was sure he could trust his uncle not to talk, and of course he would not tell him all Grandfather had said.

"You must promise not to tell Dad and Mum." Uncle Jim nodded. "Well, I'm thinking of leaving school as soon as I've got my general certificate, and going into Grandfather's business."

Uncle Jim knew Alex's father had always wanted Paul to join him.

"What's changed the situation? You always said you'd rather be a doctor."

"I still would, but I had a talk with Grandfather at Angus's birthday party. I told him I'd think about it and write to him."

"Have you written?"

"No, but I think I'm going to."

"You take my advice, and do nothing in a hurry. After all, you won't be taking that certificate for some while yet. No need to rush things."

Paul longed to explain about the money, but he felt Grandfather had trusted him to keep it a secret.

"There's a special reason for making up my mind quickly."

Uncle Jim wanted to say more, but he could feel Paul had said all he was going to say.

"Well, it's your business, old fellow, but I'm sorry. I always thought you were cut out to be a doctor."

"So did I, but other things could be more important."

"Could they? Will you let me know when you've decided?"

"You'll hear all right."

By audition Wednesday all members of the family, with the exception of Ginnie, were in a great state of excitement. Ginnie would have been interested in the audition, even though she could not imagine why anyone should want to go to one, but she thought she was being unfairly treated. The trouble was, Jane and Angus were having a holiday and she was not. She complained to Cathy and Alex, and tried to get Paul to side with her and stage a strike. Nobody took in that she felt abused; they thought she was just trying to sneak a day off from school. Because there was so much talk and fuss at breakfast on the Wednesday morning, nobody noticed that she left for school wearing an expression that a lady of the time of the French Revolution might have worn as she marched to the guillotine.

In spite of delays, last messages for Mrs. Gage, last kisses from Alex, last pats for Esau, and Angus forgetting his shoes and having to rush back for them, Jane, Angus, and Cathy arrived at the Royal Ballet School with a quarter of an hour to spare.

"Don't you think we ought to walk up and down

outside?" Jane suggested. "Won't it look rather rude if we come too soon?"

Angus was disgusted.

"Walk up and down outside! Here you've both been talking and talking, and taking hours to get ready, and there's me been waiting and waiting, knowing it was getting later and later, and thinking I'd miss my turn at the audition, and now we are here you don't want to go in."

Cathy sympathized with Jane, but however shy she felt she would not be helped by waiting.

"It won't look rude at all, darling. Besides, think what fun it'll be having time to look around, and seeing the other children who are being auditioned."

Jane looked gloomily down at her very clean, but rather old, blue cotton dress.

"I do wish Miss Bronson had said a party dress was right. I could have worn my new one. I'd have felt much more dance-ish in that."

Cathy took Jane's arm.

"Come along, goose, you look very nice. I'm glad to see you in socks. I do so much prefer them to those revolting St. Winifred's stockings."

Jane raised a foot and looked at her sock.

"You may like them, but I feel it in my bones the right clothes for a person as old as me would be tights and a tunic."

Angus was losing patience.

"Clothes, clothes, clothes! I'm just the same as usual, except for being cleaner, and you fuss, fuss, fuss about what you wear."

Cathy was feeling almost as nervous as Jane, for she had never been inside a dancing school before, so she was glad Angus was being firm with them.

"Quite right. We women do fuss, don't we? Now, come on, darlings, we're going in."

It is queer the way occasions that look as though they were going to be exciting turn out not to be, and others which sound as though they were going to be dull end up by being thrilling. Before the audition both Cathy and Jane were keyed up to expect anything, and even Angus, though he was confident the school would take him, was what Mrs. Gage called "proper above himself." But when it came to it, the audition proved a quiet, unfrightening affair. Angus was the only boy attending, so he was seen first.

Angus's account of what happened to him was that a lady, having first admired the shoes he had bought with his birthday money, told him to copy the steps she danced. Angus said he had copied the steps, and found them easy. Cathy, who had been in the room, had quite a different impression. She had seen the steps Angus was supposed to copy, and she had seen what appeared to her some very funny attempts by Angus to do so. But both she and Angus agreed about what happened afterwards. The director of the school asked Angus why he wanted to dance, and he explained in great detail what happened to his feet when he first saw a ballet. After that Angus was sent away, and Cathy was left alone with the director. She was told Angus was too young to be a full-time pupil, but he might come to classes, and if there proved to be talent, he could become a full-time student of the school later on.

Cathy was surprised and grateful at the interest taken in Jane. Miss Bronson had evidently written quite a long letter about her, for the director seemed to know just how much training she had had, her age, and that there was no money to pay fees. In a way it seemed to Cathy they took more trouble over Jane than they had over Angus. They made her take off her shoes and examined her feet, and they watched very carefully as she performed the steps she was told to do. When she had finished, the director thanked her very nicely, sent her to change her shoes, and then talked to Cathy. The director told Cathy that the school would, of course, be writing to Miss Bronson about Jane, but that naturally Cathy would like to hear something before then. The people at the school agreed that Jane appeared a talented girl but badly in need of training. If it were possible she should have proper lessons.

While Cathy, Angus, and Jane were at the Royal, Ginnie was having a bad time at St. Winifred's. She went to school deciding that if her family were mean enough to send her on a day when Jane and Angus had a holiday she would not work. "I'll just sit at my desk," she decided, "but I won't listen to a word anybody says." Of course that sort of behavior was soon noticed, and when Ginnie had been told for the third time to pay attention she found Miss Matthews, her class teacher, was not putting up with her any longer.

"You've been totally unmanageable the whole morning, and I don't intend to be bothered with you, so you can stand outside the door where I can't see you."

Ginnie felt even more martyred than she had when she arrived at school. "After all," she said to herself, "I'm not doing any harm. It's just that I'm not listening." To Miss Matthews she said:

"That suits me perfectly, thank you."

That was the last straw. Miss Matthews was a good teacher, and fond of Ginnie as a rule, but rudeness was more than she could stand.

"Does it! Well, I've no wish for it to suit you perfectly, so instead of standing outside the door you will report yourself to Miss Newton. Tell her I sent you and why."

Miss Newton! Ginnie felt her heart turn over. To stand outside the door was one thing; to be sent to see Miss Newton in her office was quite another. She gave a look at Miss Matthews to see if there was any possibility of her relenting, but Miss Matthews seemed to have forgotten her and had gone back to the class. Trying not to look frightened Ginnie opened the door and shut it gently behind her.

Miss Newton called out "Come in" to Ginnie's nervous knock. She was sitting at her desk writing. She glanced at Ginnie standing in the doorway.

"Good morning, Ginnie. What is it?"

Ginnie took a deep breath.

"I was sent by Miss Matthews to report myself."

"What for?"

"For being totally unmanageable this morning."

Miss Newton laid down her pen.

"Dear me! And have you been?"

Ginnie tried to speak bravely, but the word came out with a wobble in it.

"Yes."

"Why?"

"Because I've been meanly treated. Jane and Angus have had a holiday today, and I've been made to come to school."

Miss Newton could not, for a moment, see what Ginnie meant.

"But they're at an audition, and that's work."

"Not to them it isn't. I've said and I've said it isn't fair, but I've been sent to school just the same."

132

Miss Newton leaned back in her chair.

"I see. So you decided to be totally unmanageable."

"No, I didn't. That's what Miss Matthews said I was. I just meant to be deaf to anything anybody said to me."

Miss Newton pointed to a chair.

"Sit down, Ginnie. Have you ever tried to talk to somebody who won't listen to you?"

Ginnie did not see what Miss Newton was getting at. To her it seemed as if she was just having a nice talk. She said with fervor:

"More often than you could believe. Have you?"

Miss Newton's voice became grave.

"This is serious, Ginnie. If you've experienced such behavior you know how annoying it is."

Ginnie saw this was not a friendly talk. Miss Newton was thinking of her behavior. All the same she was certain there was justice on her side; she tried to make Miss Newton understand.

"But I did it because I was angry, and I had a right to be angry."

Miss Newton thought about that.

"Even if you have a right to be angry, and I don't agree that you have, it is your parents you should be angry with. After all it was they who ordered you to come to school this morning. If we are going to accept anyone has a right to be angry it is, I think, Miss Matthews and the rest of the staff who have that right. You have made them suffer because you were angry with your father and mother."

Ginnie felt as if she had been caught in a corner, from which there was no escape, when playing hide and seek.

"As a matter of fact, truthfully, Miss Newton, I hadn't thought of that."

Miss Newton looked at the clock.

"What would you have done today if you had been given a holiday?"

"Nothing special. Taken Esau, our dog, out for a walk, talked to Mrs. Gage, she helps Mummy, and . . ."

Miss Newton spoke crisply.

"It's now eleven thirty. You came to school at nine, and you've wasted two and a half hours of our time. You can go home for the rest of the day."

"Oh, good, thanks awfully, Miss Newton."

Miss Newton stopped Ginnie with a gesture.

"Wait. I haven't finished yet. But as you have wasted two and a half hours of our time, next Friday, Miss Matthews will give you work to take home that will take two and a half hours of your weekend time. I think that's fair, don't you?"

Ginnie was appalled.

"Two and a half hours' homework! But there's lots of things I want to do on Saturday." Then she saw Miss Newton's face, which did not look forgiving. "I'm sorry about this morning; I'll be good now. As it happens I don't want that holiday after all."

Miss Newton had a way of brushing things aside she did not want to hear. She brushed Ginnie's words aside now, just as if they had never been spoken.

"I trust you to go straight home. I shall telephone the vicarage to say you're on your way."

Cathy had decided that she, Jane, and Angus would have lunch in a coffee shop, and Alex was away for the day, so Mrs. Gage had planned what she called a proper cleaning. The last person she wanted to see that morning was Ginnie.

"Whatever did you 'ave to act up for, and get sent 'ome? If My Margaret Rose played me up this way I'd 'ave taken a slipper to 'er, straight I would. And what you're to eat I don't know. There's a bit of bacon over from breakfast, what I was goin' to 'ave, and there's a bit of 'orse meat cookin' for Esau. I suppose I could cook you a couple of eggs, but that's all you'll get."

Ginnie could usually get around Mrs. Gage.

"Didn't Mummy leave any money about? Then I could have an ice cream cone while I'm out with Esau."

Mrs. Gage very nearly smacked Ginnie.

"Ice cream indeed! I'll ice cream you, my girl. Now off you go, and you're not to put a foot in this 'ouse before one, and as soon as you've eaten your dinner, since you are 'ere, you'll make yourself useful. I'll 'ave all the bits of silver down and you can clean 'em."

The family came home. Cathy tactfully did not go into the details of why Ginnie had been home for the day— she seemed to have had punishment enough cleaning silver for two hours, and if, as Mrs. Gage said, there were to be two and a half hours' homework as well at the weekend, there seemed no need for her or Alex to interfere. Jane and Angus felt as if nothing nice would ever happen again. When Jane came in to tea she looked gloomily at the tea table.

"Isn't it odd. This most important Wednesday has turned into just an ordinary day."

Cathy knew what Jane meant.

"Feeling flat, darling?"

"So flat it's as if I were going to be a pie crust and you were rolling me out on the kitchen table."

Angus was frowning.

"I wish I could go there right away and never go back to

135

the choir school. I didn't want to go there only for dancing lessons."

Alex thought Angus was old enough to be grateful for little mercies. After all, he was very much better off than Jane.

"I don't think you've got much to grumble about, old man. These classes are quite a good idea. They'll learn then if there's any chance of their making a dancer of you."

Ginnie helped herself to a sandwich.

"You'll have to go into training, my boy. Dancers don't stuff themselves with jam sandwiches, do they, Daddy?"

Alex laughed.

"I don't know much about training for dancers. Your Uncle Alfred used to be in training when he was at Cambridge, he was quite an all-rounder."

"Really!" said Ginnie. "If you'd asked me I'd have said he was an all-fronter, for that's where he sticks out."

Cathy did not want Ginnie to get into any more trouble that day, and it was obvious she was in a mood when she could very easily be rude to someone, so she said severely, "Ginnie," and was going to change the subject when Paul, who had hurried home from school to hear the news, came tearing in.

"How did it go, Jane?"

Jane thought it was nice of Paul to be so interested, knowing, as he did, there was no chance of her going to the school.

"They don't say much. They're going to write to Miss Bronson."

Angus bounced up and down in his chair.

"I'm going to dancing classes, and then to the school later on."

Paul was disappointed. He had hoped for something much more clear-cut. He said rather crossly as he helped himself to a sandwich:

"If they didn't say much, going to this audition doesn't seem to have done much good, does it?"

Cathy thought Paul must be tired.

"Jane knew it wouldn't, but it'll be a help when Miss Bronson gets the letter. Now, Paul, we'll put all the food around you and clear the table. I think that this has been the sort of day that needs a special finishing off. I thought we might play a family game."

At once everybody felt better. Jane rushed around the table to help her mother clear.

"You are the most gorgeous mother. A family game would be exactly right. Let's play charades."

Angus thumped the table to attract attention.

"No. Let it be hide and seek all over the house."

Paul helped himself to bread and jam.

"I can't play for long because of my homework, but I could manage one game of racing demon."

Ginnie put a pile of plates on a tray.

"I suppose nobody cares what Miss Virginia Bell would like, but she thinks it would be a good evening for that blow feather game."

Alex looked at his watch.

"If you can wait until I get back from evening prayer I'll join in. I think, as you all want something different, you should let your mother choose the game."

Cathy looked around at her family, and remembered some cards she had played with as a child, which were still popular with her own family.

"What about Happy Families? It's ages since we played

that. I should like to see the Bulls, the Buns, and the Doses again."

While the rest of the family were washing up Paul tried to get some more information out of Jane.

"Didn't they say anything at this audition? I thought they would."

Jane put down the teapot she was carrying.

"It's not so much the way they say it, it's the way they look. I think they were interested, because of the way they examined my feet. I mean, you wouldn't bother to do that to somebody who couldn't dance, would you? When the director said good-bye he said thank you in an awfully nice way. I think truthfully he was rather sorry about me."

Paul had finished his tea. He got up.

"What it boils down to is that you might have a chance, if only we had the money to pay the fees."

Jane nodded.

"Quite honestly that is what I think, but I'm not going to despair. Mumsdad said it was silly to do that. He quoted something which finished up: 'Hope lost, all lost.' It sounds rather Bloggish, but I like it."

Jane carried Paul's tea things into the kitchen. The only person left in the dining room with Paul was Esau, still waiting hopefully for more pieces from his plate. Paul knelt down by him and played with his ears.

"What would you do, my boy? Mumsdad can quote what he likes about not giving up hope, but if I write that letter to Grandfather I've put paid forever to being a doctor. Fat lot of use hoping would be then."

8

Play Saturday

Every August all the family went to stay with Uncle Jim and Aunt Ann. Always it was a perfect month looked forward to by everybody. Cathy's old home, which her brother, Uncle Jim, had taken on, was a large rambling house, with heaps of room in it. It was the perfect place to have a holiday in, because Uncle Jim did not have much money, and though Aunt Ann kept everything looking as nice as she could, there was not a great deal in the house that would spoil.

The house was in Berkshire. It was right in the country where everybody could run wild and do exactly what they liked. Aunt Ann, who was a sensible sort of person, full of good ideas, had long ago started the habit of putting extra beds in Ricky's and Liza's rooms for Ginnie and Angus. These two rooms were a little cut off from the rest of the house, and so, however much noise the four made, as Aunt Ann said, "They enjoy it and it can't hurt us." This arrangement meant that, for all August, Jane and Paul had the luxury of rooms to themselves. They did not mind having Angus and Ginnie in their rooms the rest of the year—it was part of life as it was—but there was something very holidayish about having a room to yourself. As on Zoo Saturday, the families usually split up into twos. Paul often went out with Uncle Jim on his rounds. Ricky and Ginnie would disappear for hours on end, often coming back with rather a bloated look, and stains around their mouths, for when they were not eating the last of the family raspberries they visited somebody else's place. The loves of Liza's life were the family pony Thomas, colonies of guinea pigs, several hutches of rabbits, various cats, and some bantam hens. Angus thought Liza the luckiest girl in the world; every minute he spent playing with, feeding, or, in the case of Thomas, riding on, her pets, was unadulterated bliss.

"Of course picnics are simply gorgeous, Mummy," he told Cathy, "but it does seem a terrible waste to go out when there are guinea pigs, rabbits, and a pony at home."

Alex was usually so tired by the time his vacation came around that for the first week he just lay about in a deck chair sleeping. After that he enjoyed anything that was going, and best of all, he liked fishing. He did not want grand fishing, just sitting on a river bank staring at his float and better still, watching the life of the river. The only member of the family who enjoyed fishing with him was Jane. They would sit side by side for hours, seldom getting a bite, Alex watching the tiny water boatmen, the moorhens, and sometimes a heron, Jane staring into the water, seeing underneath it swirling dancers moving exquisitely in a never-ending ballet.

Cathy looked upon August as the time for filling her shelves. Together she and Aunt Ann picked windfall apples, mulberries, and marrows, and turned them into pots of jam. While the jam was cooking they talked and talked about their families. Liza's tendency to spots, Ginnie's being too fat, Ricky being a little backward at school,

140

Angus and his animals, (and this year his dancing), Jane and her dancing, Paul and his scholarship, and all the other things that mothers manage to find to talk about when their children are not there to listen.

It always seemed, when thinking about it, as if London would be unendurable when they got back, but actually each year the same thing happened. They enjoyed seeing Mrs. Gage again and telling her all about it. There was Esau to make a fuss over because it was perhaps harder for him than anyone coming home: he missed the rabbits, which he hunted every day, and to everyone's relief never caught. Even Miss Bloggs, as Ginnie pointed out, was less Bloggish when they came back in September. Then, of course, however much they grumbled about going back, there was the excitement of the beginning of a new term at school: the changes, the new pupils, and the gossip.

For Angus, leaving Liza's pets behind was made easier this year because he was starting his dancing classes. Angus starting his dancing classes was made easier for Jane because the autumn term was the one in which they had the school play, in which she was dancing the nymph. The girls of St. Winifred's were great supporters of the Invalid Children's Aid Association; they subscribed to the funds all the year, but each autumn term they gave a public performance of a play in aid of the charity, and they asked somebody of distinction to speak about it before the performance. The autumn term had hardly started before the day came when Jane and Ginnie rushed home with the most extraordinary piece of news.

"Mummy," said Jane, "you'll never, never guess the awful thing that's going to happen."

"The shame of it," moaned Ginnie. "It's the kind of

thing the school'll remember forever and ever; I shouldn't think we could possibly live it down."

Cathy went on spreading bread and butter for tea.

"What is this catastrophe?"

"We thought," said Jane, "we'd let you guess, and then we knew you never, never would. It's the sort of thing nobody could suppose would ever happen."

"Well?" Cathy asked.

Ginnie sprawled across the table.

"Miss Newton has invited Uncle Alfred to make the speech about the school charity."

Jane broke in:

"And he's said yes, but there's worse than that."

Ginnie nodded.

"It's worstish for me, really. Aunt Rose is coming too. Imagine, Mummy: I've got to present her with a bouquet."

Cathy understood how Jane and Ginnie felt, but of course she could not say so.

"I think you ought to be rather proud. After all, they generally ask someone very distinguished. It's nice to have a distinguished uncle."

Jane sounded reproving.

"That's mother talk. You don't believe a word of it."

"Besides," said Ginnie, "we don't think he's been asked because he's distinguished; we can't really think why he has been. Miss Newton said she particularly wanted him to be there, and she looked rather odd, we thought, when she said that. We think, at least my class does, that he's been asked because he's rich. We think she thinks he'll put something enormous into the collection box."

Cathy put the bread and butter on the tea tray.

"Then let's hope he does. Now listen, darlings, whatever you may think about Uncle Alfred coming to the school, you're not to say it in front of Daddy. After all, he is your father's only brother. You wouldn't like it if people were rude about Paul or Angus, would you?"

Ginnie got off the table.

"As a matter of fact, when anyone is rude about Angus I always say I couldn't agree more."

As usual when anything extra was going on, clothes became a problem. Cathy, though she had not said so, had been afraid that she was going to have to provide a dress for Jane to wear as the nymph. The clothes usually came out of the school wardrobe, but Jane said she was sure there was nothing for nymphs in it.

"Anyhow, if there was anything, St. Winifred's would probably have something made of serge or flannel, or something like that."

Cathy had laughed and said that nobody could possibly be a nymph in flannel or serge, but she had felt anxious. This chance of dancing the nymph meant a great deal to Jane, and if the school dress was too terrible she felt she would have to open the money box and buy something herself. But as it happened it was not necessary. About a fortnight before the first dress rehearsal Jane came home from school with shining eyes.

"Imagine, Mummy, Miss Newton sent for me today, and what do you think? She's having a dress made for me for the nymph. It's a simply lovely silver tunic, with a sort of cape thing over one shoulder. It's all silver, because the nymph that I play is the servant of the morning."

Cathy was delighted about the dress.

"But why do servants of the morning have to wear silver?"

Jane lowered her voice. Only Esau was in the room.

"Quite truthfully, Mummy, it's a really terrible play,

143

and I think Miss Newton thinks it is, but she can't say so because it's written by the wife of the chairman of the school governors. But my bit is lovely, because I'm all alone, and she didn't choose the music for me, I can choose what I like."

Cathy smiled. Everybody in the house knew what Jane's music was going to be, for she practiced to it every morning on her portable record player.

"If the play's very silly won't Bach's 'Sheep May Safely Graze' strike a rather unexpected note?"

Jane nodded.

"It's going to, but Miss Newton says she thinks by the time I dance the audience'll be ready for a bit of good music, and truly, Mummy, I think she's right."

For special occasions the girls of St. Winifred's had to wear what were known as "school whites." Miss Newton fought the governors at every meeting, imploring them to do away with the "school whites," but the governors refused. St. Winifred's girls had always worn white dresses since the day when the school was founded, and the governors saw no reason to change the custom. Miss Newton saw every reason. Girls in their teens are inclined to bulge, and do not look nice in white. Both parents and girls loathed the white dresses, and the girls never wore them outside the school, so any white dress would do. Usually it was passed down the family, or run up at home out of cheap stuff, and looked like it. Ginnie had just inherited a "school white" from Jane. Among the bundles of clothes for poor clergy a white evening dress had turned up. It was made of taffeta, and was rather worn, and was stained in places. But it had an enormously full skirt, and with great skill Cathy had cut out of it a really quite charming dress for Jane, with a plain tight bodice and fairly full pleated skirt. Unfortunately, what had been quite charming for Jane was anything but charming for Ginnie. What had been a tight-fitted bodice on Jane became a bursting bodice on Ginnie. Cathy let out every bit that would let out, and put buttons and buttonholes down the back, so it could not pop open, but Ginnie said she felt like a too-full hot water bottle in it, and quite truthfully that was rather how she looked. The skirt was the right length, but there was more of Ginnie behind than there was of Jane, and so it would ride up at the back.

"Just imagine how I'm going to look behind when I bow to Aunt Rose," said Ginnie. "It's lucky I match underneath, for that's the part of me the audience is going to see most of."

Cathy told Ginnie not to be a goose, she would look very nice presenting the bouquet, but to Jane she said:

"Ginnie's quite right, the dress is terrible on her, and it really is sickening she is wearing it the year the school have invited Uncle Alfred to make the speech. But thank goodness, Aunt Rose will be on the platform too. I couldn't have borne it if I thought she had her eyes on Ginnie's back view."

"Couldn't she have a new dress?" Jane pleaded. "After all, it's the first time she's done anything before the whole school."

"Oh, I do wish she could, darling. But honestly, can you think of a worse waste of money than buying a 'school white' when she already has one?"

Jane had to admit Cathy was right.

"Quite honestly I can't."

Ginnie did not much care what she wore. Except that she was afraid Uncle Alfred would embarrass her and

Jane, she quite looked forward to Play Saturday, and was willing to treat it as an ordinary day. This was a good thing, because on Saturday morning Mrs. Gage and Cathy counted on family help, but that Saturday morning Jane was no use to anybody, Angus was practicing dancing, and Paul was playing football, so all the odd jobs fell on Ginnie. First, there was answering the front door, then the shopping. There was quite a heavy basket of shopping, and Ginnie was glad to get it home. She shouted to Cathy to tell her she was back.

"Here's everything, Mummy. Goodness, it's heavy."

Cathy came down from doing the bedrooms.

"Thank you very much, darling. Would you take it to Mrs. Gage? And ask her to give you and Esau a chocolate-covered cookie each for shopping for me."

Ginnie was pleased about the cookies, but she had to be fair.

"Quite truthfully me and Esau were glad to go out. This house is terrible this morning; with Jane's practice, practice, practice, and I'm sick to death of that tune she dances to, aren't you, Mummy?"

Cathy put a finger to her lips and pointed to Jane and Ginnie's bedroom.

"She's practicing in there now. She's nervous, poor pet."

Ginnie was scornful.

"I can't think why. I'm making a speech to Aunt Rose, and I'm not nervous, only disgusted. Where's Angus? Has he stopped practicing?"

"No. But Daddy's busy, and I couldn't stand any more crashes, so I told him to go and work in the parish hall."

Ginnie thought she had answered all the day's callers.

"Daddy still busy! I let in five christenings, two weddings, six people who didn't say what they'd come about, and what looked like a family row. Once I had twelve people waiting in the hall."

"I know, darling, but Saturdays are always busy, you know. Mrs. Gage says they are worse when we have a fine Saturday after a wet week, and it has rained a lot lately."

"Poor Daddy. D'you think he'll miss the school play finishing his sermon?"

Cathy shook her head.

"He certainly won't. Even if it means staying up all night working at it, he'll be there. Besides, we promised Miss Newton we would both come. I think she thinks Jane is going to be very good, for twice she's telephoned to be sure we are coming. Now run along, pet, to Mrs. Gage, or there'll be no lunch."

Mrs. Gage was pleased to see the shopping.

"You take the cookies. My hands are wet. Only one each, mind. I'm in a rush to get on; I don't want to miss the school concert."

The chocolate-covered cookies were kept in a tin in the kitchen cupboard. They were all the same size, but Ginnie believed some had more chocolate on them than others. She chose two and gave Esau his.

"Here you are, angel boy." Then she saw there was a lot of drying up to do. "I'll dry those for you if you want to go to the school play, but you won't like it—except, of course, Jane's dancing."

Mrs. Gage handed Ginnie a dish towel.

"Thank you, ducks. Why won't I like it? Isn't it funny?"

Ginnie thought about that.

"It isn't meant to be. But seeing who are being the shepherd and shepherdess I suppose it is. They look simply terrible in their costumes, and when you think

147

they're supposed to be made of china you can't help laughing."

Mrs. Gage was cutting up vegetables. She stopped with half a carrot in her hand.

"China! Well, I never!"

"It isn't their being made of china that's funny, it's that the two girls that have to be the shepherd and shepherdess look less like china than anybody else in the school."

"Why let them take the parts then?"

Ginnie put some plates on the rack.

"Because one's head of the school, and the other's our star athlete."

"What's the piece about?"

"It's a sort of dream. The shepherd and shepherdess are in a shop and they love one another. It's that sort of idiotic play."

"I like a nice love tale."

Ginnie was very fond of Mrs. Gage, but she had discussed films with her and knew her to have what she thought regrettably bad taste.

"I know you do. But this is the worst sort of love story. You see, somebody comes to the shop and buys the shepherdess, and that makes the shepherd's heart crack. It's a good thing I've told you about his heart cracking before you see the play, or you'd never know it happened. For all the girl who is the shepherd does is to hold her front, and look as though she was going to be sick, and say in a very mimsy-pimsy voice: 'Ooh. Ooh. My heart! My heart is breaking.' Then she falls down dead, and that's the end of act one."

Mrs. Gage stopped slicing a potato.

"You got that wrong. Must be the end of the tale if the 'ero's dead. You can't go on once the 'ero's dead."

"At St. Winifred's you can. You see, the next scene is the land beyond the stars. You wouldn't know it was meant to be that if you didn't read your program, because it's just like act one, only there are roses and stars hung over everything, made by some of the older girls."

"What 'appens beyond the stars?"

"Well, it's that sort of scene that uses everybody. First, the school choir sing, dressed as sort of angels, at least they are angels' clothes in the Christmas nativity play, but they've had the wings taken off, so perhaps they aren't angels in this play. Then the best dancers, except Jane, dance. I think they're meant to be stars, but they wear the tunics they always wear at gym events, only they have stars on their heads. Then the shepherd comes back."

Mrs. Gage was trying to follow the story.

"But you said 'e was dead."

"Not beyond the stars he isn't."

"Why?"

"I don't know, it's that sort of play. The first thing that happens is he has to fight a kind of demon thing, at least he's supposed to fight it, only he doesn't really, because the teacher who produced the play was afraid somebody would get hurt. Anyway, the demon thing is supposed to be killed, so he falls down dead."

"Where's 'e go? Beyond the moon?"

Ginnie thought that very funny. When she had stopped laughing she said:

"But you mustn't laugh this afternoon, or you'll get kicked out. Anyway, after he's dead, the school choir come back and sing again. Then the stage goes black, and when the lights come on Jane's there. She's the servant of the morning."

Mrs Gage put her vegetables on the stove.

"My 'ead's goin' round. You make it sound a muddle. What's the mornin' got to do with it?"

"Nothing. And I don't make it sound half as much of a muddle as it is. There are lots of other people I haven't told you about. A cat, a dog, and a bird with a face like Miss Bloggs."

"Is Jane the end of the piece?"

"Almost, thank goodness. The shepherd comes back again, and Jane opens what are supposed to be gates, but are really pieces of curtain at the back of the stage, and there's the fat shepherdess."

"Is she dead too?"

"I don't know, but they have to kiss. It's awfully difficult not to laugh there. Then the choir sing again, and that's the end."

Mrs. Gage saw Ginnie had nearly finished the drying up.

"Better be, too, or I'll never be done in time to dress for the concert. Thank you, ducks. On the shelf you'll find some money. You take Esau with you and buy yourself an ice cream cone."

When Paul came home at lunchtime Jane was in the hall having a last practice of her dance. The record was getting worn, and her record player was old and had a tinny tone. But Johann Sebastian Bach's music could not be destroyed. The lovely notes filled the hall. Paul, climbing the stairs to change his clothes, hung over the banisters. The kitchen door was shut, Cathy was in the dining room, Ginnie and Angus out, and Jane believed nobody was looking.

Paul knew nothing about dancing. He knew Jane liked it, and people said she was good, and he thought she ought to have her chance. It was not fair that money should be spent on training him and none on training her. He was always trying to find out how good she was, but he had never thought of watching her dance, and making up his own mind. Now, as he watched her, he thought he knew the answer. He did not know how good dancing ought to look, but she certainly looked all right in the same way a good athlete looked all right. He went up the stairs on tiptoe, so as not to disturb her. In his bedroom was a microscope, and a lot of books, which would help him when he started to train as a doctor. Looking at them he suddenly pulled open a drawer in the chest of drawers, and into it bundled the books and the microscope. Then he slammed it shut. There would be no time to write the letter before the school play, but he would write as soon as he came home. It would be easier if the books and the microscope were out of sight.

9

The School Play

Because Uncle Alfred and Aunt Rose were the guests of honor, Cathy, Alex, Paul, and Angus were invited to meet them in Miss Newton's room before the school play. Only Alex thought this arrangement a good idea. Cathy had no wish to trail into the school hall behind Aunt Rose, looking, she was sure, like the poor relation that she was. Paul hated going into St. Winifred's at any time; he always felt the girls were staring at him, and the thought of making a public entrance filled him with horror. Angus would not have minded if it had not been that Veronica was going to be there.

"She's so prancy, Mummy," he complained, "and she never lets me talk. She keeps talk-talk-talking herself. I do think talking should be fair, half one person and half the other."

Her family's forebodings about their special entrance were not helped by Ginnie.

"Poor beasts! I can just see you. Miss Newton'll come first with Uncle Alfred, and all the school governors, and perhaps Daddy, then Aunt Rose looking terribly posh, and smelling so much of scent that everybody puts a handkerchief to their nose as she passes. Then Mummy, in Aunt Rose's old dress, without the roses which I think is a great pity. Then Paul, slinking like a murderer. Then Angus, and then dear little cousin Veronica, mimsy-pimsy-ing along, saying Mumsie says I look sweetly pretty in blue."

The family entrance, when they had to make it, was so very nearly as Ginnie had described it that Cathy almost laughed. The only difference was that she and Alex, with Aunt Rose and Uncle Alfred, came first, and the school governors came behind. Cathy was not a vain woman, but she could not help thinking that she must look a very shabby figure beside Aunt Rose. Aunt Rose's old black dress was still good, but it was very old, and Aunt Rose was looking resplendent. It was no wonder she was, for when Cathy said: "How nice you look, Rose," Rose looked down at herself casually and answered in her whiny way:

"It is rather fun, isn't it? But then I think this autumn's fashions are rather fun, don't you?"

Veronica, too, had new clothes. A very smart yellow coat and cap, and a fine wool dress of delicate lemon. Ginnie, sitting in the gallery at the back of the hall on the outside seat, so as to be handy to get out with the bouquet, nudged her next-door neighbor, the Alison who had had mumps.

"That's them. The fat man with the red face is Uncle Alfred. That dressed-up woman is my Aunt Rose; if you were a little nearer you could smell her. That thing in yellow is my cousin Veronica."

Alison loved beautiful clothes.

"Well, I must say Veronica looks lovely."

Ginnie was disgusted.

"She may look lovely from here, but you ought to be very, very glad, Alison, that you don't have to know her,

153

because she is the nastiest, whiniest girl you've ever heard of."

Miss Newton, Uncle Alfred, Aunt Rose, and the governors were climbing onto the stage. Miss Newton waited until everybody was seated, then she got up and told the audience what was going to happen that afternoon. She explained about the charity, and that they were very honored that Uncle Alfred had agreed to appeal for it. She said that after the appeal collection boxes would be passed around, and while this was going on everybody on the platform would come down into the front row, and then they would see the school play. She then spoke as nicely as she could about the play. She said that it had been written by the wife of the chairman of the governors, and, when the clapping about that was over, that she was not going to hold up the proceedings any longer but would ask Sir Alfred Bell to speak.

There was one thing Uncle Alfred never was, and that was short. He was one of those speakers who did not believe it was necessary to prepare a speech. He liked to know a good deal about the subject on which he was speaking, then get up and tell those who were listening all he knew about it, as well as his views on what he had learned. Because he did not prepare his speech he was apt to go on and on going round and round the same point, looking for a suitable phrase on which to end up and sit down. Sometimes finding such a phrase took him an extra three minutes or so; it did that afternoon.

"Miss Newton, school governors, teachers, girls. There is nothing that gives me more pleasure than to stand on a school platform, for I know that I am looking at young folk, with all their lives before them. You girls may not know it now, but you are living through the happiest times of your lives. . . ."

Speakers like Uncle Alfred make audiences cough and whisper. Two of the first whisperers were Mr. and Mrs. Gage. Mr. Gage had not wanted to come to the school play, he had wanted to watch football on television, but Mrs. Gage had been firm.

"I tell you you'll miss a treat if you don't come. You've never seen our Jane dance, and it's time you did. Anyway, you're comin' and that's that."

As Uncle Alfred went on and on Mr. Gage thought more and more longingly of football on television.

"We could've seen a bit of the game and then come along to watch the dancin' later."

Mrs. Gage dug her elbow into him.

"Ssh, that's the reverend's brother."

Mr. Gage nodded.

"So I supposed. Shocker, isn't 'e?"

Mrs. Gage put her mouth close to Mr. Gage's ear.

"You ought to 'ear the children lead off about 'im. Puts you in mind of a bluebottle shut in a cupboard, doesn't 'e?"

The school fidgeted, and those near enough to her looked reproachfully at Ginnie. Messages were passed down the lines of girls. "Ask Ginnie if she knows any way to shut her uncle up?" "Tell Ginnie she'll be had up for cruelty to schoolgirls." Ginnie, going over her speech to Aunt Rose in her head, looked disdainful and murmured to Alison:

"Let them say what they like. I've told everybody he'd be awful. It isn't my fault Miss Newton asked him."

Presently, after what felt to the girls like three quarters of an hour, Uncle Alfred reached the word "lastly."

"Lastly, may I say that I fully appreciate that most of you in this room have to turn every penny before you spend it. . . ."

Ginnie got up.

"Is my dress all right, Alison?"

Alison gave a pull to the skirt.

"It's pulled up at the back a bit, and it's rather creased where you've been sitting."

Ginnie looked disgustedly at her frock.

"Let's hope it stays down behind until after I've given the flowers."

Alison gave her a push.

"Go on. Mam-zelle's beckoning to you, and looking in no end of a flap."

Ginnie was not to be hurried.

"Look at the bouquet. Isn't it mingy! I knew it would be."

When Uncle Alfred at last sat down Miss Newton got up, and Ginnie, holding a small bouquet of chrysanthemums, began to walk up the hall. Miss Newton smiled politely.

"Thank you very much indeed, Sir Alfred, I feel certain that, thanks to what you have said, we shall have very full collection boxes this afternoon." Then she turned to Aunt Rose. "Thank you, too, Lady Bell. I know you are a very busy person, it has been extraordinarily kind of you to come here today."

That was Ginnie's cue. She had to climb the steps onto the stage, curtsy, and say "On behalf of the governors, staff, and girls of St. Winifred's, may I present you with these flowers. And thank you very much for honoring us by being with us today."

The curtsy had been a last moment idea, decided on as

being prettier than a bow. Ginnie hated having to curtsy and, in the excitement of the moment, forgot it and started her speech without it.

"On behalf of the governors . . ." Then suddenly she remembered. "Sorry, I ought to have curtsied first. I'll start again."

The audience, unspeakably bored by Uncle Alfred, was delighted with Ginnie. As she curtsied there was a roar of laughter. Ginnie thought the laughter was for her curtsy, which was not fair, for curtsying had never been her idea. She turned on the audience.

"If you don't mind my saying so, you oughtn't to laugh. I know the curtsy looks silly, but I didn't want to do it. Now you've put me off, and I've forgotten what I'd got to say." She turned back to Aunt Rose and shoved the chrysanthemums onto her lap. "These are for you, Aunt Rose. I know you don't need them, because your house is always stuffed with flowers, but St. Winifred's gives bouquets when people like you come, so thank you very much."

Ginnie walked back to her seat amidst roars of laughter. The school mistresses tried to look disapproving, but the girls were delighted. Alison, as Ginnie sat down, whispered:

"People clapped you sixty times harder than they clapped your uncle; he hardly got any applause at all."

The school play was very much the play Ginnie had described to Mrs. Gage. The wife of the chairman of the governors believed that lots of words, and whimsy thoughts, made a nice play for girls, and there was no need for anyone to be funny, and no need for a real plot. Ginnie had not exaggerated when she said that the star athlete and the head of the school were not well cast as the shepherd and shepherdess. Nobody, except perhaps the

157

parents of the performers, were sorry when the shepherd said that his heart was broken and fell with a crash to the floor. Uncle Alfred, who had slept through the act, woke with a jump and exclaimed in a hearty I've-enjoyed-every-minute voice: "Admirable, admirable."

Rose, on Miss Newton's other side, said:

"Very pretty."

Miss Newton, who knew the play was awful, and that Uncle Alfred had not heard a word, thanked them both politely. Then she explained how difficult it was for the drama section to find suitable plays for the school, so they were fortunate this year to have had one written for them. They would see in the next act how well this play was contrived to use the whole school. Then she smiled past Rose at Cathy and Alex, and said the big moment was when Jane danced. She was sure they would be very proud of her. Veronica, who had climbed onto her father's knee, felt enough attention was not being paid to her.

"I learn dancing. My dancing mistress says I'm very dainty, doesn't she, Dada?"

Miss Newton looked at Veronica; on her face was an expression that none of her girls would have wanted it to wear had she been looking at them.

"Indeed?"

Aunt Rose gazed proudly at Veronica.

"She's a beautiful mover, Miss Newton, but we shouldn't care for her to study ballet—so bad for the feet, I think."

Uncle Alfred's voice boomed out.

"My father's paying for my nephew Angus to train for ballet. Very impractical. There's no money there, you know."

Miss Newton felt sorry for Cathy and Alex, who could not fail to hear. She raised her voice slightly.

"Few of my girls have parents with much money." Then she changed the subject. "Where do you go to school, Veronica?"

"Minden House."

Rose smiled at Veronica. How pretty she looked in that shade of yellow, how lucky that she had managed to get shoes of exactly the same color.

"It's quite a small school."

Alfred's voice boomed out again.

"Just a few pupils, all handpicked."

Veronica enjoyed being talked about.

"Mumsie chose it because I don't have to wear a uniform. She thinks uniforms are awful, and so do I."

Miss Newton was conscious of a hush in the row behind her. She wondered what the parents were thinking. The school uniform was ugly, but it had its advantages. It prevented one girl looking better-dressed than the other. She had an almost uncontrollable longing to shake Veronica. She wondered if parents who had overheard this conversation were longing to do the same thing. But all she said was:

"Do you?"

Veronica leaned toward Miss Newton.

"When I'm old enough I'm going to a finishing school, aren't I, Dada?"

Miss Newton heard movement behind the curtain, and distant sounds of the school orchestra tuning up. Evidently the stage was set. Thankfully she raised a hand.

"Quiet, dear. I think the next act is going to begin. In a moment you will be in the land beyond the stars."

The second act went better than the first, because, as

there were more characters, so many more parents were interested in what was going on. But by the time the shepherd had killed what Ginnie had called "the demon thing," interest was again beginning to flag, for really it was a very muddling play. When the choir filed on to sing again, several members of the audience—including Uncle Alfred—had gone to sleep. Then suddenly, just as Ginnie had explained to Mrs. Gage that it would, the stage lighting dimmed, and then went out. Then, through the darkness, the first lovely notes of "Sheep May Safely Graze" filled the hall. Then, very slowly, the lights came up, and there was Jane in her silver tunic.

At all times Jane's dancing was worth watching. She needed any amount of training, much of her technique was faulty, but she was born with what is called "lyricism." When Jane danced, each step was part of the whole, and so the movements flowed into each other, and it was hard to say where one began and the other ended. Coming toward the end of a very silly play, in which not only were the words banal but the songs sung to tinkling tunes, Jane's dancing, together with Bach's music, made the audience feel as if they were looking at one real flower in a bowl of artificial ones. Even Ginnie was carried away.

"Goodness, Alison, doesn't she look marvelous?"

Cathy and Alex were transported. Paul, watching Jane, knew his decision had been right. She must have her chance. He would see she had her chance. He would write to Grandfather the moment he got home.

Mrs. Gage gave a large sniff.

"To think that's our Jane. I 'ave to cry, she dances that beautiful."

For Angus it was the night of his birthday all over

again; watching Jane, his legs knew what they ought to do.

Suddenly, the spell was broken. Veronica said in a loud voice:

"She dances rather well, don't you think, Mumsie." Her family, Miss Newton, and all the parents within hearing gave very angry shushes. Veronica, annoyed, raised her voice. "I won't shush if I don't want to."

A mother, who had shared Miss Newton's longing to shake Veronica, tapped Aunt Rose on the shoulder.

"Would you please take your little girl out. She doesn't seem to know how to behave herself."

Miss Newton spoke in a freezing whisper to Uncle Alfred.

"You will please tell your daughter to be quiet."

Alfred put his arm round Veronica.

"Ssh, Veronica pet."

Jane's dance came to an end, and she received the greatest tribute any artist can receive, a moment's complete silence before the stamping, shouting, and clapping began. There were only a few more minutes of the play, and then the curtain was down, and the cast were bowing and smiling. In the middle of the stage were the shepherd and shepherdess, but nobody, not even their parents, considered they were the stars. There was no question about it, the afternoon belonged to Jane. When the curtain had come down for the fifth time, it rose on a surprise. Standing between the shepherd and shepherdess was Miss Newton. She stepped forward and held up her hand.

"One moment, please. The school governors have asked me to make an announcement. We are not, as everybody here knows, a wealthy school, but we have a fund on which from time to time we can draw. Usually the governors give this money in grants, to assist the more brilliant of our girls to go to universities or to study some special subject. A short time ago, however, I thought it my duty to bring a case before the governors of possible brilliance, but not of the type to whom we have made grants in the past. Jane, dear, will you come here."

Jane, completely puzzled as to what was going to happen, stepped forward. The school, beginning to guess, held its breath. Miss Newton put an arm round Jane's shoulders.

"Jane, the school governors have decided to grant you a scholarship at the Royal Ballet School. You have already been to an audition there, and they are prepared to accept you as a pupil. The grant will last until you are trained or—and I feel this very unlikely—until such time as the school should decide there is no future for you in dancing." Then she turned to the audience. "You've all seen Jane dance this afternoon, and I feel sure you would like to say by your applause, God bless you, good luck, we hope you have a very successful future."

Miss Newton asked Cathy and Alex to stay to tea and meet the governors, but Cathy asked if they could be excused.

"You'll think it very idiotic, Miss Newton, but I know for the first time what it is like to cry because you're so happy. It would be a shocking thing if I cried over the governors instead of saying thank you."

Alex, too, was almost past speech. He held Miss Newton's hand.

"We shall of course be writing to the governors. . . . Will you tell them how grateful we are . . ."

Miss Newton quite understood how they felt.

"That's all right." Then she laughed. "After Jane, the star of the afternoon was your Ginnie. Don't tell her so, bad girl, but her speech to her aunt was much needed comic relief, I thought."

Cathy had another reason besides feeling emotionally upset why she wanted to get home to tea. As soon as the family reached the vicarage she shooed everybody upstairs to wash, and told them tea would only be a moment, it was all laid. When the children came down they knew why they had not been let into the dining room before. On the table was a tea as if it was a birthday party, a pink and white cake, ice cream with strawberries in it, and party favors. Cathy laughed as everybody gave pleased squeaks.

"I thought it was going to be a suitable day for a party, but I couldn't know how suitable. You know, Jane, even now I can hardly believe it."

Ginnie pulled out her chair.

"Do let's start, I'm starving. Now you know why Miss Newton asked Uncle Alfred and Aunt Rose to come, and why she kept fussing about you and Daddy coming."

Jane hugged Cathy.

"Now we know why Miss Bronson wrote the Royal Ballet School, and why Miss Newton wanted to find out if I was worth training."

Alex was looking at Paul.

"You're very silent, old man."

Ginnie helped herself to a sandwich.

"Paul's been looking like the Cheshire Cat in *Alice in Wonderland* all the way home. It's almost as if you'd had the scholarship, Paul."

Cathy was pouring out the tea.

"It's quite true, Paul, darling. You do look as if you'd won a prize."

Paul was so happy he didn't mind what anyone said. It was all over. The nightmare thought of having to give up the idea of being a doctor. There was no need to write to Grandfather ever—all his worries were over. He passed Alex his cup of tea.

"It's a bit of all right that the school will pay for Jane."

Angus was still in the same mood he had been at his birthday party, but this time he thought he understood.

"Seeing Jane dance has made me feel most peculiar."

Jane was almost too happy to eat.

"Imagine, I thought I should feel after the play that nothing nice could ever happen again. Galosh, galoosh, I feel too happy to live."

Ginnie heard Esau snuffling beside her.

"Mummy, as Jane's won a scholarship, could Esau sit on a chair at the table, and have a plate, and anything he likes to eat, just like us?"

Cathy saw eight imploring eyes turned on her, and shook her head.

"No, darlings, not even for fifty scholarships, but he shall have a slice of cake and a spoonful of ice cream on the floor."

Alex looked at Ginnie, his eyes twinkling.

"I thought Miss Virginia Bell gave a very distinguished performance this afternoon."

All the family began to laugh. Paul said:

"On behalf of the governors . . . sorry, I ought to have curtsied. . . ."

Jane took up the imitation.

"If you don't mind my saying so, you oughtn't to have laughed. . . ."

Ginnie interrupted her:

"If anybody's going to say that speech, it'll be me."

Then she paused and a slow grin came over her face. "If you want to know, Miss Virginia Bell doesn't know what she said. Was I very awful?"

Alex leaned over and patted her hand.

"Not awful at all. A little original, perhaps, but we wouldn't change her, would we, Cathy?"

Cathy looked happily round the table.

"We wouldn't change any of them. We know we're lucky parents, don't we, Alex?"

10

News for Esau

It was planned that Jane should join the Royal Ballet School in January, as there was a place open. She thought the term at St. Winifred's would drag most terribly while she was waiting for January to come, but actually it passed quicker than any other term had ever done. Everybody seemed pleased about her scholarship and were extra nice to her, then suddenly it was the end of the term, and she was flying around saying good-byes, and finding to her surprise what a lot of people there were she was sorry to say good-bye to. Ginnie, watching her, said:

"It's all very well for you, you're leaving. I suppose if I were leaving I'd find a lot of people I'd think I was sorry to say good-bye to, but when you're staying on for years and years, like me, you just know you don't care if you never see them again."

Just before the end of term the most exciting thing happened. The family were at breakfast when Mrs. Gage brought in the mail. As usual, it was nearly all for Alex, though there were two envelopes, which Alex said looked suspiciously like bills, for Cathy, and one typed envelope for Paul. Paul opened his envelope and then he made the most extraordinary sound, rather like the sort of noise a pressure cooker makes. His family stared at him.

"What's up, old man?" Alex said.

"What's in your letter, darling?" Cathy asked.

Paul's face was scarlet with excitement.

"Guess?"

It was so long since Esau's photograph had been taken that it took three guesses before Angus got the right answer.

"I know. Esau's won first prize."

Never was there such excitement. Ginnie jumped up and knelt in front of Esau.

"Darling Esau, aren't you a proud boy? I'm worshiping you."

Jane joined her and threw her arms round Esau's neck.

"You're the most exquisite dog in the world."

Angus got up and crouched down beside them.

"You gorgeous boy! Do you know you're richer than anybody else in the family this morning."

Cathy raised her voice.

"No one admires Esau more than I do, but this is breakfast time, and you three ought to be sitting on your chairs at the table."

Jane looked reproachfully at her mother.

"Such a mother to make her family stick to rules on the day their dog's won a prize."

Angus was indignant.

"It's per-post-trious!"

"If Miss Virginia Bell was Esau," Ginnie remarked, "she'd turn around and take a nip out of Mrs. Bell's leg for saying that."

As soon as the children were back in their chairs, the question arose as to how the money was to be spent.

Angus refused to budge from his point that the money was Esau's, and that he alone should decide on the spending.

"I like that," said Paul. "It's my camera, isn't it? From the way you talk you'd think Esau got himself photographed and sent it in."

"I helped bathe him for the photograph," Jane pointed out, "so I think I ought to have a little say."

Ginnie passed her cup for more milk.

"I believe it was Miss Virginia Bell who said he'd look nice on the church steps."

Alex decided that perhaps he had better make a suggestion.

"I think you'll agree, won't you, Paul, that though you took the photograph the enterprise was a family one?" Paul nodded, for of course he meant to share the money. "Then what I suggest is this. Why don't we divide the money into six equal shares, and we could each decide whether to have our share spent on us or on the house. Then each would would contribute toward a gift for Esau—enough to buy him a new lead and a new collar, and to keep him in horse meat for quite a while. Then we could . . ."

He was interrupted by loud protests from all around the table.

"Really, Daddy," said Jane, "and you a clergyman! Here it was Esau's win, and you want to give him the smallest share, and then you suggest he spend it on horse meat, which he'd have anyway."

Angus was so angry he was spluttering.

"Such meanness! Horse meat! Which he doesn't like but has to have. And a collar and lead! He simply loathes his collar and lead!"

Ginnie looked at Alex in a most reproving way.

"Take it back, Daddy. You'll never be able to look your family in the face again unless you do."

Cathy had an idea.

"I tell you what. Certainly let Esau have his share, but why not let him buy something nice for Mrs. Gage with it? After all, it was she who saw the advertisement in the paper."

In the end, after a great deal of argument, a plan was arrived at. Mrs. Gage should have a superb Christmas present, partly paid for by Esau but partly by everybody else. Cathy's share would buy her a new dress. Alex wanted to spend his on repairs to the house, but Cathy said he needed new shoes and new socks. Paul's share would buy him an overcoat.

"Please, darling," said Cathy, "your present one is so thin and old it worries me every time I see you in it."

There was no argument as to what Jane's share was to be spent on. The Royal Ballet School wore a very pretty gray and red uniform; her money would go toward that. It was more difficult deciding about Ginnie and Angus. Ginnie disliked clothes and Angus was still so angry at the family's treatment of Esau that he refused to discuss what was to be done with his money. In the end Cathy half persuaded them.

"Look, darlings. I know you think it's an awful waste of money, but you both need such a terrible lot of clothes. Would you be very generous and let me spend part of your share on each of you, leaving you each enough for Esau's present to Mrs. Gage, and for any special food for Esau that you think he ought to have?"

Christmas was always, of course, a lovely time, but that Christmas was one of the gayest and happiest. They chose a coat for Mrs. Gage out of Esau's money, and money added by all the family. Mrs. Gage always said she fancied red, but they knew her wardrobe well, and there certainly was not a red coat in it. It was a splendid red coat, with a fur collar, not, as Cathy said, a very grand sort of fur, but still fur. Mrs. Gage was thrilled. In fact she was so thrilled that for quite a time she could not say anything intelligible, only a string of things like "Well, I never!" "Chase me Aunt Fanny 'round the gas works." "Smashin' bit of fur." "Oh, wait till Mr. Gage sees this." "What I needs is an invite to Buckingham Palace."

Cathy was thrilled with her new dress. To Jane's disgust she refused to buy anything silly and garden-partyish, but it was a very pretty color, a sort of blackberry.

"Much nicer than anything Aunt Rose has," said Ginnie approvingly. "I can't wait for her to see it. I bet she'll be jealous."

Cathy said she did not think that Aunt Rose would be jealous of the dress, but it certainly made a lovely change from the old black.

The only person who did not perhaps enjoy the prize money was poor Esau himself. He always had his plate of turkey on Christmas Day, and Cathy said she thought that ought to be enough special Christmas fare. Paul and Jane felt that was being a bit mean, so they persuaded her to let him have kidneys for breakfast and a large slice of Christmas cake for tea. Mrs. Gage, to say thank you for the coat, hung up a sock in the kitchen for him, out of which stuck an enormous meaty bone. Esau ate the bone before breakfast. After breakfast, when no one was looking, Ginnie gave him a bulging paper bag.

"There's two pounds of sugar biscuits in there. You eat just as many as you like, and exactly when you like."

170

Angus took Esau into his bedroom to give him his present.

"Nobody but me thinks you've been meanly treated. I think it's terrible what's happened, so this is for you. It cost me a lot of money. You needn't take just one like we have to, you can eat them all at once if you like."

Angus's present was a large box of chocolate creams. It was noticed on Christmas evening that Esau seemed a bit drowsy, and there was no doubt the next morning that he had spent a miserable night being very, very sick.

It seemed to the children they scarcely had time to thank for Christmas presents before it was term time again. Of course to Jane the new term was more exciting than holidays, but the others did not feel that way. Ginnie particularly disliked the beginning of term. She did not want to go to the Royal Ballet School, in fact there was nothing she would have loathed more, but all the same it seemed drab going to St. Winifred's alone. Perhaps it was going there alone, still wearing the unglamorous St. Winifred's uniform, while Jane danced off in her lovely new gray and red, but something made Ginnie think about herself. This was very unlike her, for she was not at all a thinking-about-yourself person, but once she started she thought about herself in a big way. The result of her thinking was that she decided it was time she became the shining light of the family. There were Paul and Jane with scholarships, and there was Angus with a choir school scholarship, and dancing lessons from Grandfather, and there was she with nothing at all. Ginnie was not depressed by her thinking, merely determined to change the position. Somehow, some way, Miss Virginia Bell would shine, and when she did it would be such a bright shining

171

that she would become the most important person in the family.

Ginnie's first idea of a way to shine came to her as the result of a talk by one of the school governors. Miss Newton thought that particular governor a woolly thinker, and a shocking bore, but Ginnie seized on what he said, and decided it was exactly the sort of idea she was looking for. The next morning she came down to breakfast wearing an earnest expression, which she hoped her family would notice. As is the way of families, they were all thinking about their own things and never looked at Ginnie, so at last she burst out:

"Don't any of you notice anything different about me this morning?"

"Are you fatter?" Paul suggested.

Alex asked why she should look different. Ginnie paused, to be sure they were all listening.

"Yesterday we had a pep talk about service."

Angus was puzzled.

"Service in church?"

Ginnie sighed at his stupidity.

"Don't be so ignorant, my boy. Service to your country. It was one of the school governors, and he said none of us was too small to start dedicating a part of each day to service. I started dedicating yesterday."

Alex tried not to smile.

"What form did your dedication take, Ginnie?"

"I put all the money I had into the lifeboat box."

"Why did you choose the lifeboat box?" Jane asked.

Ginnie was not going to say it was the first collection box she saw.

"Why not? Somebody has to pay for lifeboats, don't they?"

"Is that all you have to do?" Jane asked. "A different little bit of service every day?"

Ginnie produced an exercise book on which she had been sitting.

"This is my dedication book. Do you see, I wrote the date yesterday, and underneath 'Dedication Day.' Then on this side I put 'Life Boat' and the amount."

"If you want something for today," Cathy suggested, "I could give you some boxes of bits to sort. I want some pieces for patching."

Ginnie closed her book.

"Sorting bits at home isn't service of the sort the man meant. I mean, it wouldn't look important enough in my book."

Paul jumped on that.

"What is it, a prize you're going in for?"

"Not a prize, just honor. The governor said that he would like to look at our books in the autumn, and see which girl had given the best service. I mean it to be me."

Ginnie kept her book faithfully, but she found it extraordinarily difficult to find outstanding service that wanted doing.

"I want to rescue someone from drowning, or catch a burglar, or something like that," she complained. "But everybody around us is so dull, they never want those sort of things done for them."

Alex was a little worried about Ginnie's book.

"This looking for dashing things to do is all wrong," he said to Cathy. "I wish she'd see there are all sorts of things which need doing under her feet, there's no need to go looking for them."

"I know," Cathy agreed; "but I think it's only a temporary craze, and sooner or later she'll give up bothering

173

with her dedication book. She's really a very helpful child; some day she'll see that helping me is just as worthwhile as catching burglars."

The Royal Ballet School was a big surprise to Jane. She had thought that in a dancing school dancing would be the most important subject and that all other lessons would come second. One week in the school and she saw how wrong her ideas were. Dancing was important, of course, but so were all the other subjects she learned.

"You can't think how ordinary a school it is in a way," she told her family. "You see, we're all only there on approval, so they want us to be good all around in case we won't make dancers."

Angus, who was not at all pleased with dancing classes only, said:

"I wouldn't call it ordinary if I could go there instead of to the choir school. I wouldn't think any school's just ordinary where I was sent to see ballet as part of things learnt, and you do have lessons every day."

But Jane stuck to her point.

"You wait until you get properly into the school, and you'll see what I mean. I suppose it's because I'm not allowed to practice at home, and because I know I'm being properly taught at school, but in some ways I think less about dancing now than I did when I was at St. Winifred's."

It was the summer term before Ginnie saw what she thought was an opportunity for a dramatic entry in her dedication book. She was waiting in the line for the bus that would take her to St. Winifred's, when Miss Bloggs got off her bicycle and stopped beside her.

"Good morning, Ginnie, dear, is your father in? I have to see him urgently."

"Not this morning, he isn't. He's gone to a meeting. Mrs. Gage said she would do his study. She said he made a fuss when he was in, but what the eye didn't see the heart wouldn't grieve about. But I know Daddy's eye will see when he gets in, because Mrs. Gage always moves something, and then Mummy has to find it."

Miss Bloggs made worried tch-tch-ing noises.

"Oh, dear! The entertainers who were coming to give my old people at the Darby and Joan Club their anniversary treat have fallen through. I don't know what to do. The old people are invited for next Saturday, and they are so looking forward to the afternoon."

"Couldn't you just give them more to eat?" Ginnie suggested. "If it was me, I'd rather have that than an entertainment."

"I daresay you would, dear, but not my old people. You see, many of them have no teeth. Still, never say die, something may turn up. But I feel a little discouraged; people are less voluntary-service minded than they were."

Ginnie stared at Miss Bloggs, while an idea blossomed like a flower in her brain. How splendid "Organized concert for old people" would look in her book. That was the sort of entry that ought to make her dedication book the best in the school. Without thinking very much she said grandly:

"Don't worry, Miss Bloggs. I will arrange the concert for you."

Miss Bloggs was amazed.

"You, Ginnie! How?"

Ginnie was uncertain how, but she was sure she could arrange it with Miss Newton.

"There's the school choir, and the folk dancers, and the verse speakers. The only thing is, it's me who has to arrange it all, or at least it has to count as me arranging it."

Miss Bloggs could hardly believe her luck.

"Really, Ginnie? You mean your school will give the entertainment? How kind."

Ginnie, carried away, sounded not only confident but regal.

"Nothing easier. Miss Newton will be pleased."

Miss Bloggs, with a sigh of relief, prepared to get back on her bicycle.

"Dear Ginnie! You'll never know what a relief this is. Still, I should have had faith. I know it's always darkest before the dawn. But I was in such a quandary. You see, I have to leave this afternoon for a niece's wedding, and I shan't be back until Friday, and the concert is the next day, so I had to leave everything planned. Oh, thank you, dear! And please tell dear Miss Newton how very, very grateful I am."

When any of her girls wished to see their headmistress they made application through their class teacher. Ginnie was called to Miss Newton's study just before morning break.

"Good morning, Ginnie. You want to see me?" Miss Newton pointed to a chair. "Sit there, dear."

Ginnie pulled the chair a little nearer Miss Newton's desk.

"Please, Miss Newton, I want the school choir, the folk dancers, and the verse speakers for a concert on Saturday afternoon."

Miss Newton tried never to let her face betray what she was thinking, but she was so surprised she looked as if she was.

"You want . . . My dear Ginnie!"

Ginnie, full of her idea for a good entry in her book, was not considering how Miss Newton looked.

"I've promised the school will do a concert, but although it's them will do the things, it has to be me who gives it all."

Miss Newton was for once almost past words.

"You promised this entertainment?"

"Yes, for Miss Bloggs—she's a person Daddy says is the cream of his parish workers. It's for her old people at the Darby and Joan Club."

Miss Newton's voice took on the sharpness and coldness of an icicle.

"Have I got this right? You, a small girl in my lower school, who is neither a verse speaker, a member of the choir, nor a folk dancer—in fact I believe unqualified to perform in any way—has promised, without reference to me, the services of half the school next Saturday?"

For the first time Ginnie appreciated she had taken a good deal upon herself.

"It sounds awful like that, but I said I'd do it because it would look so glorious in my dedication book. I thought it would make my book the best in the school."

"And what had you planned your share of this entertainment was to be?"

The bounce was leaving Ginnie.

"I promised in rather a hurry, while I was waiting for the bus. I thought I'd made a speech at the beginning, and then come on at the end like people do at concerts."

Miss Newton had a large engagement book on her desk. She opened it at Saturday.

"Saturday. Senior tennis match. Senior historical group visiting Tower of London. Junior verse-speaking classes attending open-air performance of *Midsummer Night's*

177

Dream. School choir at musical festival. Dancers attending opening round square-dancing contest." She shut the book. "I think that settles the matter, Ginnie."

Ginnie felt as if something cold was sliding down her back.

"But it can't settle it. Miss Bloggs has gone to her niece's wedding and won't be back until Friday, and then it'll be too late to tell her I can't give the concert."

Miss Newton sounded a little sorry for Ginnie.

"You've heard what the school is doing, so even if your promise had been given with the best intentions I couldn't have helped you. But I don't think it was given with the best intentions. I don't think you were trying to help Miss Bloggs, or give pleasure to the old people. I think you were just thinking how good the entry would look in your book."

Ginnie was nearly in tears.

"That man who gave us the pep talk didn't know how difficult it is to find important service to do."

"Between you and me, Ginnie, I think looking for important service is a mistake. If I was judging the best book I'd make the winner the girl who had chosen one piece of sensible service and done it every day."

"But that's so dull." Tears rolled down Ginnie's cheeks. "Goodness, what am I to do? I must have the concert. . . . I promised."

Ginnie was not looking at Miss Newton, or she would have seen she was looking sympathetic.

"You've got a lot of talent in the family. Wouldn't Jane dance? And Angus sings, doesn't he?"

Ginnie sniffed.

"Nobody plays the piano. They can't sing or dance without that."

Miss Newton leaned across the table and laid a hand on Ginnie's.

178

"If I found you an accompanist for Saturday, could you arrange a concert?"

Immediately Ginnie sprang from misery to the topmost peak of happiness. She now saw no difficulty in arranging her concert. In the eye of her mind Jane danced, Angus sang, Esau waltzed, her father recited, even Paul was performing.

"Of course I could."

Miss Newton kept her hand firmly on Ginnie's.

"But you will have to pay for the accompanist in service."

"What sort?"

"Any sort that is ordinary and useful, and you do every day. There must be plenty of people in your father's parish who need somebody to look after the baby, or something of that sort."

Ginnie's spirits dropped a point or two.

"How long would I have to look after babies?"

"How about every day for a week? That will show you how glad people are of humdrum help, and you'll find it makes quite an impressive entry in your book. Now, run back to your class, dear. Just let me know what time you need the accompanist on Saturday, and she will be there."

Ginnie meant to break the news of Saturday's concert tactfully to her family, but she had no chance. Alex came in to tea with a letter in his hand.

"Ginnie, this is from Miss Bloggs. She says you have been a very kind girl, and arranged for St. Winifred's to give the entertainment for the old people on Saturday, in the place of the concert people who've fallen through. She says she's sure you will arrange things beautifully, but as she won't be back until Friday, will I see everything is in order. Is everything in order?"

Ginnie saw there was nothing for it but the truth.

179

"Nothing's in order, except someone to play accompaniments. I did promise the school would do it, but Miss Newton said no, they couldn't." The family groaned. "Oh, Ginnie!" She turned on them. "And there's no need to 'Oh, Ginnie' me. I've said there'll be a concert, and there'll be a concert."

Cathy looked worried.

"I do hope so. Poor Miss Bloggs."

Alex spoke firmly.

"It is not going to be poor Miss Bloggs. Ginnie has promised she will provide an entertainment, so she will provide an entertainment."

"I'll ask permission to dance," said Jane. "We're not allowed to dance in pubic, but perhaps as it's only for the old people I'll get permission."

"It needn't be anything grand," said Alex. "The old people are easily pleased. I'm no great turn, but I'll sing 'Cockles and Mussels.' " He turned to Angus. "You'll sing, won't you, old man?"

"No, I won't. I abom-nate singing. If I've got to do something I'll dance."

Alex was firm.

"You'll sing. The stage isn't strong enough for you to dance on. We'll wait until you're trained for that."

"That's three things," said Jane. "What else are you going to have, Ginnie?"

Ginnie was not going to admit she had no idea. She put her chin in the air.

"Wait and see. If Miss Virginia Bell says there'll be a concert, there'll be a concert."

11

Ginnie's Concert

Not for the first time, it was Mrs. Gage who came to the rescue. On the Thursday before the concert she found Ginnie looking worried, and asked her what the trouble was.

"If I tell you," said Ginnie, "will you absolutely promise not to tell anybody?"

Mrs. Gage was putting on her hat to go home. She paused and looked in a come-off-it way at Ginnie.

"That time you thought you 'ad the mumps and didn't, did I tell anybody anything? It's the concert, isn't it?"

"Yes. Angus is going to sing, though he doesn't want to. Daddy's singing 'Cockles and Mussels.' Jane's being allowed to dance twice, but that's all there is. I told Daddy there were two more things happening, but there aren't."

"You didn't ought to 'ave done that."

"It was true. I thought Paul would lecture on cricket, but he won't."

Mrs. Gage laughed.

"Good job too. Can't see the Darby and Joans fancyin' that, po'r old dears. What was the other turn?"

"I thought Esau would waltz, but he won't learn, even though I bought him chocolate biscuits for prizes. He won't even try. So all that's happening is I'm dressing him up as a baby and pushing him across the stage."

Mrs. Gage was not a person who held back her thoughts.

"That won't look much. Like as not they'll take 'im for a real baby, and see nothin' in it."

"I'm afraid you're right, so I've got to think of something else. I said there'd be a concert, so there's got to be one."

Mrs. Gage suddenly slapped a hand on the table.

"What am I thinkin of? What the old people like is choruses. You know, 'earin' the old songs what they've always known. You give 'em those, they'll be a riot."

"But who's to sing them?"

"Me, of course. On the bus on an outin' I always leads the choruses."

Ginnie never looked for in-between troubles. To her, if Mrs. Gage could sing choruses, then the accompanist would know all the songs. Her concert was arranged. She hugged Mrs. Gage.

"Darlingest angel Mrs. Gage. Oh, goodness, you can't think how nice I feel. Here I've been worrying and worrying, and all the time I only had to ask you."

Mrs. Gage made clucking disapproving noises.

"There you go, proper rush and tear as usual. No good me sayin' I'll sing unless the lady piano player what Miss Newton sends knows the songs. You better find out tomorrow."

Ginnie frowned and kicked at the kitchen table.

"Quite truthfully, I didn't want to see her again before Saturday. You see, she's made me pay for the accompanist. I've got to look after somebody's baby every day for a week and put it in my dedication book as service. I don't know when she meant me to start, but I haven't yet, because I've been so busy with the concert."

"You 'aven't far to look for a baby. The verger's wife is 'avin' teeth out Monday. You offer to take 'er baby for a bit after school, and they'll be ever so grateful. You tell Miss Newton that, and she'll understand. Well, so long, ducks, I must be off, or Mr. Gage will make a fuss."

Ginnie saw Miss Newton the next day. She quite understood about the verger's baby, and said waiting until Monday was a good idea. Then Ginnie explained about Mrs. Gage.

"She helps Mummy, and she's simply marvelous. I like her better than anybody who isn't family."

"What sort of songs does Mrs. Gage want to sing?"

"Tunes like 'Daisy, Daisy, Give Me Your Answer Do,' and all those."

"I see, just the old favorites. My pianist knows all those."

"Angus is singing 'Cherry Ripe' and 'Matthew, Mark, Luke, and John,' and if he's encored, and he always is, 'I'll Walk Beside You' and 'There Was a Lady Sweet and Kind.' Daddy is singing 'Cockles and Mussels,' but no encore because he doesn't know another song."

"She can certainly play those. What's Jane dancing to?"

"First 'The Sugar Plum Fairy,' and then the tune she danced to in the school play."

"What's she wearing?"

"Just ordinary clothes, I think. She hasn't anything else."

"Come and see me before you go home; I'll have her silver messenger tunic packed. I expect she'd like to borrow it."

Ginnie gazed at Miss Newton in amazement.

"Goodness! If you don't mind my saying so, you've

been a great surprise to me. I thought you were very mean about the concert, and now you're helping."

Miss Newton laughed.

"You'll find that people do surprise you when you get to know them."

Ginnie turned to go. Then she remembered the babies.

"I shan't like the verger's baby, for it's got a very sneering face, but I'll be extra nice to it, because you've been nice about my concert."

Saturday was very hot. Cathy had tried to please the family by preparing a cold breakfast. She had made a brawn. Mrs. Gage was the first to see it.

"What ever's that, dear?"

"A brawn. Chopped and molded pig's feet. I read in a paper that it was easy to make, and all the family would love it, but it doesn't seem to have turned out right somehow."

Mrs. Gage looked at what seemed to be a cross between cold soup and a half-jellied jelly.

"Put's me in mind of jellied eels. What are the bits of solid? Look chewed to me."

Cathy shuddered.

"Don't, Mrs. Gage, dear. I had already taken a dislike to it, but now it makes me feel sick."

Mrs. Gage peered again at the brawn.

"I couldn't fancy it meself, but maybe it seems worse in one piece. Perhaps it won't look so bad slopped out onto different plates."

Cathy put the brawn on the breakfast tray.

"Let's hope so, for it's all there is, and the family have a busy day in front of them."

Angus came down to breakfast very worried. As soon as Alex had said grace he turned to him.

"I don't think one of my caterpillars is well, Daddy. You can't see much of a caterpillar's face, but what I can see looks rather white."

Alex was consoling.

"I expect it's the weather. The pavements are red hot this morning. My word, makes us think of Berkshire, doesn't it?"

"Only six weeks and two days before we go," said Ginnie. "It makes it nearer when you scratch the days off on a calendar."

Cathy put the brawn in front of Alex.

"Doesn't it. I scratch the days off in my engagement book. I don't know why, but I seem to need a holiday more than usual. I think it's been extra dusty in London."

The family had their eyes on the brawn. Jane asked in rather a weak voice:

"What's that, Mummy?"

Cathy tried to sound fond of her effort.

"A brawn."

"I thought brawns stood up," said Paul.

Cathy thought her brawn looked worse in the dining room than it had in the kitchen.

"So it should. Do try and eat a little of it, darlings. The recipe said it was very nourishing, and the perfect breakfast for a hot morning."

Alex, with a spoon, put brawn on everybody's plate. For a little while nobody spoke. Then Esau put a paw on Angus, asking for breakfast. Angus tried to whisper so quietly that only Esau would hear, but he was not very good at whispering.

"You wouldn't like it. It's not at all nice."

Jane laid down her spoon.

"Don't wear your suffering-martyr face, Mummy. We

185

FAMILY SHOES

know you meant it to be a nice cold breakfast, but darling, we can't eat it, honestly we can't."

Paul tried to say something kind.

"The meat bits aren't too bad; it's the jelly that's so awful."

Ginnie pushed away her plate.

"To me it looks as if it was something somebody had eaten, and . . ."

Alex spoke sharply.

"Ginnie!" Then he turned to Cathy. "How about letting Esau have this? It's very hot—none of us needs more than bread and butter."

That shocked Angus.

"Daddy, how mean! Poor boy, he doesn't want pot-o-maine poisoning."

"He's quite right, Mummy," Jane agreed. "Esau's such a polite dog he'd probably eat it out of good manners, and then be frightfully sick afterwards."

Cathy heard Mrs. Gage outside, and called her in.

"Would you take this brawn away."

Mrs. Gage had the mail. She laid it all down beside Alex.

"Nasty lookin' lot." She picked up the brawn. "I'll put it in the pig bucket. The bluebottles are somethin' fierce this mornin', and I wouldn't wonder if this finished them."

Cathy looked at Alex's letters.

"Go through them again, Alex. I'm sure there's one for me from Ann."

Alex turned over his letters.

"There isn't. As Mrs. Gage rightly said, they're a nasty looking lot, mostly typed, and one at least is going to need a long difficult answer. Is it important?"

"About the holidays, of course. Ann and I write almost

daily now. I saw a new kind of jam jar top advertised, and I sent the advertisement to her, and suggested I bought some."

"Jam tops!" said Jane. "I like hearing you talk about them. I can see you and Aunt Ann picking mulberries, and me and Daddy fishing. It's almost as if we were there."

Paul got up.

"I must be off. I wonder if I'll get a chance to play cricket for the village, like I did last year."

"Don't be late," said Ginnie. "My concert begins at four o'clock, and you've absolutely promised you'll be there."

In spite of the heat the old people enjoyed their tea. Jane was changing for her dance, but the rest of the family except Ginnie helped Miss Bloggs serve refreshments. Ginnie had tried to help, but she was too anxious to pay attention to what she was doing, so after she had upset a plate of buns and given an old lady two cups of tea at the same time, Cathy told her to give up.

"You can't think of two things at once, darling. You go and stand in the door and wait for your accompanist."

Ginnie was grateful.

"Thank you awfully, Mummy. Of course I never did a concert before—you can't think how fussed you feel. Miss Bloggs keeps saying how everybody's looking forward to it, and she's sure it's going to be splendid, but quite truthfully I'm not sure. Miss Newton's absolutely promised the person who plays the piano will know all Mrs. Gage's songs, but if she doesn't it'll be simply awful, for there's hardly any concert at all."

Cathy laughed and kissed her.

"Don't worry, pet. I'm sure Miss Bloggs is right, and it will go splendidly."

Long before the accompanist was due to arrive Ginnie was hopping first on one foot and then on the other. Suppose Miss Newton had forgotten? Suppose the accompanist had been run over? Then a small car drove up to the curb, the door opened, and out stepped Miss Newton herself.

Nobody at St. Winifred's would have known Miss Newton that afternoon. She climbed up on the platform and settled down at the piano as if it were an old friend. She was pleased to see Jane, talked to all the family, and to Miss Bloggs, and had a grand discussion with Mrs. Gage on old songs, but never once did she forget it was Ginnie's concert.

"Let me know the order of the program. Are you making an opening speech?"

Ginnie had given up that idea.

"No. I thought I would just do it at the end."

"I don't want to interfere, but I think I'd just say a word of welcome if I were you."

Ginnie was so startled to find Miss Newton there at all, let alone treating her so respectfully, that she would have agreed to stand on her head if Miss Newton had suggested it. She stepped to the front of the platform.

"How do you do? I can't make a proper speech—I'm not any good at it. This is Miss Newton, she's my headmistress, and she's playing the piano for everybody. Paul's going to announce the names of the songs. Jane's going to dance, Angus is going to sing and so is Daddy, and Mrs. Gage is going to do community singing, like she does at outings."

188

Jane, standing at the side of the stage in her silver tunic, gave Paul a nudge.

"Even though I've left St. Winifred's when I see Miss Newton I still feel like Alice in Wonderland. You know: 'Curtsy when you're thinking; it saves time.' "

Paul looked at Miss Newton.

"Seems a good type to me."

Jane limbered up.

"I think schoolmasters and schoolmistresses always seem good types to people who don't go to their schools."

Miss Bloggs, while Ginnie was making her speech, whispered to Miss Newton:

"Please play just the dear old favorites ... the nice ones, you know. We mustn't forget this is the parish hall. Mrs. Gage could, I think, be very easily carried away."

Miss Newton nodded as if in agreement, but privately she was sure Mrs. Gage would sing exactly what she wanted to, without asking her advice. And she was quite right. Mrs. Gage opened the concert, and right away she was a riot. She had only to sing a line, and she had all the old people singing with her. She would have taken up all the concert time, only Miss Newton gave some very loud finishing chords and called out:

"That will have to be all for now, Mrs. Gage, or my hands will drop off. Who's next, Ginnie?"

It really was a most successful concert. The old people enjoyed every moment of it, and when it was over it was not Ginnie who made a speech to the old people but an old man in the audience who made a speech to her. He was a very distinguished-looking old man, and he started with a grand bow.

"On behalf of all here I wish to give our most heartfelt thanks. We understand this concert was arranged for us

189

by the little lady they call Ginnie. I can assure you, Miss Ginnie, from the bottom of my heart, that we have had a real treat this afternoon, and we would like to show our appreciation to you and all who entertained us in the usual way."

Then the old people clapped and clapped and the concert was over.

The whole family, Mrs. Gage, and Miss Bloggs saw Miss Newton to her car, and tried to thank her, but she would not be thanked.

"I've enjoyed myself enormously. Hearing Mrs. Gage sing is a tonic. I thought you sang beautifully, Angus, and 'Cockles and Mussels' is an old favorite of mine, Mr. Bell. As for you, Jane, I'm proud of you. I'm glad we gave you that scholarship, for you are a credit to us. But of course, top praise is for you, Ginnie. It was a lovely concert."

Having said good-bye to Mrs. Gage and Miss Bloggs, the family, tired but pleased with themselves, trailed back to the vicarage. It seemed to have got stuffier while they had been in the parish hall, for a hot wind had arisen and blew bits of grit around in an irritating way. Cathy paused on the doorstep and looked around her.

"I've been so happy in this vicarage that often I forget how hideous it is here. Imagine, not a tree in sight! If this were August, and we were in Berkshire, this wind would make leaves rustle."

Jane put her arm through her father's.

"Wouldn't it be a gorgeous evening for us to fish?"

Ginnie sighed.

"Ricky and me would be lying under raspberry canes, and eating and eating."

Angus hopped as he remembered Liza's pets.

"Oh, goodness, why isn't it August now?"

190

Alex patted Esau.

"No one wishes that more than you do, old man. You'd rather chase rabbits than be dressed up as a baby at a parish concert, wouldn't you?"

In the letter box there was a telegram. It was addressed to Cathy. She tore it open, then stood staring at it.

Alex was worried.

"Anything wrong, darling?"

Paul had a horrid thought.

"Mumsmum or Mumsdad aren't ill, are they?"

Cathy pulled herself together.

"Nobody's ill. It's from Uncle Jim. It says: 'Bad fire. House completely burnt out. Writing. Jim.' "

12

A Busy Morning

At first the Bells were so sorry for Uncle Jim, Aunt Ann, Ricky, and Liza that they did not see what the fire meant to them. But Uncle Jim's first letter made the position perfectly clear. The fire was started by a fuse in the cellar. Everybody was out, and the fire had a good hold before anybody noticed it. A neighbor had rushed in and saved as much medical equipment as he could out of Jim's office, and Aunt Ann had managed to rescue a lot of clothes and bed linen, and a certain amount of furniture had been pulled into the garden, but they had more or less lost everything. Fortunately, they were fully insured, but he doubted if the old house would be worth repairing. What they would probably do was to build a small house, which would be much easier to run. In the meantime they had rented rooms in the village inn, and he had borrowed a room in the vicarage as a temporary office. Then he wrote:

"We feel so badly about all of you. Where will you go for August? We've tried to see if we could find a room for you and Alex, and the children could camp, but everything seems booked up."

Cathy felt miserable. She had been brought up in the

house: it was hateful to think what was left of it was to be pulled down, and a little, new, probably ugly house put up in its place."

"Of course it's the sensible thing to do," she told Alex, "but oh, dear, how I hate to think of the house disappearing. Not only because I loved it so when I was a child, but for all those glorious Augusts we've spent there."

August in Berkshire was so much part of family life that at first it was almost impossible to take in that there was not only not going to be any Berkshire that year, but quite probably there would never again be a family holiday there. Then slowly, like the tide coming in, it swept over the children, that not only was there not going to be any Berkshire, but unless something wonderful turned up, they would not be going away at all.

Every sort of scheme was put up. Alex put an advertisement in a church paper, offering to exchange parishes for a month with a country vicar, but even as he wrote the advertisement he told Cathy it was a waste of money.

"It's much too late. Anybody who wants to come to London has arranged an exchange months ago."

"And anyway," Jane pointed out, "I can't see why anyone would want this vicarage. If only we lived in a nice part of London we might have a chance."

"Anyway, I don't want Daddy swapping parishes," said Cathy. "He's arranged for somebody to do his work in August and he's going to let him do it. He needs a holiday."

Paul thought of Christmas.

"If only we'd known Uncle Jim's house was going to burn we could have saved Esau's prize money. Think of the splendid holiday we could have had with that."

Alex laughed.

"Well, we didn't know, and even if we had it's very unlikely we'd have managed to hold on to it until now. But your mentioning that money, Paul, has made me think. It's difficult for you children, but I don't want you to talk about what's happened. People around here have hearts of gold, and it would be only too easy for some kindhearted person to start a fund going to send us away. Well, we don't want that. Nobody in these parts has much money, and anything they have should go on holidays for themselves. You'll have to ask Mrs. Gage to say nothing, Cathy."

Mrs. Gage, when she heard what Alex had said, was furious.

"I never 'eard such nonsense! Carries goodness too far, the vicar does. There 'e is lookin' like a piece of string what somebody's chewed and spat out, and everybody sayin' 'ow bad 'e needs 'is 'oliday, and how 'e's not goin' away, and nobody isn't to know. Enough to turn the milk sour, it is. There's many would be glad to 'elp, and some I can think of wouldn't miss the money."

"All the same," said Cathy, "he's trusting you to say nothing, so you won't, will you?"

Mrs. Gage sniffed.

"You know me, proper clam when asked. But it turns me up, and it isn't only the vicar. There's Paul too tall by 'alf, and too thin, and not eatin' like 'e ought. There's Jane a proper disgrace. I was only sayin' to 'er yesterday, get any thinner and you'll slip down with the bath water. Angus could do with a bit more color. And as for you, dear, you're a nasty sight, put me in mind of a cabbage leaf what's been left lyin' around and gone soft. The only one of you lookin' properly 'erself is Ginnie. She's like my

194

Margaret Rose, never offer food and a proper dragon for sleep."

However Ginnie looked, she was finding the days after her concert heavy going. The verger's wife was delighted by her offer to look after her baby.

"Oh, it is kind of you, dear. I feel completely knocked out by my teeth. If you'd just push the pram up and down outside the church, he loves a ride in his pram, don't you, ducks?"

Ginnie did not think the baby a "ducks." She thought it a very disagreeable baby. It would lie on its back, staring at her in what she thought was a very rude way, and when it was not staring at her it blew bubbles. Her only comfort was her entries in her dedication book. "Spent from tea to nearly bedtime taking the verger's baby out in its carriage," looked, she thought, more imposing service than she had expected.

Only two nice things happened to lighten the family gloom. Jane had a very good report from the Royal Ballet School, and Alex had a letter saying that Angus could go as a full-time pupil.

"I suppose I'm pleased," Angus said, "but you can't really be pleased about future things. I like everything to happen now."

Alex laughed.

"You're an ungrateful boy. Think how miserable you would feel if they had written to say they wouldn't take you."

Angus looked scornful.

"It couldn't happen. My legs know they are learning very well indeed."

"I wish my legs were sure" said Jane. "Everybody seemed fairly pleased, but now that good report has come I feel

195

as if a load had fallen off my back. I think I'd die if they had written and said I'd never make a dancer."

Because they could not go away, Paul found the worry about joining Grandfather's business nagging at him. He had written to Grandfather soon after Jane won her scholarship, saying that he had decided to be a doctor. Grandfather had written back and told him he was a fool, but he could always change his mind.

"Any time you write to me promising to come into my business I will keep my word, and settle an allowance on you."

That allowance! In bed, and at odd moments during the day, Paul would see it in his mind's eye. He could see more. He could see himself saying to the family: "Don't worry, you're going to have a holiday after all. I've fixed it for you."

Then, on the Wednesday after they had heard about the fire, Jane beckoned him into her bedroom. She shut the door in a very secret way.

"Do you know any boys at your school who earn money at weekends and in the holidays?"

Paul sat on Ginnie's bed.

"Why?"

"Because, even if it's only for a week, Daddy must go away. He looks simply awful, and so does Mummy."

"I don't believe we could earn enough for that."

"Why not? I've heard of an agency. It's called the Helping Hand. I'm going there on Saturday to see if I can get some baby-sitting or something like that."

Paul laughed.

"Doing Ginnie out of a job?"

"That's only for her dedication book and she isn't paid,

196

but proper baby-sitters are. I don't see why I shouldn't be one."

Paul was remembering a chance conversation.

"There's a chap I know who did some work at home of some sort, which brought in quite a bit. I know it must have, because he bought books with the money he made, and they were jolly expensive books."

Jane's eyes shone.

"Good. Well, see him and find out what it was. I'm going to tell Ginnie and Angus we're going to try and earn just in case there's any way they can help, but I shouldn't think there is, they're too small to be much use."

As if the cancelation of their holiday was not enough tribulation for one week, Aunt Rose rang up to say that she, Uncle Alfred, Veronica, Grandfather, and Grandmother would like to come to tea on Saturday.

"We're off to France, you know," she said in her whiny voice. "Alfred's father and mother want to see you before we go. We're driving as far as Folkestone on Sunday, and going on to Dover on Monday morning in time to catch the boat. Alfred says can we all come to tea with you on Saturday?"

Cathy could feel Rose did not want to visit them the day before she left, and she did not blame her. But she knew Alfred: if he said a thing was going to happen, it happened.

"We'll love to have you of course. Lucky you going to France."

Rose sounded more whiny than ever.

"It's a terrible drive to St. Jean de Luz. We'll all be exhausted by the time we get there. Alfred wanted to fly,

197

but it was hopeless, you can't take much on a plane, and you need such a mass of clothes in a place like St. Jean."

Cathy tried to imagine St. Jean de Luz.

"I suppose you do."

"And talking of clothes," Rose went on, "my maid has turned out a lot of things of Veronica's and mine that we'll never wear again. The chauffeur's dropping the parcel in on you this morning. Good-bye, dear. See you on Saturday."

As usual, when she needed comfort, Cathy turned to Mrs. Gage.

"There's a parcel coming from Lady Bell. I ought to be grateful, but I don't feel like sorting clothes in this heat."

"Funny, I seen a parcel in me teacup at breakfast." Mrs. Gage thought Cathy looked paler than usual. She was washing up, but she left the sink to pull a chair away from the table. "Come and 'ave a nice sit-down. We don't 'ave to unpack Lady Bell's parcel just because she sent it, do we?"

Cathy sat and, which was very unlike her, drooped despairingly.

"But we do. She, Sir Alfred, Veronica, and the vicar's parents are all coming to tea on Saturday; they're just off to France for a holiday. We must unpack it before she comes, so at least I know what she's sent."

Mrs. Gage, in her mind, threw her washing-up water at Aunt Rose.

"Makes you mad, don't it? Sorry to speak rough of the vicar's relatives, but they're swank-pots—no good sayin' different. France! I'd France them. Goin' off where they like, and there's you all needin' a 'oliday so bad, gettin' a parcel of old clothes."

Cathy half got up.

"I'll start the beds."

Mrs. Gage jerked her head in a commanding way.

"You'll stay right where you are till I done 'ere. Nothin' like a bit of comp'ny when you're down-'earted."

Cathy rested her head in her hands.

"I don't mind admitting I'm downhearted. Of course, I'm worried about my brother, but I'm still more worried about my family. They simply must get away for a bit. If only it hadn't been so sudden. I could have fixed something. And you know how it is, Mrs. Gage: when you're going away you feel things can wait, but now we're not going, I see how much needs doing. The dining room's a disgrace, there's a piece of paper coming off the hall wall, the big armchair in the drawing room has an enormous hole. I simply can't let the family see the house like this on Saturday. I must do something to tidy it up."

Mrs. Gage had finished the washing-up. She patted Cathy's arm.

"Don't you worry, dear. I'll take some paste to the paper in the 'all, and you can run around with a brush of paint. And I'll give the 'ouse such a cleaning by Saturday, whatever else Lady Bell and that Sir Alfred find to turn their noses up at, it won't be our vicarage."

Cathy was in the kitchen when Mrs. Gage staggered in with the parcel from Aunt Rose and put it on the table. Mrs. Gage gave an imitation of Uncle Alfred's chauffeur, Hodges.

"This parcel is from 'er Ladyship for Mrs. Bell."

Cathy laughed.

"Get the scissors, and let's see what she's sent. Perhaps I can find something to cover the drawing-room armchair."

Aunt Rose's parcels were always beautifully packed by

her maid, but as a rule there was not much in them that was exactly what was wanted. This parcel was no exception. There were frilly dresses of Veronica's, which were too small for Jane and wrong for Ginnie. There were lace evening dresses, and chiffon blouses that would go with nothing, elaborate housecoats and smart hats. The plain clothes, which would have been a godsend, seldom came in the parcels, for when they were in good condition Aunt Rose sold them or gave them to her maid. It was only now and again something really useful, like the black dress, came to Cathy. In this parcel the most useful thing was a garment made of brown velvet. Cathy thought it was a housecoat, but Mrs. Gage thought it was an evening dress. Whatever it had been, it had an immensely wide skirt, and Cathy fell on it with a cry of joy.

"Look at that!"

Mrs. Gage looked.

"Well, I must say velvet's classy, but it's very worn. Will it cut up for Jane?"

Cathy hugged the garment to her.

"It won't, she'd look awful in this color. It's going to recover the armchair."

Mrs. Gage was holding up Veronica's dresses with coos of approval.

"Sweetly pretty, aren't they?"

Cathy laughed.

"Don't say that to Ginnie. Put everything on my bed, but leave the velvet with me. I'm going to have a grand afternoon's upholstering."

On Friday, when Ginnie went to fetch the verger's baby in its baby carriage, she heard he was going away with his mother the next morning. She was most annoyed, and as she pushed the baby around the church she told him so.

"You are the miserablest baby. You've looked sneering every day, you've blown bubbles at me, and now, on the very last day of my week, you're going away, so I've got to look for a different baby tomorrow. You see, I promised Miss Newton it would be a baby every day, and tomorrow isn't a day when I've time to look for babies, because the relations are coming to tea."

On Saturday morning before he went to school Paul talked to Jane.

"That chap I told you about is going to take me to see the man who gives him work. If I'm late for lunch and Mum flaps, say you knew I might be late, because I'm seeing someone."

"I'm going to the Helping Hand agency this morning, after I've done the beds. Let's hope we both get a job. If I can get some baby-sitting I'll start tonight after the relations have gone. I hope your friend finds something sensible for you. I mean, if it was to do with a drugstore or something like that, it would help with being a doctor, wouldn't it?"

The hot weather made Paul feel tired and cross.

"If I ever am a doctor."

Jane looked at him witheringly.

"What do you mean, Paul Bell?"

"Well, sometimes it all seems so hopeless. Especially now we can't go to Uncle Jim's. If I was to work for Grandfather . . ."

Jane was really shocked.

"That would be selling your soul for a mess of pottage; you're a lily-livered loon to think of it. I hate seeing

Mummy and Daddy looking tired as much as you do, but if you think I'd give up dancing and go into Grandfather's wool business because of earning money, you're wrong. I wouldn't."

"Oh, all right, don't nag. It's only a thought. Good luck with the Helping Hand people."

The Helping Hand agency was a small business in unimposing premises. But although it did not look grand, Jane hung about quite a while outside, trying to get up courage to go in. She hoped she was not looking too young. She had tied her hair back, because she thought it seemed more grown-up that way, and put on her longest cotton dress, but it did not hide the fact that she was wearing socks and what she called little-girl shoes. She could only hope she would sit to be interviewed and then her legs would not show.

Inside the agency there was a counter, and behind it sorting cards was a brisk-looking woman with gray hair. She looked up as Jane came in.

"Good morning. What is it, dear?"

Jane tried to sound as if she was used to agencies.

"I've come to see if you have some work I could do."

The woman looked amused.

"We've no work for children."

"I'm not a child. I mean, I'm much older and stronger than I look, and I'm honest, sober, and hard-working."

The woman laid down her tray of cards.

"Come and sit down." Jane sat. "Now, who are you? I want your name, age, and address."

Jane had not thought of having to give her address.

"If I tell you, will you keep it a secret? I mean not ring up Daddy, or anything like that?" The woman nodded. "Well, I'm Jane Bell. My father is vicar of St. Mark's."

The woman was very good at listening, and very kind. She seemed really sorry about the fire, and quite understood that Jane wanted to help. When Jane had finished talking she asked her to wait while she went to the telephone in the back room. She thought she had just the right work for her, which she could do at home in her spare time.

While Jane was in the agency, Ginnie was out doing the family shopping, but at the same time she was looking for a baby to be kind to. Oddly enough she could not find one; there were plenty of babies, but none of them had mothers who looked as if they needed help in looking after them. Then suddenly, just as she was giving up hope, she saw what she was looking for. There was a baby carriage in the full glare of the sun, and the baby was screaming like a parrot in the zoo. Ginnie pushed the carriage across to the shady side of the road.

"Don't cry, baby," Ginnie whispered. "I'm going to take you for a walk in the shade. It's a shame leaving you in the sun, you look red and most peculiar, rather like bacon that's been too much cooked." She jolted the carriage up and down, and the baby, glad to be out of the sun and pleased with the motion, smiled. Ginnie was enchanted. "You're much nicer than my other baby I took out for service. If I had any money I'd buy you an ice cream."

It was just as Ginnie was whispering those words that the screaming began. High, hysterical screams on the words "My baby! My baby! Somebody's stolen my baby!"

Ginnie turned the carriage again. "Silly woman!" she thought. "Why couldn't she shop a little longer? I wonder if Miss Newton would count this teeny walk as looking after somebody's baby? It's not my fault that mother wants it back."

Ginnie turned the carriage to cross the road, and as she did so the baby's mother, and the friends of the baby's mother, saw her and rushed across to her.

"You dirty little thief," the mother sobbed, dragging Ginnie's hands off the carriage. "How dare you steal my baby!"

Ginnie was amazed at such stupidity.

"I wasn't stealing it. I was taking it for a walk for service."

A red-faced woman joined in.

"That for a tale!"

An old lady shook her head at Ginnie.

"I don't know what children are comin' to. No sense of responsibility."

The mother sobbed louder and louder.

"Only left 'im for a moment . . . then I found 'im gone . . . really upset me, it has."

The red-faced woman put an arm around the mother.

"Come and sit down a minute, dear. It's the shock, that's what it is."

More people crowded around, all telling each other what had happened.

"Stealing the baby . . ."

"Only left 'im for a moment."

"What 'er Dad'll say I don't know."

"Ought to know better, seein' 'oo she is."

"Ought to be locked up."

Then, above the noise, came a slow, solid-sounding policeman's voice.

"Now, now. What's all this?"

Everybody tried to tell him, but the policeman fixed a stern eye on Ginnie.

"What 'ave you got to say?"

Ginnie still thought everybody was being very silly.

"Of course I didn't steal the baby. I have to look after a baby each day this week for service, and the verger's baby's gone away, so I took this one for a walk."

Everybody started to shout at that.

"That's what she says."

"Oughter know better."

"Properly upset the poor mother. Looks like she's about to faint."

The policeman thought it would be easier to find out the truth when fewer people were talking. He beckoned to Ginnie.

"You come along with me to the station."

Miss Bloggs, passing on her bicycle, saw the crowd and thought there had been an accident. She stopped to see if she could help.

"Has there been an accident, Constable?" Then she saw Ginnie. "Hallo, dear. What's happening?"

The policeman, who was new to the district, did not know Ginnie or Miss Bloggs.

"Is this your child, madam?"

"No, no. This is little Virginia Bell. Daughter of the vicar of St. Mark's."

The voices rose again.

" 'Er Dad won't 'alf give 'er a hidin'."

"I'd take a strap to 'er if she was mine."

The policeman's voice rose above the noise.

"Quiet, please." Then he turned to Miss Bloggs. "This child was found with this lady's baby." Then he took out

205

his notebook and looked at the mother. "Are you charging this child?"

The mother was still crying.

"I don't want to be 'ard, but . . ."

Miss Bloggs opened her purse and took out some money.

"Would one of you go with this lady and see she has a cup of tea."

That somehow cleared the crowd. There was still a good deal of muttering about how bad Ginnie had been, but everybody moved away, and only the policeman, Ginnie, and Miss Bloggs were left. The policeman shook his head at Ginnie.

"You were lucky the mother didn't charge you. Rightly I ought to take you to the station. Still, maybe it will be enough if I see your father."

Miss Bloggs felt it would be very upsetting for Alex and Cathy if a policeman brought Ginnie home.

"Her father must, of course, be told, but if I might suggest, I know the family well, perhaps you would allow me to tell him."

The policeman looked gravely at his notebook. Then he shut it and put it in his pocket.

"Very well, madam, but it's a serious offense. She's very lucky not to be in bad trouble; her father should know that."

Miss Bloggs looked like a frightened hen.

"Quite right, Constable. He shall know, and I can promise you Ginnie will be punished."

When Paul came in lunch was over, so he had his by himself in the dining room. Hearing Jane come in with Esau he called her in.

206

"What on earth's up? Ginnie's howling in the study with Dad, and Mum's shut in the drawing room."

Jane closed the door and sat down at the table.

"Ginnie's such a fool. You know she's looking after a baby for service—well, the verger's baby has gone away, so she stole one this morning."

Paul could not help laughing.

"What happened?"

"She nearly went to the police station, but Miss Bloggs rescued her. She promised the policeman Daddy would punish her."

"So that's what's happening. Poor old Ginnie—but she is a prize fool. What luck with the agency?"

Jane was ashamed to be pleased with so much gloom around, but she could not help being.

"I've got some work. It's in my bedroom. What about you?"

Paul, too, was pleased.

"So have I. I've got mine over there."

Jane looked where Paul was pointing.

"Boxes!" Then a thought struck her. "Paul Bell, you aren't being paid for addressing envelopes, are you? That's what I'm doing."

"I am. The man said you can get awfully quick when you're used to it. How are we going to explain being in our bedrooms so much?"

Jane leaned on the table.

"I was thinking about that while I took Esau out. I thought I'd tell Mummy I was making something as a surprise; you could say the same thing. We'll have to tell Mrs. Gage what we're doing, because she'll stop Mummy being too interested. I won't lie—I'll say it's something for Daddy, which is true, and she'll think it's for his birthday,

207

as it's in September. I think I'll see her now, and sort of plant the idea."

In the study Alex had been trying to make Ginnie understand what she had done.

"This was a very wrong thing you did, Ginnie, taking that poor woman's baby."

"I keep telling you, Daddy, I didn't take it. It was meant for niceness."

Alex's voice was stern.

"It was meant for nothing of the sort, and you know it. I suppose what really happened was that you'd lost the verger's baby, and you wanted to get your baby-minding over, and snatched at the first baby you saw."

"Not the first. There were hundreds of babies out this morning."

"Anyway, you took a baby without asking the consent of the mother, which you knew to be wrong. That's the truth, isn't it?"

Ginnie stopped prevaricating.

"Yes, Daddy."

Alex sighed.

"You know how Mummy and I hate punishing you. But now I've got to."

"One of the people who shouted said you ought to take a strap to me."

"I don't see how taking a strap to you fits the crime of frightening a poor mother by taking away her baby."

Ginnie leaned against Alex.

"Do you think you could decide on my punishment fairly soon? I absolutely hate things hanging over me."

Alex put his arm round her.

"I'll try to. It'll hang over me too, you know."

Ginnie flung her arms round Alex's neck.

"Poor Daddy. I'm sorry, truly I am. But it's so hot, and I'm so tired of looking after babies. I wanted to get the last baby over, and never look after a baby again. I was thinking such a lot about that, that I forgot it was wrong just to take a baby and not ask its mother."

Alex held Ginnie to him.

"I'm sure that's true. But you must learn that nothing must ever so fill your mind you forget to think what is right and what is wrong. I'm going to give you a punishment to help you to think about that."

"What's it going to be?"

Alex spoke slowly.

"You took something that didn't belong to you. Is that right?" Ginnie nodded. "But your share of the next family treat does belong to you. Is that right?"

Ginnie began to see what was coming.

"Yes."

"Well, when the next family treat turns up, you must give your share of it away. I don't mind who you give it to, but you have to give it away without any reminder from me."

"What sort of treat? It might be something simply gorgeous."

"I'm sure the poor mother thinks the baby you took simply gorgeous."

That was when Ginnie started the crying Paul had heard.

"It's all that beastly dedication book. I don't think 'looked after baby' is grand enough service. I wanted to get it over, and do something else."

Alex gave Ginnie his handkerchief.

"I've not quite understood why that dedication book is

209

so important. There are plenty of other honors at St. Winifred's Miss Virginia Bell could win. She has always seemed quite happy without them. Why is having the best dedication book so vital a matter?"

That was the last straw. A howl of woe came from Ginnie.

"Silly Daddy! I don't want to be top at lessons, or anything like that: I want to win something I'm the only one in the family can do. All the others are good at something. I'm not good at anything at all." Tears choked her. "You'd hate to be the only one who wasn't good at anything, wouldn't you, Daddy? You know you'd hate it. Oh, that beastly baby, I wish I'd never seen it and its horrid carriage."

Jane found Cathy kneeling by the armchair, fixing its new cover.

"Goodness, Mummy, when did you make that?"

Cathy stood up and looked at her handiwork.

"It was a housecoat of Aunt Rose's. It came in that last parcel."

Jane walked around the chair.

"It's an awful color, isn't it?"

"It is to me," Cathy agreed; "but I don't think it can be really. Aunt Rose's clothes all come from the best places, and I shouldn't think they make clothes in awful colors at the best places."

Jane put her arms around Cathy and hugged her.

"Oh, Mummy, how I wish I could jump suddenly from me learning to dance, to me being able to dance properly, and earning money for you and Daddy. I'd buy you everything, and you'd never, never again have to spend

210

hours in hot weather cutting up a beastly old velvet house-coat to cover a chair."

Cathy kissed Jane.

"Darling, don't be so silly. Do you think I'd miss one minute of watching my children grow up for all the money in the world?"

Jane felt as if quite easily she could cry.

"I don't mind us being poor, we have more fun than any other family I know. It's only now, when we can't have a holiday or anything, and when the relations come, that I feel low-spirited. When Aunt Rose and Uncle Alfred are here everything's spoilt. We all fuss how the house looks, what we're going to wear, and what we're going to eat."

Cathy spoke gently and quietly.

"Jane! Don't get worked up, darling. You worry too much. You're worrying now about what Aunt Rose is going to say about that chair, aren't you?"

"Only because she'll look despisingly at you."

"But I don't mind if she does. I'm too glad of her old brown velvet to cover the chair. It was a disgrace as it was."

Jane swallowed the lump in her throat.

"I'm a silly fool to mind, and you're an angel not to."

Cathy knelt down again to put in another nail.

"They won't stay long, as they're leaving tomorrow. That's one comfort. I don't know what punishment Daddy is giving poor Ginnie, but if he doesn't send her to bed early, perhaps we could take supper to the park. It'll be cool there."

It was a lovely idea. Then the piles of envelopes in her bedroom came to Jane's mind.

"I'm sorry, Mummy. Paul and I can't go out tonight. We're working at something."

Cathy hammered in another tack.

"Are you? What at?"

"A secret. I'll just tell you it's to do with Daddy."

Cathy laid down her hammer.

"Is it? Now, I wonder what you're giving him?" Then she saw her watch. "Oh, goodness, look at the time! Send everybody to wash and change, the relations will be here in half an hour."

13

The Relations

The relations had the pleased-with-themselves feeling that comes with being sure that, at great personal inconvenience, you are doing the right thing. It was very hot, Alex's vicarage was in an unattractive, extra stuffy part of London, and they were going away tomorrow, but they were not allowing any of these things to put off the visit. As they drove along they congratulated each other.

"It wouldn't seem right somehow, going to foreign parts without saying good-bye to Alex, Cathy, and the children," said Grandmother.

"They would have felt it if we hadn't gone to see them today," Grandfather agreed.

Rose fanned herself.

"I hope they're grateful, because really in this heat it is rather an effort."

Alfred was sitting in front with the chauffeur. He turned around.

"Never mind, Rose. You'll soon be lying by the sea in one of those fancy beach getups."

Veronica felt she was being forgotten.

"And so will I, Dada."

Alfred smiled proudly at the thought of what a picture Veronica would be in her beach clothes.

"So you will and all. Dada will be glad to see the roses back in those pale cheeks."

Grandmother looked at Veronica and thought she looked remarkably healthy.

"I don't think Veronica looks pale, and she certainly looks cool all in white."

"It's quite a plain dress, though," Rose said. "I don't like to dress her up when she's meeting her cousins; it seems hardly kind."

Grandfather and Grandmother exchanged looks. They thought a lot of things were said in front of Veronica which never should be said, for they made her more affected than she was already.

"Oh, well," said Grandmother, "Jane's one of those children who looks nice in anything she wears, and Ginnie, bless her, doesn't care what she puts on."

"And I reckon," Grandfather added, "they'll have every bit as good a time with Cathy's relations in Berkshire as we'll have in France, so they're in no need of pity from us."

Alex, Cathy, Esau, and the children were waiting outside the vicarage for the relations. Cathy said, looking particularly at Ginnie and Angus:

"Don't forget, darlings, no one is to say we aren't going away. If the subject comes up of course they've got to know about the fire, but not that we've no other plans. Just say where we're going is a secret, or something like that, but with any luck you won't have to say anything, for they'll take it for granted we're going to Berkshire as usual."

The children had been told several times they were not to say they were not going away, and they were bored by the subject. They were particularly bored by it as they

214

thought it was silly of Alex and Cathy to be so secret about their troubles.

"It isn't as though they'd help," Paul said to Jane. "Grandfather said Dad should never have a penny of his brass, and he's stuck to it, but at least it might make them talk less about what they're going to do in France."

Jane agreed with him.

"It might even make them feel sort of ashamed. If I had relations much poorer than I was, I'd feel a mean dog going to France leaving them stewing in London."

The relations' arrival was something of a sensation, for Alfred had just bought a new car. He always had big cars, but this one was bigger and shinier-looking than usual.

Alex, as he kissed his mother, said:

"Alfred's cars put our stock up in this neighborhood. No one else around here has cars of this size outside their door."

In the drawing room, just what Jane had been afraid would happen, did. As soon as they got into the room Veronica started to giggle.

"Oh, look, Mummy!"

Rose looked.

"Good gracious! My old housecoat!"

"I hope you don't mind," said Cathy; "but the chair needed covering so dreadfully badly."

Rose had a very tinkling sort of laugh.

"Of course I don't mind. I'm just amused, that's all. So funny seeing one's old clothes as a chair cover."

Jane's face had flushed. Grandmother, who had been looking at her, held out a hand and drew her onto the sofa beside her.

"You're a lucky girl, Jane, to have so clever a mother. Is that dancing school too hard? You're looking thin."

Jane felt soothed by Grandmother's praise of Cathy.

"Of course it's not too hard, it's gorgeous. I love every second. But it's been a bit hot, hasn't it, and I expect I look rather end-of-termish."

Grandmother nodded.

"That'll be it. When do you go to your brother's, Cathy?"

Out the story had to come. The relations were horrified.

"Burnt down!" Grandmother exclained.

"I hope they were fully insured," said Alfred.

Alex was glad to be able to answer that satisfactorily.

"They certainly were. Jim's thinking of building an entirely new house on the old site."

Grandfather had noticed that when Grandmother had asked Cathy about going to Berkshire the children had exchanged looks. He scented a mystery.

"If you aren't going to Berkshire, where are you going for your holiday, Alex?"

Alex shook his head at his father.

"That's something you can't ask. It's a family secret."

Cathy felt they were on dangerous ground.

"Ginnie, Angus, and Veronica, it's very dull for you up here. Why don't you show Veronica your caterpillars, Angus, and, Ginnie, tell Mrs. Gage we're ready for tea."

Grandfather was no fool. He watched Ginnie, Angus, and Veronica run out of the room. He listened while Cathy, rather carefully he thought, took the subject away from holidays. Then to himself he said: "Something's oop."

Over tea Paul asked Uncle Alfred about the new car, what it would do, how long it would take them to motor to Folkestone, and how long from Calais to St. Jean de Luz. Grandfather laughed.

"The person you want to talk to, Paul, is Hodges. He's doing the driving, not your uncle."

Grandmother had an idea.

"Why don't you let the children have a drive around after tea, Alfred? They could go by the river, the air'll do them good, and maybe there's somewhere nice where they could stop for ice cream."

Paul, Jane, and Angus looked at Uncle Alfred, who, after a moment's thought, nodded.

"I don't see why not." He smiled at Veronica. "Would Dada's little sweetheart like that?"

"Well, they mustn't be too long," Aunt Rose whined. "We have a long day tomorrow, remember."

"Nonsense, Rose," said Grandfather. " 'Tisn't every day I get a chance of a talk with Alex. It isn't half past four yet; if they're back by six it will give us time."

"Six!" thought Cathy. "Oh, goodness, I suppose Alex will take his father and Alfred into his study, and what I'm to do with the other two I don't know. Alex's mother is all right, but an hour of Rose!" Then she looked at her children, and gave herself a mental slap. What a selfish mother she was, thinking only of herself. Of course the children wanted to go out in the new car.

"How lovely," she said to Grandmother, "to have a real long time together. Hurry up, children. You'll have time to go to Greenwich and back. It'll be lovely there today."

Ginnie's heart sank lower and lower. The first treat! The new car! Ice cream! It was more than could be endured. She looked at Alex, and her eyes asked a question. "Must it be this treat?" Alex's face was sorry, but a punishment was a punishment. He answered by nodding his head. Ginnie got up.

217

"Can I tell Mr. Hodges, Mummy? He's in the kitchen having tea with Mrs. Gage."

Hodges was delighted to hear the children were to have a run by the river, for he was proud of the new car, and they were a much better car audience than Uncle Alfred, Aunt Rose, and Veronica. But he was still more pleased when he heard Ginnie invite Mrs. Gage.

"Would you like to go for a drive in Uncle Alfred's posh car?"

"Me! Well! If only I'd known, I'd 'ave come in me best 'at. I hope Mr. Gage sees me, 'e won't 'alf get a shock. But what's your Mum doin' about the clearin' and washin' up?"

Ginnie had not thought of that, but she was fond of Mrs. Gage and if somebody had to have her share of a treat she was glad it was her.

"I'll do it."

Mrs. Gage started to ask why Ginnie was not coming. Then she remembered the stolen baby. She gave her a kiss.

"Thank you, ducks. Sorry you aren't comin', but I shan't 'alf enjoy meself."

Ginnie could not bear to see the others drive away without her, so she told Cathy she would clear the table, and shut herself in the dining room. The relations, of course, noticed she was not in the car.

"Why didn't Ginnie go?" asked Rose.

Cathy knew Grandmother would guess Ginnie was being punished for something, so she gave her a meaningful smile as she answered:

"She stayed to help me."

Rose saw nothing odd in Ginnie staying behind. She supposed, in a more or less servantless household, one of the children would have to stay behind to work.

"I'm glad that woman of yours has gone with them. If they get out, I don't want little Veronica running about getting hot and tired, and of course the woman will see they stop at a nice clean place to have ice cream."

Alfred, too, saw nothing in one of the children being kept at home to work, but Grandfather thought it odd. Instead of following Alfred and Alex into the study he went into the dining room.

"So this is where you've got to, young Ginnie. I hear you stayed behind to help your mother. Very kind of you."

Ginnie grinned.

"I bet you didn't believe it. You know I'm not the sort to give up driving in a gorgeous car, and having ice cream, if I didn't have to. I'm being punished."

Grandfather sat down and lit his pipe.

"Are you now. And what might you have been up to?"

Ginnie sat down and told Grandfather all about her dedication book, and paying for the concert with looking after babies, and what had happened that morning.

Grandfather was a very good audience. When Ginnie had finished he did not say anything about the baby stealing, for he thought, as she had been punished, there was no need for him to rub in how badly she had behaved. Instead he said:

"Where's this place you are going for your holiday?"

Ginnie got up and piled plates on a tray.

"Daddy told you it was a secret."

"I know he did, but I was always curious. I can't bear a secret. I just have to find out what it's all about."

Ginnie was enchanted.

"Do you? Then that's why I'm so curious. I always have to find things out." Then she remembered that this was

219

something Grandfather could not find out, but it seemed mean to leave him guessing. "Well, actually . . ." Then she paused, trying to think of somewhere lovely to pretend they were going, and an idea came to her. "We're going to a posh hotel. It's by the sea. One of those very big hotels that you see on films."

Grandfather took a match and pushed some tobacco into his pipe.

"One of those places with large verandas overlooking the sea?"

Ginnie was quite carried away by her fairytale hotel.

"Yes, and there's a skating rink . . . oh, and a fun fair in the garden, where everybody can go on everything, even the giant racer, without paying."

"And free ice cream by just pressing a bell?" Grandfather suggested.

Ginnie skipped with pleasure.

"Of course, every sort and kind, and every color, only you don't press a bell. It's in a shop thing in the hall, with a notice on it saying 'Help yourself.' And beside it there's a candy shop where you help yourself too. Oh, it's a stupendous place. I can almost see it."

Grandfather had tidied his pipe.

"When do you leave for this posh hotel?"

Grandfather saying that brought Ginnie back to earth with a bump. She piled the rest of the plates onto her tray.

"I'm not absolutely sure, and if you don't mind, Grandfather, I've got to go and wash up."

14

The Earners

The weather changed. It became wet and muggy. Then a boisterous, gritty wind blew the wet away. Then, of all unkind things, just about the time the family would have been leaving for Berkshire, it turned hot and sunny again.

When people need a change of air, and do not get it, they are inclined to become cross. As the days grew hotter, the Bells got crosser—even Cathy was short-tempered. Alex never got really cross. He thought it wrong to be cross, and so struggled to keep that he was feeling cross to himself. Jane said Alex's keeping feeling cross to himself was worse than snapping out as ordinary people did, who were not parsons. She thought trying hard gave him a martyred face, which made other people lose their tempers looking at it. Cathy was in despair about her family. Luckily for her she had Mrs. Gage to talk to, for Mrs. Gage, on hearing the family could not go away, said she would not go away either.

"I would 'ave gone if you was all goin', but seein' you're not, I'd just as soon take a day 'ere and there."

"But what about Mr. Gage?"

"Oh, 'im! I said to 'im, you can take an 'oliday when

221

you like, so you'll take it when the vicar goes away. Like it or lump it."

Cathy sighed.

"When the vicar goes! Poor Mr. Gage, I'm afraid that's not going to be this summer."

Mrs. Gage thought of the piles of addressed envelopes leaving the house, and the money they were earning.

"Never say die. You never know your luck."

"Hope you're right," said Cathy; "but I can't think how it's going to be managed, for we can't clean ourselves out of savings. But, oh dear, the children look pale. Jane's a perfect disgrace; she's a greenish color, and nothing but skin and bone."

Mrs. Gage tried to cheer Cathy up, but she, too, was shocked how wretched Jane looked.

"Jane's one 'oo's looks pity 'er. My Margaret Rose was the same, always 'avin' me along to the school they were, askin' what she ate. Malnutrition, that's what they call it. I said to the doctor, 'I'll malnutrition you! I'll 'ave you know my Margaret Rose eats enough to keep your 'ole 'ospital goin'. Don't ask me where it gets to, all I know is it goes down. I can't 'elp it if what goes in don't show when it gets inside.' "

Cathy was cooking lunch. She gave some fish she was preparing an angry slap.

"I wish Paul and Jane would give up this secret they're working on. I think it's something for their father's birthday, but it isn't good for them, shut up in their bedrooms hour after hour. If only they would go out we could do some nice things. I've offered them days at Hampton Court, Kew Gardens, Hampstead—anywhere they like. If only they would take a day out, the vicar would probably come too—he promised he would take a holiday even if he was at home, but he isn't. It's always something; one of his pet parishioners is ill, or in trouble, and off he goes."

Upstairs Paul had gone into Jane's room.

"I've just finished. I shan't start another hundred before lunch."

Jane raised her head wearily.

"My people have such awful names, yours are much easier, just plain Mr. or Mrs. I do think I ought to get extra money for writing names like Brigadier Wildensea-Prothero, C.V.O., O.B.E., D.S.O. Oh, Paul, shall we ever earn enough? I'm so stupid this morning, I keep getting the names wrong, and have to scratch them out, and then the envelopes look awful. . . ."

Paul thought the envelope Jane showed him looked so awful the agency would not accept it.

"You've got some spares: You should use those."

"I've used them."

"Well, I've got some you can have. It's no good sending this one as it is."

Jane was nearly in tears.

"I couldn't have believed there was such an awful, awful thing to do as addressing envelopes. If only I could do something with my feet, instead of with my hands. I wouldn't mind dancing the same exercise over and over again, but addressing envelopes. . . ." She broke off as a sob choked her.

Paul looked at her in a worried way.

"You better give up. It's no good getting in a state."

Jane was really angry.

"I wouldn't mind if we had nearly finished, but it takes such thousands of envelopes to earn any decent amount, and when they're all Right Honorables, or The Dowager Lady Something-or-other, nobody could write fast."

"Tell you what. You take an afternoon off, and I'll put in a bit of extra time after tea, and do some of yours."

Jane cried worse than ever at that.

"That'll mean you'll have addressed envelopes every single minute of the day. Of course I can do mine; it's only I feel so stupid today."

Paul sat down on Jane's bed.

"I've been thinking. If we get rooms for Mum and Dad for a week somewhere, we might manage to camp."

"What in? We haven't any tents."

"No. But Dad was going to spend something on our holiday, so he might manage to hire two for a week. I say, you do look awful. Do leave the beastly things for now, anyway."

Jane had the stubbornness people get when they are overtired.

"I won't till the gong goes. I'm going to finish this hundred. Here's another beast—Sir Alexander and Lady Corfu."

Paul did not know what to do. He hated to see Jane crying and looking so ill.

"Pack it up, do. I tell you, I'll do them for you."

Jane blew her nose and tried to choke back a sob.

"I won't. It's just as bad for you as it is for me."

"If you could see yourself."

That made Jane even more stubborn.

"Oh, shut up, and don't natter."

Paul decided to use force. He put an arm around Jane and with his free hand held her pen.

"Now will you stop? I shan't let you go until you do."

Jane struggled, and threw Paul off his balance. Before

he came in she had refilled her fountain pen, and forgotten to screw the cap back on the ink. There was a splash, and the ink bottle fell into the box in which were her finished envelopes.

With a howl Jane freed herself from Paul, seized some blotting-paper and knelt on the floor mopping furiously.

"Oh, look what you've done! You've put ink all over my finished envelopes, they won't pay me for them now, and I'll have to pay for new envelopes to make up, and the carpet's sopping. . . ."

Paul knelt beside her, scrubbing at the ink patches on the carpet. Then, as he worked, he came to a decision. It was nonsense going on like this. The money they earned would go nowhere—they all needed more than a week's change.

"I say, Jane. Pack up the beastly envelopes. Put away your pen. I'm going to send a telegram. When I get the answer to it, there'll be enough money for a holiday for all of us."

Jane was crying so badly she could hardly speak.

"Don't be silly! A telegram where? Oh, goodness, I shouldn't think it would be possible to be unhappier than I am now. It's so hot, and everybody's cross. Do you suppose anything nice will ever happen again?"

Paul paused in his mopping.

"Listen. I really can send a telegram. I'm not supposed to tell anybody, but I know I can trust you. . . ."

As they cleared the floor, Paul told Jane of the conversation he had with Grandfather in the theater the year before. He told her how he had decided to accept his offer on the very day she had won her scholarship. Of how he had written to Grandfather, and the offer was still open. When he had finished, Jane was no longer crying; instead she was angry.

"Paul Bell! Don't you dare to send that telegram, or ever, ever think of Grandfather's business again. Just now, because of no holiday, being poor seems to matter, but it doesn't really, and you know it doesn't. Just imagine what you'll feel like when you're old, thirty or something like that, and because of upsetting some ink now, you're working in the wool business forever and ever, instead of being a doctor."

Paul gave a last dab at the carpet.

"I think that's the best we can do with the floor. Being poor doesn't matter to me, but it's all of you."

Jane got up and faced him.

"I suppose you see yourself as a Christian martyr, being thrown to the lions. Well, I don't see you like that at all. I think you're being a coward."

"I like that!"

"It is cowardly, just for a holiday, to give up doing what you know you can do, for something you'd hate and be terrible at. And another thing, you've no right to throw yourself to the lions for your family without asking your family if they want you to be eaten for them. The least you can do is to ask them first, and I know what we'll say."

"I hadn't thought of that."

"Well, think now. How would you like it if secretly I gave up being a dancer to give you a holiday? Just imagine, whenever you looked at me, thinking: 'If I hadn't had that holiday Jane might have been dancing at Covent Garden.' Well, that's how we'd be about you. We'd think if we hadn't had that holiday you might have been Sir Paul Bell, surgeon to the Queen."

Although he had written to Grandfather, the idea that he might have to go into his business was always at the back of Paul's mind. Also, he now knew, at the back of his mind he had seen a grateful family saying thank you. Now what Jane said was like a window opening and letting sunshine into a dark room. She was right. He could never accept Grandfather's offer, because the family would hate it if he did. It was a lovely releasing feeling to think that never again would the possibility of writing that letter crop up.

"You're a fool," he told Jane, "but you're perfectly right. You'd all loathe it if I said yes."

While Paul and Jane were talking, Ginnie had been sent up to wash before lunch. She had been going into her bedroom, but outside the door she heard Jane crying. Then she heard her say: "I wouldn't mind if we had nearly finished, but it takes such thousands of envelopes to earn any decent amount." Looking thoughtful, Ginnie tiptoed into the bathroom. Presently, as she washed, she spoke a thought out loud. "And me and Angus earning nothing! But somehow we'll earn something this afternoon."

Although Paul accepted he could not write to Grandfather, he did not agree that Jane could do any more envelopes that afternoon. In this he was supported by Mrs. Gage. Jane called her to ask her advice about the ink on the carpet, and at once she took charge.

"On the carpet! As far as I can see, there's ink everywhere. Look at your dress, Jane. Lucky it's your blue. Take it off, dear, and I'll get the worst out with a drop of milk. What 'appened?"

"I was trying to stop Jane working," Paul explained. "I

227

said she looked awful, and ought to have an afternoon off."

Mrs. Gage looked at Jane.

"Awful's not the word. She looks like somethin' the cat dragged in. If you ask me, you're both actin' silly, earnin' a bit is all right but never goin' out is foolishness, and you're worryin' your poor Mum to death. Now you both go for a walk after your dinner, and then when you come back you'll feel ever so much fresher. Sittin' cramped over the table, write, write, write, it's carryin' things too far, that is."

Jane gave Mrs. Gage her dress.

"But the envelopes . . ."

Mrs. Gage gave Jane a friendly push.

"Go on, give your face a wash. You don't want your Mum to see you've been cryin'. And drat the envelopes. You'll do 'em twice as fast when you've 'ad a breath of fresh air."

Paul and Jane wanted to take Esau out with them, but Ginnie begged so hard for him to go out with her and Angus that they gave in. Angus was puzzled.

"Why do we want Esau? As a matter of fact, I wasn't going out this afternoon."

They were on the upstairs landing. Ginnie beckoned him into his bedroom and shut the door.

"Angus, my boy, Miss Virginia Bell has had a simply gorgeous idea. She and Mr. Angus Bell are going to earn holiday money."

"How?"

Ginnie lay across Paul's bed.

"How would you like to go to Paul and Jane, and throw down simply pounds and pounds, and say we earned that for our holiday?"

Angus knew Ginnie's ideas. He felt cautious.

"How could we earn pounds and pounds?"

Ginnie lowered her voice.

"It's not perhaps a way everybody might think the best way, but it's a way, and really, Angus, it's time we earned. There's Paul and Jane slaving and slaving, and us doing nothing."

Angus was looking at his caterpillars.

"What would we do?"

"Well, first we make Esau wet, and don't dry him."

Angus thought that mean.

"Poor Esau! I think the miserablest thing is a wet dog."

"It's very hot, so it won't hurt him, and being wet will make him look thin, and that's part of my plan. Then we're going by bus, to where there are rich people. I think near St. Winifred's will do. There are lots of grand houses there, where rich people live, and they won't know us nor that I go there to school, as I'm not in my uniform."

Angus left his caterpillars and came over to the bed.

"When we get there what do we do to get pounds and pounds?"

Ginnie turned over on her back and spoke in a don't-be-a-silly-little-boy voice.

"You sing, Esau shivers because he's wet, and I go around with a collection box, and people fill it with money because we're poor and hungry."

"But we aren't poor and hungry."

"Don't argue, my boy. People who can't go for holidays are poor, and by the time we get there we'll be hungry because it will be a long time since lunch."

Angus could feel that Ginnie was in a determined mood.

"I shan't like singing in a road."

Ginnie rolled over on her chest and frowned.

"Miss Virginia Bell hasn't noticed that you mind dancing in the road."

"That's because my legs feel like dancing, and not because people are going to give me pounds and pounds."

Ginnie was disgusted.

"You're a poor weak creature, Angus. Here's me with a simply gorgeous way for us to earn money for a holiday so that Paul and Jane stop looking scorn at us, and all you do is to say you wouldn't like singing in a road."

Angus was weakening.

"But I won't like it, and Esau won't like sitting in the road while he's wet."

Ginnie got up. With a wave of her hand she dismissed Angus.

"Very well, if you and Esau don't mind poor Mummy looking so dreadfully tired everybody's talking about it, and poor Daddy looking so thin that, as Mrs. Gage says, you can see through him when he's in the pulpit, I suppose I can't make you. But me, I'd be proud to put in my dedication book for today's service 'Collected money for needy family to have holiday.' "

"I want Daddy and Mummy to have a holiday as much as you do—it's only I don't want to sing. Still, if it's only one afternoon, and I didn't have to sing for very long . . ."

"You'll have to sing just as long as people give us money. Now, we'll go downstairs very quietly into the kitchen. There's no one there. Then you take Esau outside the back door, and for goodness' sake hold him tight, because I'm going to pour jugs and jugs of water over him."

Though Ginnie and Angus did not know it, as they went out the back door Miss Bloggs was coming in at the front. She knocked on Alex's study door.

"Can I come in, Vicar?"

Because it was supposed to be holiday time Alex had been reading a thriller. Rather sadly he put it down and opened the door.

"Of course."

Miss Bloggs came in, talking as she came.

"It's that holiday camp for French students at St. Winifred's. I went up there, as I promised you, but I cannot make the director of the party understand about the special service for them on Sunday. I spoke very distinctly, but I fear my French is a little rusty."

Alex pulled a chair forward for Miss Bloggs.

"I expect mine is too."

Miss Bloggs sat down.

"I said *église* several times, and *dimanche*, but the director spoke so fast that I'm afraid I did not quite follow what he said. I wonder, could you spare the time to come up with me this afternoon?"

If Cathy had known what Miss Bloggs was saying, she would have been very cross with her. But Cathy was in the dining room ironing, so Alex, looking as if going to the holiday camp at St. Winifred's was the one thing he wanted to do, went out with Miss Bloggs.

Miss Bloggs and Alex walked part of the way to St. Winifred's, because, as Miss Bloggs said, there was nothing like a lungful of God's good air. Alex privately thought God's air was not smelling good in southeast London that afternoon, but he was quite glad of a walk.

In the garden at St. Winifred's Alex met the very charming director in charge of the holiday camp, and in no time fixed up with him for the service on Sunday.

"Now, you know my telephone number," Alex said as he turned to go. "If you want me, don't hesitate to call."

"It is a pleasure," said Miss Bloggs in English, "to do anything we can. We are all brothers under the skin."

The director was puzzled and he turned to Alex.

" 'Ow is that, m'sieur?"

Alex wished Miss Bloggs would not say things that were so difficult to translate. He fumbled for words.

"*M'zelle Bloggs dit nous sommes frères audessous de peau.*"

From the way the French director looked at Miss Bloggs, Alex could see he had not made a success of that translation, so he changed the subject.

"What are your young people looking at over the gate there?"

The director looked across the tennis courts.

"*Ah, c'est drôle.*" He beckoned to Alex and Miss Bloggs to follow him. "*M'sieur regardez, c'est comique ça.*"

Alex and Miss Bloggs followed the director across the tennis courts to the side gate. At first they could not see what was happening, for half the students were hanging over it. Murmurs came from them. "*Ah, les pauvres petites!*" "*Regardez le chien.*" Then an English voice in the road said: "I'd like to give that dog a decent meal; doesn't look as though he'd eaten for a week." Then Alex saw Ginnie. Her back was to him, but what was she doing was perfectly clear. She had a money box and into it people were dropping coins. What she said was perfectly clear too.

"Thank you so much. Actually, Esau isn't really hungry, but every penny helps."

The voices around rose.

"It's a shame, that's what it is." "Nicely spoken too." "*Ah, le pauvre petit chien.*" "Poor little scrap." "Terrible to see kids reduced to this sort of thing." "*C'est malheureux, n'est ce pas?*"

Then Alex heard Angus's voice.

"I've sung everything I know, Ginnie."

"Sing a hymn. You haven't done that yet."

The crowd moved a little, and Alex could see Angus. Ginnie had done her best to dress him for the part: his face was dirty, his hair hung over his eyes, and he was wearing a torn shirt. His voice rose clear and true, and silenced the talkers.

> *"All things bright and beautiful,*
> *All creatures great and small.*
> *All things wise and wonderful . . ."*

On the word "wonderful" Alex had pushed through the students and was standing beside Angus.

"Stop singing, Angus."

Ginnie was furious.

"Oh, Daddy, what are you doing here spoiling everything?"

"I think it's more a question of what are you doing here, Ginnie?"

Alex went back to the director and asked him in French to move his students away. He explained that Ginnie and Angus were his children. This caused a sensation. Eyebrows and hands flew into the air. The people in the crowd told each other the news.

"Ce sont les enfants de M'sieur le curé." *"Ah, ce n'est pas possible!"* *"Mais c'est tout à fait extraordinaire."*

The director spoke in a loud voice.

"Depêchez-vous, tout le monde."

Everybody drifted away, except Alex and Miss Bloggs. Alex was really angry, but he tried hard not to show it.

"Have you taken money from all those people, Ginnie?"

Ginnie shook her box.

"Everybody who would give me anything. One person gave me half a crown."

Alex thought perhaps Angus would explain better.

"Why were you singing?"

Quite suddenly, from being part of a splendid enterprise, Ginnie saw that she was in disgrace.

"It was nothing to do with Angus—it was me who thought of it. You see, we had to earn money."

"What for?"

"I'm sorry, Daddy, we can't tell you that. It's a secret, isn't it, Angus?"

Alex's voice was stern.

"I'm afraid this can't be a secret. You've taken money under false pretenses."

Ginnie thought Alex was being unfair.

"There was nothing false about it. We are poor, and anyway, Esau did most of it really, he looks so miserable when he's wet."

Miss Bloggs was sorry for everybody.

"Oh, dear! Most distressing!"

Alex took Ginnie by one arm and Angus by the other.

"We're doing no good standing here. The best thing we can do is to catch a bus home. Perhaps on the way you will explain to me what has been happening."

But on the bus, Alex got no nearer understanding, for Ginnie and Angus would only say they needed money and would not say what it was for. After Miss Bloggs had got off the bus, Alex remembered Ginnie's dedication book.

"Was it anything to do with service for that book of yours?"

"Well, I was putting it in my book, but that wasn't the reason we were doing it."

Alex tried to be patient.

"What exactly were you entering in your book?"

Ginnie, too, was losing patience.

"I keep telling you and telling you I can't tell you, Daddy. If I did, you'd know our secret."

"It isn't only Ginnie's and my secret, it's Jane's and Paul's too," Angus explained.

Alex gave up.

"All right, I'll wait for my answer until I get in and can have a talk with Paul and Jane. Whatever this secret may be, if it means that you and Angus do what you know to be wrong it's got to finish."

But when Alex, Ginnie, and Angus reached the vicarage, there was no talking to Paul and Jane. Jane, after her walk with Paul, had meant to go back to her envelope addressing, but climbing the stairs she felt peculiar. Mrs. Gage heard her fall, and came running to her, calling for Cathy.

Cathy knelt beside Jane.

"Jane! Jane, darling!"

Mrs. Gage lifted Jane's shoulders onto Cathy's knees.

"There we are, dear. Ups-a-daisy."

"Whatever happened to her?" Cathy asked. "Did she hurt herself?"

"No, dear. Just come all over like."

Jane opened her eyes. Mrs. Gage smiled at her.

"You lean against your Mum, while I fetch a drop of water."

Cathy stroked Jane's hair.

"My poor pet. You've been doing too much."

Jane was still feeling peculiar.

"Everything's going 'round and 'round."

Mrs. Gage came back with the water.

"Drink this, dear, but from the look of you you could do with a nip of something stronger."

Paul came running down the stairs.

"What's up?"

Cathy answered.

"Jane's turned a little faint. There, darling, I'll just dab some of this water on your forehead."

Paul leaned over the banisters.

"She ought to have her head between her knees."

Mrs. Gage made clicking sounds with her tongue.

"You do look terrible, Jane, and no mistake. If you were in a grocer's I shouldn't know you from a lettuce."

Cathy felt the right place for Jane was bed.

"Do you think if Paul and I helped you, darling, you could get up to your room? You ought to lie down."

Jane tried to move, then lay back again.

"In a minute. Everything's still a bit come-ish and go-ish."

It was at that moment that Alex, Ginnie, and Angus came in. Alex was across the hall in three strides.

"What's happening?"

Cathy was glad to see him.

"It's Jane. She's a little faint. I think she ought to be in bed. I was just saying Paul and I could help her upstairs."

Alex stooped down and picked Jane up.

"I'll carry her."

Jane wriggled.

"Put me down, Daddy. I'm much too heavy."

Alex marched up the stairs.

"You weigh nothing at all. It's many years since I've carried you, but it doesn't seem to me you've grown much heavier."

Jane rubbed her cheek against his sleeve.

"It's a good thing for a dancer to be light."

"But not so light we can almost see through her."

At the top of the stairs Jane struggled to get out of Alex's arms.

"Please put me down here, Daddy. There's things in my bedroom I don't want you to see."

Cathy saw Alex was going to argue. She laid her hand on his arm.

"It's this awful secret they're working at. Put her in our room."

Alex laid Jane on the bed and stroked the hair off her forehead.

"There you are, darling. Would you like some brandy?"

Jane managed a half laugh.

"Of course not. I'm quite all right now. It was only that everything was a little bit fuzzy."

Alex was terribly worried and looked it.

"Very fuzzy I should think. The best thing for you is to stay quiet. Perhaps a cup of tea when you feel like it."

The meeting that should have taken place in the study took place in Alex and Cathy's bedroom after tea.

"I'm sorry," said Alex, "to have a family council when you're not well, Jane, darling, but a little clearing of the air is needed."

"You sound very solemn, Alex," said Cathy.

Alex sighed.

"I feel solemn. Ginnie, put that money box on the dressing table."

Alex told Cathy, Paul, and Jane what had happened that afternoon. Cathy, though she was shocked, could not help finding the story funny.

"Begging! Oh, dear!"

Paul looked despairingly at Ginnie.

"Of all the blithering idiots."

Jane raised herself up on her elbow.

"We told you not to bother."

Alex turned to Paul.

"Ginnie and Angus won't tell me what they were collecting this money for—they say it's a secret. Is that true?"

Paul nodded.

"I'm afraid it is, Dad. But we never thought of anything so idiotic as begging." Then he turned to Ginnie. "You're absolutely hopeless."

Cathy thought of the hours Jane and Paul had spent shut up in their bedrooms.

"Must it go on being a secret, Paul?"

Paul hesitated. He looked at Jane.

"Seems silly to tell them now. After all, we don't know it'll come off." Then he turned to his father. "It isn't anything you'd disapprove of, Dad. I mean, what Jane and I are doing isn't. It's only that idiot Ginnie . . ."

Ginnie put her chin into the air.

"Everybody always says 'Oh, Ginnie!' Miss Virginia Bell thought it a very good idea."

Alex's face was grave.

"That isn't true, Ginnie. What happened was, you wanted something, and snatched at the first idea that came into your head that would give you what you wanted. You knew it wasn't right to beg, didn't you?"

Ginnie was not admitting anything.

"I said to Angus that it wasn't perhaps the way everybody would think the best way."

Alex turned to Angus.

"And what did you say?"

"I said I didn't want to sing in the road, but it wasn't because of begging."

Jane leaned over the bed to pat Esau.

"The worst thing was making Esau wet. Poor blessed boy, he must have hated it."

"If you want to know," said Ginnie, "he got more money by looking miserable than Angus did by singing."

Alex sounded sad.

"I'm afraid, Ginnie and Angus, you did something you knew was wrong, and so you will have to be punished."

Paul tried to make Alex understand.

"Begging was absolutely idiotic, but the idea behind the begging was all right."

"I daresay," said Alex, "though the end may have been right, the means was disgraceful, and both Ginnie and Angus are old enough to know it. The money that has been collected will go into the General Purpose Fund box in the church. But as it was collected under false pretenses . . ."

Ginnie could have stamped, she thought Alex was being so stupid.

"It wasn't false pretenses. We are poor, and it was quite a long time since lunch, so we might have been hungry."

Alex went on as if Ginnie had not spoken.

"As it was collected under false pretenses, Ginnie and Angus will spend tomorrow earning money honestly. There are several hundred old hymn books in the parish hall, which need sorting to see if any pages are missing. When they have been sorted you will each be given some money to go into the poor box, and you must put in this week's pocket money as well." Glad talk of punishments was over Alex came across to Jane. "As for you, you bad girl, you ought to be punished, too, for giving us all a fright by fainting this afternoon. Mummy and I have been talking things over, and we've decided the trouble is that you need a holiday. We are sending you away."

Jane sat up.

"What! Just me? I won't go by myself, I simply won't."

Cathy sat on the bed beside her.

"You will. Daddy and I have decided that we'll ask Uncle Jim and Aunt Ann if you can share Liza's room in the inn they're staying in."

Jane was appalled.

"Silly Mummy, it'll cost an awful lot of money, and I don't want to be the only one having a vacation."

Cathy kissed her.

"You won't be. We're going to try and get Paul into one of those fruit picking camps, and when they get back from France, we're going to ask Grandfather and Grandmother if Daddy and I, Ginnie and Angus can stay with them for a bit."

Jane knew how much Cathy disliked staying at Bradford. She almost got off the bed.

"Mummy, if you think . . ."

Cathy put a hand on her.

"Lie down, darling."

"I can't lie down when you say things like that. You know I'd simply hate going to Berkshire all alone." She gazed imploringly at Paul. "Say something. You know I won't go."

"It looks as if we'll have to tell them," said Paul.

Jane nodded.

"That's what I thought."

Cathy was pleased.

"It's the secret? Oh, darlings, do tell me. Like Kipling's Elephants' Child I've been dying of ''satiable curtiosity.' "

Together, one telling one bit, and the other another, with small interruptions from Ginnie and Angus explaining how they too had tried to help only they could not find a way, Jane and Paul told the whole story of the envelope addressing.

"Oh, Mummy," said Jane, "it is the most dreadful way of earning that you ever, ever thought of. And you don't get any more money for one tiny little name with four letters in it than you do for dowager marchionesses, and people like those."

Alex held out a hand to Ginnie.

"So that's what you and Angus were up to."

Jane said:

"Only Ginnie would ever think of begging by the side of the road, while Angus sang."

"But you do see it was partly our fault why they did it?" said Paul.

Jane turned to Ginnie.

"Had we been looking proud and despising because we were earning and you weren't?"

"Not exactly," said Ginnie. "More miserable. Angus and me felt mean dogs not to be doing anything."

Jane lolled against Cathy.

"It's been a failure though. We never earned much because we wasted such a lot of envelopes. We wanted to get you a room somewhere for a week, and we've only barely got enough for a weekend."

"It's going on doing it for hour after hour that makes you slow," Paul explained, "after five hundred you make the most awful mistakes."

Cathy gasped.

"Five hundred envelopes! I should think you would make mistakes. It was lovely of you, darlings, but the money won't be wasted: you'll both have some to spend while you're away."

Jane was so disgusted she nearly bounced off the bed.

241

"Do you think we slaved our fingers to the bone, worse than that, slaved them nearly off, to spend the money on ourselves? We earned that money for you and Daddy, and it's going to be spent on you and Daddy, isn't it, Paul?"

Mrs. Gage opened the bedroom door.

"Sorry, all, but I was just 'ome, an' sittin' down to me tea when it come over me that as young Jane was doin' 'er faintin' act a letter comes for young Ginnie. I put it in me pocket."

"Dear Mrs. Gage," said Cathy, "you shouldn't have come back."

"Well, I wouldn't 'ave, only there was some for you, Vicar, which might be important. I put them in the study." She nodded at Jane. "Good night, dear. Try and look a bit less like a tired cucumber in the mornin'."

The children were looking admiringly at Ginnie's letter. It was typed, and had a French stamp. It was not often that Ginnie had a letter; she took her time opening it.

Cathy let Ginnie enjoy the grandeur of being the only one to have a letter, until it was properly out of its envelope. Then she said pleadingly:

"Would you read it out loud, Ginnie? We're all dying of curiosity."

Ginnie, from complete gloom, because of the punishment tomorrow, and not being allowed to keep the money in her money box, was now bursting with happiness. She looked in the proudest way around the family.

"Very well, as you've asked me, Mummy, I will." Then she smoothed out the letter. Because it was typed it was easy to read.

242

DEAR GRANDDAUGHTER,

You will, I think, be leaving shortly for that posh hotel by the sea, of which you told me. I shall enjoy thinking of you going around endlessly on the free giant racer, every now and again pausing to help yourself to the free ice cream, standing in the lounge. I feel, in spite of all the luxury that is to be yours, there may still be a few pleasures which you could enjoy more fully with money in your purse. If you will look in this envelope, you will find something which may be of use to you. With every best wish for a most enjoyable holiday, from your affectionate

GRANDFATHER

Everybody was so startled by the letter that nobody spoke. Ginnie, who was almost too excited to know what she was doing, picked up the envelope off the floor where it had dropped. At first there did not seem to be anything inside it; then she drew out a piece of pink paper. Ginnie did not know what it was, so Paul took it from her. It was a check for three hundred and fifty pounds.

15

Holiday by the Sea

Ginnie wanted to stay in a posh hotel, but she gave up the idea when Alex told her how much posh hotels cost. He said:

"I think it was your choosing so very grand a hotel that made Grandfather guess you could not really be going to stay in one."

Ginnie, of course, told the family exactly what she had told Grandfather, but it was very difficult to get the story out, they laughed so much.

"Free ice cream in the lounge," said Jane. "Oh, Ginnie, what a gorgeous idea!"

Paul laughed so much he had to lie on the floor.

"A fun fair in the garden! Free rides all day long on a giant racer!"

But of course, though Grandfather's check would not take the family to a posh hotel, it would take them somewhere. Nor would that be all; besides paying the fares Alex could manage to add a bit, and of course there was Paul and Jane's envelope money. Still, the largest part of the money was Ginnie's, so it was for her to decide where they went.

"Has Miss Virginia Bell any idea where she would like to go?" Alex asked.

Ginnie shook her head firmly.

"No, Daddy. You'll be surprised, because having this check is much the grandest thing which has ever happened to her, but Miss Virginia Bell doesn't want to be the only one to choose."

"But somebody has to choose, darling," Cathy pointed out.

"I know," said Ginnie. "But I think we'll all choose somewhere, and then we'll draw the places out of Daddy's hat to see where we go."

Jane chose the Sussex downs. Paul Devonshire, somewhere on Exmoor. Ginnie wanted Blackpool.

"There isn't anything else there, except giant racers, and those motor cars that whizz round, and things like that. I think a place that is nothing but a fun fair is the most perfect place for a holiday."

Angus chose a farm anywhere. Alex wanted Cambridge. He had never been back there since his undergraduate days. Cathy was the last to make up her mind.

"When I was little I had measles, and I was taken to Kent to stay at Hythe. I don't know what it's like now, but I remember a great bay with miles and miles of sea. Oh, and there were donkeys giving rides on the sea front, and scarlet poppies everywhere. I should like to go to Hythe."

When Alex had written the places he passed the hat to Ginnie and told her to pick out one. The paper had Hythe written on it. Cathy had won. Angus went mad-doggish with excitement.

"We're going away! We're going away! The Bells are going to Hythe!"

Perhaps because they had not expected to go away, or

245

perhaps because they all so badly needed a change, none of the family ever forgot their holiday in Hythe. They stayed in lodgings quite near the sea. Their landlady, who was made in two bulges like a cottage loaf, was called Mrs. Primrose. Before Mrs. Primrose had married Mr. Primrose she had been a children's nannie, and nothing made her happier than when her rooms were taken by a family with children. She was a wonderful cook, and her great idea was to see the family swell out. By using every penny that could be spared, they managed to stay with her for three weeks, and by the third week the change in them all was startling.

"When you came," Mrs. Primrose said in her cozy voice, "it was as if six ghosts walked in. Now look at you! Why, even Jane has plumped up, which I thought she never would."

The weather was kind, and the family practically lived on the beach, and in the sea. They did a few special things. A trip on the smallest railway in the world to Dungeness, across land reclaimed by the Romans when they occupied England. One never-to-be-forgotten evening, they splurged and bought tickets to Hythe's Venetian Fête. They did not know until they got to Hythe there would be a Venetian Fête, but Mrs. Primrose talked about it so much they felt they had to see it, and how glad they were that they had. It was like a fairy story come true. Float after float drifting by, either beautiful to look at or very, very funny. Angus laughed so much at one of the funny floats that he fell off his chair and very nearly dropped into the canal. Sometimes Alex and Jane went to the canal to fish. They caught nothing, but it was lovely sitting on the bank, watching dragonflies and, when they were lucky, seeing a heron fish for his lunch. Ginnie found a really magnificent hotel called the Imperial. It had a wonderful garden, tennis, croquet, and a golf course.

"Nothing," she said to Alex, "could look posher than this hotel. I shall send Grandfather a post card of it. I won't tell a lie and say we're staying there; I'll say 'This is a lovely place,' which is true, and might mean the hotel, or just mean Hythe."

One of the most exciting things about the holiday in Hythe was that Ginnie discovered she had a talent. At St. Winifred's the girls went swimming once a week, and if they liked it they could go on Saturday mornings. Ginnie had learned to swim, and had often been told by the swimming instructor that she could be a fine swimmer if she worked. Somehow what he said had never sunk in, and Ginnie had spent most of her time at the pool fooling around and ducking her friend Alison. But now, swimming in the open sea, she found that swimming was a gorgeous thing to do. She was like a little porpoise in the water, turning over and standing on her head, but every day she swam farther, and she swam better. Paul was amazed.

"I say, Dad, Ginnie's really good. I know I'm not much of a swimmer, but I could beat Ginnie when we first got here; now I can't."

Alex had noticed Ginnie too.

"If she keeps it up when she gets back to London I think she's going to be outstanding. She cuts through the water like a torpedo."

Ginnie, when Cathy spoke to her about her swimming, took it quite for granted.

"I think I'll be the sort of girl who swims the Channel."

Alex laughed.

"What about the Olympics? Or do you despise them?"

Angus's great joy was the donkeys. Every day he rode them up and down the sea front. He christened his favorite Balaam, and refused to change the name when Ginnie pointed out his mistake.

"Such ignorance for the son of a vicar! Balaam *rode* on an ass, my boy—it wasn't the ass's name."

Nobody enjoyed the holiday more than Esau. He would go prowling off by himself along the beach. Very often he ate starfishes on his walks, which made him dreadfully sick, but, as Alex said, everybody must enjoy themselves in their own way.

Then suddenly it was the last day. The suitcases came out from under the beds. Fairly tidy clothes for traveling were laid out, and of course the last of everything had to be done. The last swims, the last donkey ride, the last ice cream at the kiosk, and of course, final present buying. Nobody had much money left, but two people simply had to have presents, one was Mrs. Primrose and the other Mrs. Gage.

For Mrs. Primrose, after much thought, and a lot of arguing, they chose a vase; for Mrs. Gage all the family chose different presents. Ginnie bought her a little box trimmed with shells. Jane a cup and saucer with fishes on it. A man on the beach had taken a family group with Angus's camera, which was better than Paul's, so Paul had a copy framed in a near-silver frame. Angus chose the most surprising present, a bowl of goldfish. Cathy looked rather gloomily at it when she saw it.

"Are you sure you want to give her that, Angus? It's such a splashy present to travel."

The train back to London left in the late afternoon, so the family came home for an early lunch, and last packings. It was as they were sitting down to lunch that the awful thing was found out. Esau was missing. They tried to remember who had seen him last.

"He went back to the house with you, didn't he, Ginnie, when you went to fetch your dedication book?"

As a last gift to Hythe Ginnie had thrown the dedication book out to sea.

"I shan't need it now I'm going to be a champion swimmer."

It had been fun at the time, and all the family had laughed, but no one laughed now.

"He wouldn't come," Ginnie explained. "I called him, but he was digging and digging for something on the beach."

Jane got up and looked out of the window.

"I expect he's coming. He's such a different dog here to the one he is at home. He doesn't expect anyone to look after him, he just goes where he likes."

Usually Esau was very conscious of mealtimes. Alex got up.

"He may be hunting on that waste ground."

Paul stopped him.

"He isn't. I came home that way."

Cathy tried to sound cheerful.

"There's nothing to worry about. He never goes near the sea, so there's no danger of his being drowned."

Jane looked at Cathy.

"You've got your let's-keep-calm-at-any-price face. You think he's lost, don't you?"

Cathy struggled to sound confident.

"Of course I don't. But I wish he was here. It'll be a worry if he's late today, just as we're going."

"He'll come," said Alex. "I expect he's found an especially

249

juicy dead starfish, and he will honor us by being sick in the train."

Mrs. Primrose had provided an extra special last lunch. Chicken, bread sauce, peas, potatoes, and a trifle to follow, and she was not going to have her food wasted for any dog.

"Don't let his being late spoil your dinners. I'm not having my chicken wasted. If he's not in by the time you've finished I'll send the boy next door on his bicycle to the police station. This isn't a big place; if he's been found wandering, or anything's happened to him, they'll know."

"Are there many dog thieves here?" Jane asked.

Mrs. Primrose gave a warm chuckling laugh.

"Dog thieves! In Hythe! Whatever next."

Angus felt Esau was not appreciated.

"He's a valuable dog. He won a prize last year for being the most beautiful dog in Britain."

"And no wonder," said Mrs. Primrose cozily. "But being so handsome everybody would notice him. A common dog no one might see, but Esau is a dog that stands out. You leave it to the boy next door. He's a boy scout, he'll be back with him all right."

Mrs. Primrose made the family feel less worried. Her cozy voice, which Cathy said made her feel about four years old, was the sort that gives confidence. But when the chicken was taken away and the trifle was on the table and there was still no Esau, fright gripped them again. And when, after lunch, the boy next door came back and said the police had not seen Esau, and nor had anyone else, the family began to despair. They split up to search the nearby streets. The boy next door found some fellow boy scouts and searched the farther-off streets. Angus

250

walked all the way up the sea front in both directions, in case Esau was on the beach. But only a short time before they had to leave everybody was back at the house, and none of them had seen or heard anything of him.

"If we don't find him we can't go back," said Angus.

"Of course we can't," Jane agreed. "Blessed angel, imagine him coming here and finding us gone."

Ginnie's voice was truculent.

"This is my holiday, and Esau was part of it. I say nobody can go home until he's found."

Cathy was as miserable about Esau as anybody, but she had to be firm.

"I'm sorry, darlings, but Esau or no Esau, we're all going back to London this afternoon."

Jane was nearly crying.

"We couldn't, Mummy. We simply couldn't."

Angus flung himself at Alex.

"Daddy, you won't make us go without him, will you?"

"It seems awful to leave him, Dad." said Paul.

Alex put an arm round Angus.

"The trouble is, we shan't do any good hanging about here. Esau's loss has been reported to the police, and we're on the telephone. I've arranged he's to be sent home the moment he turns up."

Mrs. Primrose backed Alex.

"Your father's quite right, my dears. The police'll let you know as soon as there's any news. But I've a feeling in my bones you'll find him before you go."

Ginnie put a hand into one of Mrs. Primrose's.

"Are your bones reliable?"

Mrs. Primrose squeezed Ginnie's hand.

"Never known better. When I feel in my bones something happens, it happens. My bones feel now Esau travels back with you."

In Hythe there is the best station bus system in the world. The bus meets every train and then wanders around the town dropping passengers and their luggage at their front doors. Going away, the bus calls for passengers at their houses. Though they were still protesting, and Ginnie was quite crying, and Jane very nearly, the Bells and their suitcases were waiting for the bus. Mrs. Primrose, still holding in a pleased way the vase they had given her, came to the door to see them off.

"Good-bye, dears. Come again. It's been lovely having you. If I hadn't the rooms booked I'd have had you another week for nothing, I would. Smile now. Try not to worry."

The bus driver, who also took the fares, and helped with the luggage, was a cheerful man. He remembered the Bells, and beamed at them over his shoulder.

"I drove you when you came. Had a good time?"

Jane was nearest to him, so she answered.

"Absolutely perfect, but it's all spoilt now. You see, we've lost our dog."

The driver began to remember Esau.

"Spaniel, wasn't he?"

Ginnie got up and came to the front of the bus.

"A very valuable one. Last year he won a competition for the most beautiful dog in Britain."

The driver wore a thinking face.

"Is he a red spaniel?"

"Almost orange," said Jane. "Like an autumn leaf."

"Usually," Ginnie put in; "but he's been out a lot since he's been here, so he hasn't been brushed much, so he's darker than ordinary."

There was a little silence, then the driver said:

"I know where he is."

The family gasped. Then they got up and surged to the front of the bus.

"Where?" "You know?" "Have you seen him?"

The driver was not a man to be hurried.

"When I come home for my dinner, my wife says to me she'd been down to buy a bit of fish from the boats as they came in. She said the fishermen were laughing fit to burst, on account of a red dog. When the boat went out this morning, up comes this spaniel, and jumps in without a by your leave, and sits down as if he'd bought the boat. So they took him out with them."

Alex was feeling in his pockets.

"Quick, Paul. Here's your ticket and Esau's. Will you stop, driver. If you miss the train, Paul, come by the next."

The train was making leaving noises. The family had almost given up hope. Then streaking up the platform came Esau dragging a breathless Paul on his lead. Everybody shouted. Just in time they opened the carriage door. Paul and Esau fell in.

St. Mark's Vicarage looked friendly, welcoming, and as Jane said, almost Hythe-ish when they reached home. Mrs. Gage, with a grin that split her face in half, was waiting on the doorstep.

" 'Ere you are at last. Lovely to see you all again. And don't you look well, ever so brown. Look at you, Jane, proper fat lady at the fair."

Everybody tried to tell her their news at once. How Esau was lost. What they had brought her. Ginnie's swimming, and how she had thrown away her dedication book. About the Venetian Fête, the small railway, and Mrs. Primrose. Mrs. Gage managed to understand quite a lot.

"Fancy you losin' Esau! My word, you must 'ave been in a state. That's a dear little box, Ginnie, look lovely in me front room. Fancy you a swimmer! Well, I never! Thank you for the cup and saucer, Jane dear. I'll keep it on the shelf 'ere for me mornin' cuppa. Don't want Mr. Gage drinkin' out of it. Goldfish! Well, I never, Angus! Mr. Gage was always fond of a bit of fish, give 'im a treat, these will."

But it was Paul's present that truly thrilled her. He said:

"I'm afraid the frame isn't really silver, it only looks like it. A man on the beach took it with Angus's camera."

"Look at you all! Isn't it smashin'! Doesn't your Dad look funny without 'is clergyman's collar? There seems more of your Mum undressed, some'ow. Jane looks sweetly pretty. Look at you, Paul, quite the film star. Oh, there's young Angus, with his arm round Esau. Look at Ginnie, proper little barrel she looks." Then, to his surprise, she gave Paul a smacking kiss. "Thanks ever so, ducks. It's just what I'd fancy. My Bell family, large as life, and twice as 'andsome, standin' on me table for always."

Mrs. Gage made all the family go and tidy up for supper.

"It's on the table, and you should be ready to eat, so get a move on now." When they came down again she flung the door open with an air. "Welcome 'ome all."

No wonder Mrs. Gage wanted them tidy for supper, for never was there a more beautiful meal. There was a large cold ham, and a cold chicken, fruit salad and an enormous ice cream, and to Ginnie and Angus's great joy, the table was loaded with party favors—the kind that explode when you open them. Cathy was so surprised she could only stare at the table.

"Am I dreaming? Where did all this glory come from, Mrs. Gage, dear?"

Mrs. Gage whipped out a letter she was holding behind her back and gave it to Alex. He read it out loud.

"A mark of appreciation from all your friends in St. Mark's parish."

"The 'am's from the butcher," said Mrs. Gage, "the cake from the choir. Miss Bloggs coughed up the chicken. The rest came in dribs and drabs. Oh, and the children of the Sunday school sent a woppin' great bone for Esau."

At first everybody was so busy eating nobody spoke. Then Jane said:

"Do you know, nothing looks as shabby as it did when we went away."

"That's the best of going away," Cathy explained, "home seems so nice when you get back."

"And it's still vacation time," Paul pointed out, "and we've none of those awful envelopes to address, so we could do some nice things."

"Let's make a plan," Cathy suggested. "Nice things not only for vacation but for all the rest of the year."

"You mean we all make a plan?" Ginnie asked.

Cathy nodded.

"Everybody. Mr. Paul Bell, Miss Jane Bell, Miss Virginia Bell, Mr. Angus Bell, and Mr. Esau Bell."

"In fact," said Jane, "a combined operation by the Reverend Alexander Bell and family."